MW00849209

SONGBIRD'S SECOND CHANCE

ASHLEY FARLEY

Copyright © 2024 by Ashley Farley

All rights reserved.

Cover design: damonza.com

Editor: Patricia Peters at A Word Affair LLC

Leisure Time Books, a division of AHF Publishing

All rights reserved. No part of this book may be used or reproduced in any manner without written permission from the author.

This book is a work of fiction. Names, characters, establishments, organizations, and incidents are either products of the author's imagination or are used fictitiously to give a sense of authenticity. Any resemblance to actual persons, living or dead, events, or locales is entirely coincidental.

ALSO BY ASHLEY FARLEY

Matters of the Heart

Road to New Beginnings

Stand Alone

On My Terms

Tangled in Ivy

Lies that Bind

Life on Loan

Only One Life

Home for Wounded Hearts

Nell and Lady

Sweet Tea Tuesdays

Saving Ben

Sweeney Sisters Series

Saturdays at Sweeney's

Tangle of Strings

Boots and Bedlam

Lowcountry Stranger

Her Sister's Shoes

Magnolia Series

Beyond the Garden

Magnolia Nights

Scottie's Adventures

Breaking the Story

Merry Mary

ONE
HARPER

I feel all eyes boring into me, watching me, waiting for me to make a wrong move. I'm an imposter, a wedding crasher, the newcomer in a small town where everyone knows everyone else. Bowing my head, I slump down in the white wooden folding chair. From beneath my brow, I peek at the guests around me. To my relief, no one is paying any attention to me. They're too engrossed in the ceremony. The bride and groom are center stage, standing with the minister under an arbor of blue hydrangeas with the cerulean waters of Catawba Sound glistening in the background. They strike a handsome couple—she in a midi white chiffon dress and he in a pale gray linen suit.

I haven't yet met the couple. But the groom, Will Darby, owns Tracy's Threads, the women's clothing boutique where I recently started working. The boutique's manager, Mollie, invited me to be her plus-one for the wedding when her boyfriend bailed on her at the last minute in favor of a bill-fishing tournament up the coast in Mount Pleasant. I jumped at the chance to visit Marsh Point, the Darby family's ancestral home, a graceful Lowcountry-style house set amid a backdrop of the sweeping Carolina marshland.

I slip a scrap of paper from my vintage beaded clutch and read the message written in my mother's hasty handwriting. *Darby Baby. January 9th. Marsh Point. One hundred Pelican's Way. Water's Edge, South Carolina.* My adoptive mother, Victoria Boone, died eight weeks ago, at the beginning of April, from a brain aneurysm. Ten days ago, while searching her desk in her home office for her life insurance policy, I found a sealed envelope beneath her hanging files in the bottom drawer. Either my mother had hid it there, or it had slipped through the hanging files. Along with the address, the envelope also included a remnant of a baby's blanket—yellow flannel printed with baby ducks. January 9 is my birthday. If my suspicions are correct, one of the two women seated in the front row on the groom's side is likely my biological mother.

Returning the paper to my purse, I shift in my seat to get a better view of the Darby sisters, but with several rows of people separating us, I can only see the backs of their heads. While their hair is the same golden honey color, one sister wears hers in a pixie cut and the other in long, layered waves. An attractive man sits tall and erect beside the sister with short hair. Is he her husband? Where are her children? Do the bored-looking flower girls and ring bearer belong to her? Seated beside the other sister are two teenagers—a boy and a girl—with hair the same mahogany shade as the man with them, who, I assume, is their father.

The minister pronounces them husband and wife, the couple kisses, and the crowd cheers. Following the migration of guests to the food tent, I spot the Darby sister with the pixie cut waiting at the carving station for a slice of beef tenderloin.

I step in line behind her. "Lovely wedding. Your family's home is gorgeous."

When she turns to face me, confusion replaces her smile. "I'm sorry. Have we met?"

I extend my hand. "Not yet. I'm Harper Boone, the new sales assistant at Tracy's Threads. I'm Mollie's date for the wedding. Her boyfriend was unable to attend at the last minute."

She shakes my hand. "In that case, welcome to Marsh Point. I'm Ashton Darby, Will's eldest sister."

"Nice to meet you, Ashton." Looking more closely at her, I detect no similarities in our features. We both have blue eyes, but mine are deeper, the color of the ocean, and hers are more gray. Her face is oval-shaped, mine is round.

The guests standing in front of Ashton step away, and the carver hands us small plates with juicy tenderloin on yeast rolls. As we move down the table to the condiments, Ashton asks, "What brings you to Water's Edge?"

"I landed here by accident, actually. After my mom died in April, I needed to get away from Raleigh, where I'm from, for a change of scenery. I was headed to Hilton Head for a week at the beach when I stopped at Corner Coffee for some caffeine. I spotted a sign advertising for help in the boutique's window and applied for the job on a whim. And here I am. I needed a change more than I realized." I fake a laugh. Ashton must think I'm a nutcase. What kind of person accepts a job in a strange town where she knows no one?

"I'm sorry for your loss. My mother died last summer." When she looks up from spreading horseradish on her tenderloin, someone in the crowd catches her attention. "Excuse me. I need to speak with a friend. It was nice meeting you, Harper."

I watch Ashton make her way toward an athletic-looking middle-aged man. Is he a friend? A business associate? What line of work is she in?

Someone says, "It's not you. My sister is rude to everyone." I turn to see the long-haired Darby sister beside me.

"She wasn't being rude. She wanted to talk to her friend."

The sister presses her lips together. "Mm-hmm. That's Carter Leach, Ashton's private investigator. She's been spending a lot of time with him lately. The matter Carter was helping her with has long since been solved. Which leads me to believe whatever is going on between them now is personal."

I look back at Ashton, who now has her head pressed together with the man, deep in conversation. *Why does Ashton need a private investigator?*

The sister goes on as though she were gossiping with a friend instead of a total stranger. "I spotted them having lunch together at The Nest the other day, whispering to each other like they are now. I wonder if Ashton's boyfriend knows about them."

Ashton's boyfriend? He must have been the one sitting with her during the ceremony. I study the sister out of the corner of my eye. She's a softer, rounder version of her sister with the same gray-blue eyes. I see nothing of myself in her physical features. Maybe my suspicions are wrong after all. Perhaps I wasn't adopted.

"You look so much alike. Are you twins?" I ask her.

She lets out a humph as she tears her eyes away from her sister. "Ashton would not be happy to hear you say that. I'm younger by two years. I overheard you say you're new to town. How do you like working at Tracy's Threads?"

Did she happen to overhear? Or was she eavesdropping? "So far, so good. But I've only met a few customers. Do you shop there often?"

Her brow shoots up. "I can't afford the outrageous prices."

I'm not surprised to hear this from the looks of her outdated pink ruffled dress. "Then you're in luck. I've convinced Mollie, the manager, to have a summer clearance sale."

Her face lights up. "Great! My daughter will need some new things when she goes off to Chapel Hill in August."

"I'm a Carolina girl myself." I locate her mahogany-haired daughter over by the food table. She has a pretty face and a trim figure that will look good in anything. "Is she interested in joining a sorority? I was a Kappa. I'm happy to write a letter for her."

"That's kind of you. The rush process is daunting."

I pull out my phone. "If you give me your contact information, I can text you when we decide on the dates for the sale," I say, making a mental note to see if the store has an email list.

"That would be great. I'm Carrie Wilson."

As she calls out the number, I enter it into my phone. "It was nice to meet you, Carrie. I'll be in touch soon."

I grab a glass of champagne from the bar and search for the groom. When I locate Will, I approach him with outstretched hand. "Mr. Darby, I'm Harper Boone, your new sales assistant at Tracy's Threads."

Recognition crosses his face as he offers a calloused hand. "Of course. Mollie told me about you. She mentioned you would be coming today. Nice to meet you, Harper. And please, call me Will."

The older of the two flower girls tugs at his coattail. "Daddy, can we change now? This dress is so itchy." She shakes all over to emphasize her discomfort.

I kneel to her. "But your dress is gorgeous," I say about the ivory lace and tulle tea-length dress. "And you look like an angel. Why would you want to take it off?"

The child beams. "Do you think so, really? Maybe I'll leave it on."

"My name is Harper. What's yours?"

"Caroline." She sweeps an arm at her sister. "And this is my sister, Sophie."

"Both beautiful names." I finger one of Sophie's stray corkscrews. "You're a curly top like me." When Caroline's lips turn downward, I smooth a hand over her golden head. "And your lovely locks are the color of sunshine."

This brings the smile back to Caroline's face.

"You're good with them," Will says. "By any chance, do you babysit?"

I straighten to face him. "I used to babysit all the time. I even nannied a couple of summers during college. I currently have plenty of time. Being new to town, I haven't yet made any new friends. Give me a call. You know where to find me."

Will's brilliant blue eyes sparkle. "I'll do that."

A thought occurs to me, and my heart skips a beat. Is it possible Will Darby is my biological father? Only the Darby surname is written on the slip of paper. I naturally assumed one of the Darby's unwed teenage daughters put me up for adoption. But it could've just as easily been his girlfriend. He's attractive and fit with a full head of light brown hair. But he appears much younger than his sisters. Around forty, if I had to guess. And I just turned thirty, which means he would've been way too young to father a child.

Noticing an older couple waiting to congratulate the groom, I say goodbye to Will and his daughters and step away. Downing the last of my champagne, I deposit my empty glass on an abandoned serving tray and sneak away from the reception.

Suspecting Mollie would want to stay longer than me at the reception, I had insisted we drive separate cars. I've accomplished the first step of my mission. Now that I've met the Darby siblings, I can begin insinuating myself into their lives.

TWO
SAVANNAH

I have little use for a computer. I use the desktop in the office at the tavern where I work when I order something from Amazon or stalk my sister on social media. I don't dare follow Ashton, but I check her Facebook profile periodically to see what's new in her life. I'm on my lunch break on Sunday afternoon when I come across pictures my sister posted of my brother's wedding yesterday. Will's wife has been dead less than a year. He certainly didn't waste any time in finding someone new. But who am I to judge? I don't even know my brother. Outside of social media, I haven't seen him for thirty years.

I click on a photograph and study the faces of the bride and groom. Will's bride, Julia, is lovely with short dark hair and doe-brown eyes. I might not recognize my brother on the street if not for the piercing blue eyes I remember from our youth. I always felt as though he could see my soul.

I click on the image of our entire family and roll the mouse over each of their faces. My sisters, Ashton and Carrie. Carrie's husband and their teenage daughter and son. Will, Julia, and their three children—his two daughters and his new wife's little boy. My father and May May—my mother's best friend and surrogate mother to us Darby siblings.

Longing tugs at my heartstrings as I scrutinize our family's home with its double-decker porches and the blue-green water of Catawba Sound glistening in the background. I remember my carefree childhood summers at Marsh Point. The long days spent frolicking on the sandy beach. Diving contests off the dock's pilings. Lazy afternoons on the porch. Unfortunately, the ugly memories of my mother's drunken tirades mar those happy times.

I exit the Internet browser and push back from the desk. Rinsing out my salad container, I return to work behind the bar where two regular customers sit at opposite ends. To my right is Donny, a bona fide alcoholic who will drink himself blind before calling an Uber to drive him home to his empty apartment. And to the left is Glenn, who will sip the same drink until he can no longer avoid going home to the wife he refers to as The Shrew. Glenn and I have become friends over the years. He confides in me about his problems. He's made passes at me before, but married men aren't my type. Even if their marriage is on the rocks. Besides, I gave up on finding a man nearly a decade ago.

As I go about my work, my thoughts drift back to my family. My mother's been dead for a year now. Nothing is keeping me from going home to South Carolina to visit my siblings. After thirty years, I've finally grown accustomed to the Pacific Northwest. But I miss the Lowcountry like a sailor misses the sea.

The sound of Glenn's voice interrupts my thoughts. "What's troubling you, Savannah? Have you been looking at social media again?"

I look up from wiping the bar. "How'd you know?"

He eyes the rag in my hand. "You're rubbing at that spot so hard you're gonna wear a hole in the wood."

"You know me too well, Glenn." I toss the wet rag into the sink behind me and move down the bar to him. "My brother got married yesterday. My sister posted the pics on Facebook. Seeing my family all together at Marsh Point made me nostalgic."

"Then get on an airplane and go visit them." Glenn shakes the ice in his lowball glass. "Be a dear and pour me another."

My eyes narrow as I stare at the empty glass. "You're joking. In all the years you've been coming here, I've never known you to have two drinks in one afternoon."

"I need more courage than usual to face The Shrew."

Taking the glass from him, I dump out the ice and mix him a fresh whiskey sour. "Trouble in paradise?" I ask, sliding the fresh drink across the bar to him.

His shoulders sag. "We had a nasty argument last night. She's threatening to leave me. I wish she would."

"If you truly feel that way, why don't you leave her?"

"The same reason you refuse to visit your family," Glen mumbles.

My face turns to stone. "Touché."

Signaling our conversation has ended, I open the dishwasher and unload the clean glasses onto the shelves. Glenn and I are cowards. The Shrew is the mother of his two middle-school-aged children. He's afraid of tearing his family apart. And I lack the courage to face the past, the dreadful event that forever changed my life.

I've finished with the dishwasher and moved on to slicing limes when Doug emerges from the back to attend to a table of newcomers. The dark circles rimming his hazel eyes are evidence of his concern about the future of Mariner's Lantern. A host of newer, more upscale establishments are attracting our customers. When flocks of tourists arrived in town for Memorial Day last weekend, we saw an uptick in business but not the usual surge. In response, Doug has scaled down his waitstaff and picked up the slack himself. We've weathered through slumps before. Locals are naturally curious when a new restaurant opens up in Fairhaven.

They've always come back to us before, but a sick feeling in my stomach tells me this time is different.

When I arrived in Fairhaven thirty years ago, Doug was the only restaurant owner willing to hire a kid under eighteen. Only ten years my senior, we became fast friends. But he has also been a mentor to me, helping me through some tough times. He insisted I get my GED and even offered to help pay for my college. I once dreamed of studying music and becoming a country music star. But that dream went down the drain with all the others.

I've had my share of lovers along the way, including a brief affair with Doug that ended when he met his wife. He fell head over heels in love with Margaret. And understandably so. She's the most kindhearted person I've ever met. She and Doug are my family.

Joining me behind the bar, Doug nudges me out of the way as he pulls draft beers and mixes drinks. "Why don't you knock off early? It's a beautiful day. Spring clean your house. Plant some flowers. Write a song. Margaret and I will cover for you."

I give him a curious look. Things must be really bad if he's cutting back *my* hours. But I'm not one to argue. "Okay. As long as you promise to call me if you get slammed."

"I promise," he says with a sad smile. We both know a sudden rush isn't likely to materialize. Doug lifts his tray of drinks off the bar and returns to his customers.

"Looks like I've been dismissed," I say to Glenn. "Are you ready to close out your tab?"

"Sure." Glenn tugs his wallet out of his back pocket. "I should get going too." He stares down at his full glass. "I wish I hadn't ordered the second drink."

"I can fix that." I pour it down the drain and only charge him for one drink. In response, he gives me a bigger tip than usual.

Untying my apron from around my waist, I deposit it in the dirty linen bin and retrieve my belongings from the back. On the short walk home, I consider Doug's suggestions for how to spend the afternoon hours looming ahead. My house is already spotless —I'd tackled my chores yesterday morning—and the containers flanking the columns on my front porch currently display fresh pink geraniums. Maybe I will write a song. It would be good to get this tune that has been playing in my head for a while onto paper. As the music returns to me, I float the rest of the way to my tiny rental house.

The music comes to an abrupt halt, like a screech on a vinyl record, when I discover my landlord placing a For Sale by Owner sign in my postage-stamp front yard. He doesn't hear me approach and startles when he notices me standing over him. "What're you doing, Bennie?"

"Hey, Savannah. I was hoping I'd run into you." He makes sure the sign is secure in the ground before straightening. "I've decided to put the house on the market. In this economic environment, I can no longer afford the mortgage. I figured this would be a good time with your lease coming up next month."

"Why sell? Why not just raise my rent?"

"I wish it were that simple." His pained expression tells me this is a last resort. "I've decided to move to Texas. I'm looking to make a career change, and Austin is an up-and-coming tech hub. Since my brother lives there, I figured I should give it a shot."

"But what about me? Where will I go?"

"You'll have plenty of time to find a new place. Unless you want to make me an offer," he says with a sparkle of mischief in his moss-green eyes.

While the location is prime, the house needs a complete overhaul. "No thanks. I'm not interested in buying a house."

"Why not? Think of all the money you've flushed down the drain by paying rent. If you'd bought a house when you first moved to town, you would've paid off your mortgage by now."

"Don't remind me," I say, unlocking the door and letting us in.

The problem is I never intended to stay in Fairhaven this long.

Every year, when I signed a lease— for this house and two others before it—I thought it would be my last year in Fairhaven. Yet I'm still here, and the years are passing me by at a rapidly increasing pace.

Bennie looks around the living room and sticks his head in the kitchen. "The place looks good, Savannah. I know I can count on you to keep it clean and tidy for potential buyers. For your inconvenience, I'm giving you a fifty percent discount on your last month's rent."

"How generous of you," I say in a sarcastic tone.

"I'm sorry it has to be this way, Savannah." Bennie rakes his fingers through his milk chocolate hair, and I'm struck, as I often am, by his good looks. *If* only he weren't ten years younger than me. *If* only I hadn't sworn off men. I wonder why nobody has snatched him up.

"Don't worry about it, Bennie. I'll find something else. Interest rates are high, but this is a desirable location. You'll probably have a bidding war on your hands. Ideally, when would you like to close?"

"As soon as your lease is up."

"In other words, I need to find somewhere to live fast."

His lips curve in a sympathetic smile. "I'm afraid so."

I draw myself to my full height. "In that case, I'll get right on it."

After seeing Bennie out, I change into more comfortable clothes and take my guitar outside to the metal rocker on the tiny front porch. The lyrics spill from my lips as I pluck out the chords. I work on the song for hours. When I'm satisfied with the finished product, I transfer the lyrics and notes to the staff paper in my music composition book. Like others I've written over the years, this song tells the story of a young woman on a journey home to her family.

THREE
HARPER

I'm sorting clothing items in preparation for our clearance sale next week when Mollie floats through the door with a dreamy expression on her face and her left hand extended. "I'm engaged," she says, wiggling her fingers as she flashes her sparkling diamond ring.

I drop the armload of clothing on the checkout counter and rush to her. "That's wonderful, Mollie! Congratulations. Let me see." Taking hold of her hand, I study the solitaire diamond. "This is gorgeous. How did he propose?"

"He took me on a picnic to a deserted beach area on Sandy Island." Wrenching her hand free of mine, she holds the ring up as she admires it. "He surprised me. We've only been dating for six months. I figured we'd get married one day, but I had no idea it would be this soon." She drops her hand. "He's moving to Charleston, and he knew I wouldn't go with him unless we were engaged."

My mouth falls open. "Wait! What? You're moving? When?"

"At the end of June."

I narrow my eyes. "But that's only a few weeks away."

"I know." Brushing past me, Mollie walks through the clothes racks to the checkout counter, storing her belongings on the shelf underneath. "I've already gotten a tip on a job. A women's boutique on King Street is searching for a manager."

I move to the counter, standing opposite her. "I'm thrilled for you. But who's going to manage Tracy's Threads?"

"We'll have to hire someone." She flashes me a sly grin. "Unless you're interested in the job."

"Me?" My hand lands on my chest. "I've only been working here a week."

Mollie hunches a bony bare shoulder. "So? You're extremely creative. I love your ideas for painting the walls, rearranging the displays, and broadening our accessory offerings."

"Will Darby will never go for it. He'll want someone with more experience."

"This store is a noose around Will's neck. He'll sell it to the first interested party who makes him an offer. That person hasn't yet presented themselves, but they will in time." She play-slaps my arm. "Who knows? Maybe you'll end up being the new owner."

"Ha! Let's not get ahead of ourselves." I've considered many potential occupations for myself over the years, but shopkeeper was never one of them.

"Okay, fine. But I still think you should take over for me as manager. I can convince Will."

"But I have zero experience in managing a store." Grabbing a red pen, I begin marking the price tags on the sale items.

"It's not a hard job, Harper. I can teach you everything you need to know in a few weeks. You'll earn more money, and you can hire your own sales assistant. Will you at least think about it?"

"Sure. Why not?" I say in a half-hearted tone, but the potential promotion is all I think about for the rest of the day. What does an English major with eight years of experience as a paralegal know about running a clothing store? Then again, I'm committed to staying in Water's Edge until I connect with my biological mother, and that could take months, maybe longer. While this isn't my dream job, I don't mind it so much. As the manager, I can implement the changes I'm sure will bring in more business. But I still have some lingering doubts, which I discuss with Mollie when she brings up the subject again at the end of the day.

"Before I can make such a big commitment, I have some things I need to sort out back home in Raleigh."

"Like what?" she says as she tallies the day's sales receipts.

Like officially resigning from my other job, I think to myself. "Like getting the rest of my clothes and putting my mother's house on the market. I'd planned to do those things in time, but getting away from the store won't be as easy if I'm manager." I haven't told Mollie about my mission to find my biological mother. As far as she knows, my impulse decision to take this job was about my needing a change after losing my mother.

"I can hold down the fort for a few days while you're gone. When would you want to go?"

"Hmm." I tap my chin, thinking. "Since we're not open on Sunday, I could leave after work tomorrow and be back in time for the clearance sale on Tuesday morning."

"You'll need more than two days. Take tomorrow off too." Mollie paperclips the receipts and slips them in her bank bag. "In the meantime, if you want, I can talk to Will about promoting you."

"I'm not sure. Maybe float it by him to see what he thinks. But I'm not ready to commit just yet. I need to get my life in order. I'll give you my decision on Tuesday morning."

"Fair enough." Mollie reaches under the counter for my purse and brings it around the counter to me. "Now go. You need to pack for your trip." Taking me by the arm, she walks me to the front of the shop. "Don't hesitate to call if you have questions about the position." When we reach the door, she stops me. "And Harper, I wouldn't recommend you if I didn't think you were an ideal candidate for manager."

I give her a quick hug. "Thanks for your vote of confidence."

Leaving the boutique, I walk two blocks east to my apartment. A hair salon occupies the first floor of the converted warehouse. The upstairs is divided into four equal-sized apartments with scrumptious pine floors, exposed brick walls, and floor-to-ceiling windows. So far, my only furnishings are an air mattress, a plastic milk crate, and a cheap lamp. The space is a blank canvas for me to create my first home. Despite spending hours on Pinterest, I've yet to identify my decor style. There are many to choose from— contemporary, coastal, rustic, and Boho, to name a few. I hate wasting money on cheap furniture when my mother has a house full of the good stuff. Victoria Boone never did anything halfway. She hired top designers to keep her home updated and fashionable. Unfortunately, her decor is too sophisticated for my liking.

With no plans to occupy my Friday evening, I grab my cosmetics bag and head out on the nearly five-hour trip to Raleigh. Once I'm on the interstate, my mind returns to the decision at hand. Should I take the manager position? I don't necessarily need a salary increase. My mother left me enough inheritance to last my lifetime. But I'm not the life-of-leisure type. Although I learned from Victoria the importance of being productive, there's a vast difference between her and me. She loved her career, and I have yet to discover my true passion.

———

AFTER MY MOTHER'S FUNERAL, I moved out of the swanky furnished apartment I was sharing with a friend and back into my childhood home. My heart ached for Victoria and being near her possessions helped ease my pain.

I wake early on Saturday morning but linger in bed, luxuri- ating in the Egyptian cotton linens. As I nestle deeper beneath the covers, my eyes travel the room from the posters of my idol— guitarist and vocalist Joni Mitchell—to the various instruments I learned to play growing up—guitars, electric and acoustic, saxophone, and violin. While she indulged me by paying for my lessons, my mother thought my interest in music was frivolous. My voice coach found my soulful timbre distinctive, and when he began pressuring me to pursue a career in the industry, my mother insisted I quit music and focus on building my resume for college. Victoria dreamed of me becoming an attorney and practicing at her law firm. But I found the law boring. I despised my job as a paralegal. I kept postponing taking the LSAT. Now my mother is dead, and I'm off the hook.

Throwing back the covers, I plod on bare feet to the recently renovated chef's kitchen for coffee. Seated at the island with my laptop, I send emails to the top-selling real estate agent in the area and the managing law partner at my mother's firm. I schedule an appointment with Jennifer, the Realtor, for first thing Monday morning and make a date with Mr. Wells for brunch tomorrow at eleven. I call several reputable moving companies, but only one has a representative available on Monday.

Finishing my coffee, I roam around the house, surveying my work ahead. All of my mother's personal items will have to go. I inspect the handsomely tailored wardrobe in her extensive walk-in closet. But there's no way I can wear her clothes. She was much taller and leaner than me. I'll consign most and donate the rest to charity.

As a whole, the furnishings are too elaborate, but my mother had impeccable taste, and there are several pieces I can use for my apartment in Water's Edge. These include the soft taupe velvet sofa, alabaster table lamps, an Oriental rug in muted shades of blue, and a few contemporary works of art that I'd never paid attention to, but now find fascinating.

Changing into jeans, I brush my hair back in a ponytail, locate a pile of abandoned cardboard boxes in the attic, and set to work. I sort and pack and make trips to the consignment store and to Goodwill.

By six o'clock, I'm exhausted but encouraged by my progress.

I'm rummaging through the freezer for dinner options, my hair still wet from the shower, when my next-door neighbor, Miss Bea, bustles through the back door with a casserole dish. She sets the dish on the island and draws me in for a hug. I collapse in her plump arms, the warmth of her soft body comforting me. This is what coming home feels like. I never experienced this kind of tenderness from Victoria.

My mother considered Miss Bea her closest friend. They got along remarkably well, considering my mother was the quintessential professional woman, and Miss Bea was a stay-at-home mom turned grandmom. Miss Bea picked up the slack for Victoria by bringing us well-balanced meals several times a week and taking care of me after school when I was too young to stay alone.

She pushes me away to look at me. "Where have you been, sweet girl? I've been so worried. You left so suddenly, and I had no way of contacting you."

I furrow my brow. "What? Don't you have my cell number?"

When she laughs, the loose skin under her neck jiggles. "Surprised me too. I guess I never needed it. Whenever I wanted to talk to you, I just walked on over." Letting go of my arms, she gestures at the casserole. "I brought you your favorite hot chicken salad."

"You're the best. There's nothing in the freezer." I place the casserole in the warming drawer. "Can I interest you in a glass of wine?"

"Sure. But I can only stay for a minute." Miss Bea loves her afternoon wine time. Saying she'll stay for a minute means staying for at least two glasses.

Removing a chilled bottle of white from the refrigerator, I pour two glasses and hand one to her. "Let's go outside," I say, leading the way to the wrought iron lounge chairs on the back patio.

I sip the wine and set down my glass on the coffee table. "I'm glad you came over. I want to discuss something with you, the reason I left town so suddenly. Did you live next door before I was born?"

"Yes, I did. I beat your parents to the neighborhood by five years. Why do you ask?"

I twirl a curl around my finger as I consider how to broach the subject. "Did you know I was adopted?"

Miss Bea lowers her gaze to her wine glass. "I assumed that was the case, although I never discussed the matter with your mother. I don't have to tell you how private a woman Victoria was. She would not have confided in me if she was trying to start a family. Then one day, out of the blue, you appeared in her arms. A slim woman like your mother wouldn't be able to hide a pregnancy. How did you find out?"

"I found an envelope in her desk." I tell her about the scrap of paper with my birth date, *Darby baby,* and the Water's Edge address.

"And this is why you left town?"

I nod. "On a whim, I drove down to Water's Edge. Once I got there, I realized I couldn't just barge into their lives. So I took a job at the Darby brother's boutique while I figure out which of his sisters is my biological mother."

Miss Bea blinks hard. "You're working for someone in the family?"

"Yep. And I attended his wedding. You should see Marsh Point, their family's home. The property is spectacular, a beautiful old Lowcountry-style house on the Catawba Sound in Water's Edge, South Carolina."

"When do you plan on telling them?"

"I'm not sure. I guess I'll know when the time is right." I look away, staring out across the backyard. In the short time I've been gone, weeds have taken over the flower beds. "I was stunned when I found the envelope, but now everything makes perfect sense. It explains why my mother and I are so different. She wanted me to be like her, and I fought her every step of the way." My throat thickens. "I'd give anything for more time with her. For another chance to be a better daughter."

Miss Bea reaches for my hand. "You were a wonderful daughter, sweetheart. And Vicky was so proud of you."

I smile at her use of my mother's nickname. Only Bea could get away with calling her *Vicky*. "I appreciate you saying that, but we both know you're lying. Becoming a lawyer would've made her proud."

Bea grunts. "Vicky put too much pressure on you to follow in her footsteps. I told her that many times. You had such musical talent. I was heartbroken for you when she made you quit."

"I know. But she did what she thought best." I pick at a loose thread on the chair cushion. "Part of me feels like I'm betraying her by looking for my birth mother. But I can't help myself. I've always sensed something missing in my life, and now that I know what it is, I urgently need to find it."

"You would be betraying yourself if you don't." She shifts in her chair to face me. "But, Harper, this is about more than genetics. You've been suppressing your need to create for years. Give yourself permission to reconnect with your creative side. That is where you should start your journey of self-discovery."

A comfortable silence settles over us, and I ponder her words as I finish my wine. *My journey of self-discovery.* Is that what I'm doing? Is that what this driving force I feel is about?

"I'm putting the house on the market, Bea." I don't look at her for fear of the disapproval I might find in her face.

"Don't you think it's too soon? They say you shouldn't make any drastic changes for at least a year after a significant loss."

"I'm aware. This might be hard for you to understand, but to fully commit to my so-called journey of self-discovery, I need to rid myself of everything tying me to the past. I wanna be free to stay in Water's Edge if I decide to do so. If things don't work out with my birth mother, I may get a wild hair and take off for Nashville, try my hand at becoming a country music star."

"Are you serious?" Bea asks in a hopeful tone.

I laugh out loud. "No way! I'm past my prime. But I'd like to visit Nashville one day for fun."

I look past Bea at the back of the house. The awnings overhanging the french doors are in desperate need of power washing. While the house is lovely, the upkeep is constant. If I was married with children, I might feel differently about living here, but I don't want that burden at this stage in my life. "I imagine a young family will move in here, and you'll have a new crop of little children to spoil."

"No one can take the place of you in my heart. You must promise to stay in touch." Bea pulls out her phone. "Give me your number right now."

I call out my number as she enters it into her phone. I wonder what the future holds for Bea and me. Will we fall out of touch, or will we make the effort to call each other occasionally? Once I sort out my life, I may move back to Raleigh. Although something tells me, that's not likely to happen. I'm starting over, beginning anew. And this time, I'm the only one in the driver's seat.

FOUR
SAVANNAH

Bennie parades an endless stream of potential buyers through my home. I'm shocked at the exorbitant rental rates when I take time off work to look for somewhere to move. With the reduced tips I've experienced lately, I can't afford a one-bedroom in the new upscale apartment buildings. The houses I can afford, I fear, are rodent-infested.

I'm scrolling through Zillow on my phone Saturday midafternoon when one of the bartenders at Fir and Tide—the swanky new establishment across the street responsible for stealing our customers—comes in for a late lunch.

Jessica plants herself on a stool. "I see your business has slowed to nonexistent."

I ignore her jab because I'm in no position to argue. She's the first customer we've had all day. Even Donny and Glenn haven't been in lately. "What can I get you, Jessica? Are you drinking or eating?"

"Eating. We've been busy all morning, and I have to work until closing. I need a break to refuel my body and collect myself." She glances at the menu. "I'll have the burger, cooked medium, and a glass of sweet tea."

Taking the menu from her, I walk to the kitchen and submit the order to Marco, who is seated on a stool reading a paperback mystery novel. In a joking tone, I say, "If you can spare the time, I need a burger, cooked medium."

He sets down the novel and slides off the stool to his feet. "Coming right up."

When I return with Jessica's tea, she says, "Seriously, Savannah. The Lantern is a ghost town. If the rumors are true, Doug and Margaret are on the verge of shutting down the place. We're hiring bartenders if you're interested. I'm happy to put in a good word with Gina for you."

"Thanks for your concern, but I'm not worried. We're just going through a slump. Our patrons will return once they tire of paying your outrageous prices."

Margaret would not have flown to Florida to visit her family if the situation were that desperate. However, now that I think about it, her trip was sudden and unplanned. She never even mentioned it to me. Doug is the one who told me about it on Thursday when she failed to show up for work. I assumed she'd be gone for at least a week, and I'm surprised when she arrives for the evening shift around five. Her haggard appearance further escalates my concern.

"How was your trip? You weren't gone long."

"It wasn't a vacation. I had some business to work out with my family."

"Are the rumors true, Margaret? Are you and Doug closing The Lantern?"

Margaret pinches the bridge of her nose. "That is not what we want, Savannah."

And that is not the reassuring answer I was hoping for.

Around six o'clock, the front door bangs open, and a boisterous group of Bellamy family members and their friends file in. The four Bellamy brothers always celebrate their birthdays at The Lantern, which averages out to be one every quarter.

Steve, the youngest brother, says, "I'm sorry, Savannah. I

forgot to make a reservation. But it looks like we don't need one," he says, sweeping an arm at the empty tables in the pub.

I smile at him. "You're fine. We'd fit you in even if we were crowded."

Margaret and Doug come out of the back to greet their valued customers. The three of us slide tables together to accommodate the party of twenty, and for the next two hours, we hustle to meet their drinking and eating needs. They've finished eating and are working on a fresh round of drinks when Steve calls out to me, "Hey, Savannah! How about some music?"

I dismiss him with a wave of the hand. "Not tonight. I haven't performed in ages."

"Puh-lease. It's my birthday. Just one song." Coming behind the bar, Steve takes me by the hand and leads me to the cozy corner in the back, where a small stage is set with a sound system, a single microphone, and a lone barstool. Leaning against the stool is one of my old guitars. I leave it here for such occasions.

Lowering myself to the stool, I spend a few minutes tuning the guitar. I play one of my original slow songs that I know to be one of their favorites. When the song ends, I break into a lively version of "Happy Birthday," and everyone at the table sings along. Next is the Eagle's "Hotel California," followed by several popular rock tunes from that era. The world slips away, my concerns about the future of The Lantern forgotten as I lose myself in the music. When I look up again an hour later, the group is paying their tabs and saying their goodbyes.

"See! We still have plenty of loyal customers," I say to Doug and Margaret in an upbeat tone as we clear the table.

"The Bellamys were our only party tonight," Margaret says. "We're usually crazy busy on Saturday nights."

I set a stack of dirty plates in the gray bus bin. "Live entertainment always draws a crowd. I could go back to performing a few nights a week. Or we can host a karaoke night. We haven't done that in ages."

Doug shakes his head. "Karaoke won't save us this time, Savannah."

"What are you saying, Doug?"

Doug and Margaret exchange a look that prickles my skin. Margaret hurries into the kitchen with the bus bin, and Doug locks the front door, turning the sign to Closed.

He motions me to a barstool. "Sit." He goes behind the bar and pours two shots of whiskey, setting one down in front of me.

I eye the shot glass. "I'd rather not."

"You're gonna need it," he says, downing his shot.

I swallow the golden liquor in one gulp. The whiskey burns my throat and warms my belly. "You're closing The Lantern, aren't you?"

Doug hangs his head. "We have no choice, Savannah. Things have been bad for longer than you think. Margaret and I have fought a hard battle, but we can't make ends meet." He pours himself another shot and holds the whiskey bottle out to me. "More?"

"No thanks," I say, placing my hand over the glass. "What will you do?"

"Margaret went to Florida to ask her father for a loan. He refused to give us money, but he invited us to join his business," Doug says, referring to his in-laws' successful seafood restaurant in Islamorada in the Florida Keys. "Her parents are approaching retirement age. He offered us a deal we can't turn down."

"Good for you." I'm genuinely happy for my friends. I only wish I knew what would become of me.

"Believe me, Savannah. Margaret and I would much rather stay here. Fairhaven is our home. But in this economic environment, we don't have any choice."

"When are we closing?" I expect him to say the end of the month, and I'm floored when he tells me tonight.

Tears well in his eyes as he gestures at the front door. "I just closed that door for the last time."

"This sucks," I croak out past the lump in my throat.

"Yes, it does." Doug comes from behind the bar and sits down next to me. "I'm giving you a generous severance package."

I hang my head. "You don't have to do that."

"Yes, I do. You've been a model employee for a very long time. And I feel awful for not giving you more notice." He reaches over the bar for the whiskey, taking a long chug straight from the bottle.

"*More* notice. You didn't give me *any* notice," I say, unable to keep the anger out of my voice. I remind myself this isn't his fault. He's worked hard to try and save The Lantern. I wish he'd trusted me enough to let me in on their problems.

"Honestly, I'm excited about this next chapter in our lives. I'm relieved to be getting rid of this burden," he says, his eyes darting around the dismal empty restaurant.

"You should be! You're moving to sunny Florida." I place my hand on his forearm. "I'm going to miss you guys."

He smiles over at me. "You have no idea how much we're going to miss you. I've spoken to a number of the neighboring restaurant owners on your behalf. You'll have your choice of jobs if . . ." His voice trails off.

I jerk my head up. "*If* what, Doug?"

"If you decide to stay in Fairhaven. I think you should use this opportunity to go home to South Carolina, at least for an extended visit with your family. Money isn't an issue. I happen to know you're sitting on a fat savings account."

"Not *that* fat." I straighten, holding my head high and chin up. "But I have enough to tide me over until I figure out my next move."

He stands and pulls me to my feet. "If all else fails, as a last resort, you can come to work for us in Florida."

"Gee, Doug, don't sound so excited about the prospect."

He kisses my cheek. "I would love to have you. But I don't want you to use us as a crutch. You've been hiding out in Fairhaven long enough. The time has come, Savannah. You and I both know what you have to do. You can do this. You're stronger than you think."

Feeling close to tears, I bite down on my lower lip. "Do you mind if I come back tomorrow for my things? I need to be alone right now. I'm sure you and Margaret do too."

"Of course. Whenever it's convenient for you. We'll be around the rest of the week, closing up The Lantern."

He lets me out the door and gives me a warm parting embrace. "Take care of yourself, Savannah."

"You too, Doug."

Pushing him away, I head off on foot toward home. I'm nearing the corner when a rowdy group of young people causing a commotion as they spill out of Fir and Tide gets my attention. I smile to myself as they pile into an Uber. That driver will soon be hearing an earful. Uber drivers and bartenders are alike in that regard. We're the flies on the wall. We see all. If only our customers knew.

I wander over and peek in the window at the packed house inside Fir and Tide. While I'm not a partier, the infectious energy of the live entertainment and the uninhibited joy of the young dancers on the floor captivate me. Maybe I will talk to Gina about a job. The servers are probably making a killing, which means I could afford the rent on the one-bedroom apartment. I'm not opposed to hiding out in Fairhaven for a few more years.

As I turn away from the window, Doug's words come back to me. *You and I both know what you have to do.* He's the only person I've ever confided in about my secret. He gives me too much credit. I'm not strong enough to face the past.

FIVE
HARPER

Buford Wells is already seated when I arrive five minutes late for brunch. Tazza Kitchen is packed, and I'm grateful he remembered to book a reservation. He stands to greet me with a peck on the cheek. "You left town so suddenly. I've been worried."

"That's one of the things I wanted to talk to you about." I hang my purse over the back of the chair and sit down opposite him at the table for two. "How is Stacy?" His daughter was my classmate in high school. A gifted actress, she has made a name for herself on Broadway. "When I left town, she was waiting to hear back from an audition. How'd it go?"

He nods curtly. "Very well. Thanks for asking. She got the part. And she also got engaged. We're planning a wedding for next summer."

"How exciting." I can't help but feel envious of Stacy. Everything is going well for her—dream career and now marriage. Meanwhile, I've no career, no family, no significant other, and an empty apartment in a town where I know only a handful of people.

Stop feeling sorry for yourself, I tell myself, and sit up straighter in my chair.

Lifting the menu, I observe Mr. Wells over the top as I peruse the offerings. He's a handsome man with silver-streaked hair and a healthy glow from spending time at his house at Wrightsville Beach. It hardly seems fair that he's enjoying his summer while my mother is buried in City Cemetery.

When the waitress appears, we order Bloody Marys with chips and guacamole.

Mr. Wells waits until she leaves before asking, "So, what is it you need to talk to me about?"

I set down the menu and fold my hands on the table. "Are you aware I was adopted?"

His face tightens, but he does not appear surprised. "I never discussed it with Victoria. But she was certainly never pregnant. You had to come from somewhere."

"Do you know if the firm handled the legal work for the adoption?"

"We did not. At least, I did not. Someone else may have. Have you known about this? Or is this a recent discovery?"

I remove the scrap paper from my purse and slide it across the table to him. "I found this in Mom's desk at home. January ninth is my birthday."

"Is this where you've been? In Water's Edge?" he asks, tapping the paper.

I nod. "I should've called you. But I left town in a hurry."

"Your mother's death was so sudden. I figured you needed some time to yourself," he says, handing me back the slip of paper.

"There are two Darby sisters. One of them is my biological mother. Finding my adoption papers would solve the mystery."

"Good luck with that. I wasn't sure when you were returning, so I took it upon myself to pack up Victoria's office. Everything is in storage if you want to go through her personal effects. But I've sorted through all her files. I did not find any adoption papers."

I tug at my bottom lip. "Maybe she had a safe deposit box. I'll look around at home for a key." I let go of my lip. "Since Mom was a criminal attorney, wouldn't she have hired someone with adoption experience to handle such an important matter?"

He frowns. "Maybe. As you know, we're a full-service firm. She could've consulted with one of our family attorneys. If you like, I can ask the other partners if they know anything. I'll be discreet, of course. Victoria may have given the documents to one of them for safekeeping."

"That'd be great if you don't mind."

The waitress arrives with our drinks and appetizer. Mr. Wells digs into the nachos and guacamole while I sip my Bloody Mary. "I hate to leave you in a bind, Mr. Wells, but I've decided to stay in Water's Edge until I figure out about my birth parents."

"Good for you. And don't worry. We can easily find a replacement."

My eyes widen. "Gee. I may not be the best paralegal, but I didn't realize I was that bad."

Mr. Wells chuckles. "You're a fine paralegal, Harper. But the law isn't your passion like it was your mother's." He reaches across the table for my hand. "I've known you all your life, young lady, and I will miss having you around the office. But I haven't seen you truly happy since you starred as Maria in *West Side Story* your senior year. You sparkled like a brilliant-cut diamond that night."

"That's kind of you to say, but I would never have gotten that role if Stacy hadn't been sick with mono."

"I wouldn't be so sure about that. You really wowed the audience. My daughter is a talented actress, but her vocals don't hold a candle to yours. Whether it be music or something else, you owe it to yourself to find the *thing* that brings back the sparkle."

THAT NIGHT, I dream about my performance in *West Side Story*. I'm singing my heart out on the stage while my father watches from the front row, a bouquet of red roses draped over his lap. The performance ends, and the audience erupts in cheers. Dad waits for me backstage, and we exit the auditorium into the balmy early April evening. The sweet fragrance of the Carolina jasmine growing nearby fills the air. Spring is upon us, bringing with it the promise of fresh beginnings.

My father turns to me, handing me the bouquet of roses. "I'm so proud of you, Harpie. You've become a lovely young woman with a spectacular voice."

Our surroundings change like the stage props, and we're no longer standing outside the school. We're on the beach in front of the cottage we rented at Bald Head Island every summer.

Dad takes my hand, and we stroll with our feet in the surf. "Your mother meant well, but she couldn't help herself. She desperately wanted you to follow in her footsteps. But she's gone now, and you're on your own, free to follow your heart."

Then, in a flash of bright white, he vanishes.

I wake with a start, my heart pounding against my rib cage. My father died when I was eight. Most of what I remember of him is from old photographs. But he seemed so real, so lifelike, in the dream. My dad is the only one who's ever called me Harpie.

I snuggle under the covers, but my brain is too wired to fall back asleep. At daybreak, I give up, get dressed, and spend several hours cleaning. The house is pristine when the real estate agent arrives at nine, and I'm relieved when she assures me it's in good enough shape to put it on the market immediately.

"I'll need a couple of weeks to take photographs and develop marketing materials." Jennifer pulls out her phone and looks at her calendar. "If all goes as planned, the listing will go live the last week in June. You'll do well with the sale, Harper. Your neighborhood is one of the most desirable in Raleigh, if not *the most*, and the inventory for homes of this caliber is slim."

"That's good news. I certainly hope you're right. My new apartment in South Carolina is bare. Would it be possible for me to take a few pieces of furniture with me now? Unfortunately, they are some of the more visible items." When I tell her which pieces, she appears unfazed.

"No worries. Take whatever you want. We'll move things around so no one will notice."

I give Jennifer a key to the house and the alarm code. She's backing out of the driveway when the representative from the moving company arrives. Thomas Bankman is a likable man, not much older than me. And he's incredibly accommodating.

"I'll take good care of your mother's possessions. We'll store them for you until you're ready for them."

"Even if that's years away?"

"As long as you don't mind paying the monthly storage fee," Thomas says, giving me a ballpark amount that makes my jaw drop.

"Why so much?"

He laughs. "In case you haven't noticed, there's a lot of stuff in this house to store."

I let out a low grumble. "I may be looking for a house sooner than I thought."

After calling his scheduler, Thomas reports that he can deliver my small load to South Carolina by the end of the week."

"Excellent. Thanks so much."

We discuss a few more details before Thomas sees himself out. I spend the next hour loading my clothes, accessories, and a few small household items into my 4Runner. When I go next door to tell Miss Bea goodbye, she convinces me to stay for lunch.

Seated at her worn pine kitchen table, we eat egg salad sandwiches and discuss old times. After devouring thick slices of pound cake for dessert, she loads up a Styrofoam cooler with the contents of her refrigerator and bids me a tearful goodbye. By two o'clock, I'm on the highway, heading back to South Carolina. During the long drive to the Lowcountry, I debate whether or not to take the manager job at Tracy's Threads. Voices from the past two days play on auto-rewind in my head.

Miss Bea telling me to permit myself to reconnect with my creative side. *That is where you should start your journey of self-discovery.*

Mr. Wells complimenting me on my performance as Maria in *West Side Story. You sparkled like a brilliant-cut diamond that night. . . . Whether it be music or something else, you owe it to yourself to find the thing that brings back the sparkle.*

And my father. *She's gone now, and you're on your own, free to follow your heart.*

By the time I reach Water's Edge, I've decided. I'll accept the position. I have nothing to lose and everything to gain. Managing a boutique may not be my endgame, but I'll learn something about myself. And it may very well set me on the path toward discovering my passion.

SIX
SAVANNAH

A loud banging on the doors wakes me on Sunday morning. I roll over to look at the clock on my bedside table. How can it be nine o'clock already? For the first time in years, I didn't set my alarm. Why get up early on Sunday morning when I have nowhere to go? I no longer have a job. No bestie to meet for brunch. Nothing to show for the past thirty years spent in Fairhaven.

The persistent knocking jolts me out of bed and onto my feet. Slipping on my robe, I hurry to the door to find an irritated Bennie with his balled fist poised to knock again.

"Geez, Bennie. What's with the four-alarm fire?"

"Sorry for the intrusion." He brushes past me into the house. "I have a couple who wants to see the house again before making an offer."

I shake my head to free it of sleep cobwebs. "You mean now?"

"In ten minutes." He flicks his wrist, shooing me back to my bedroom. "Go! Throw on some clothes. Make your bed. Do whatever you need to do. But hurry."

I glare at him, dumbfounded. "Seriously, Bennie? You're pissing me off right now."

"I realize I'm inconveniencing you. I promise the couple won't be long. You can wait at the coffee shop down the street. Please, Savannah. These people are serious buyers."

"Ugh." I stomp my bare foot on the hardwood floor. "Okay. Give me five minutes."

Retreating to my bedroom, I slip on exercise clothes and quickly make my bed. I'm brushing my teeth when Bennie knocks on the door. "Are you ready? They're here."

"I'm coming already. Can't a girl brush her teeth?" Leaving my bedroom, I grab my purse from the kitchen and slip out the back door as the potential buyers enter the house through the front.

I race-walk two blocks to Cascade Brew and order a large black coffee. The cafe is crowded, but I get lucky and snag a small table on the sidewalk. Sipping the strong coffee, I consider my dilemma. My time is running out. If these buyers don't make an offer, someone else soon will. Fairhaven has been my home for the past thirty years. Why would I leave? My life is here, however pathetic that life is.

Pulling out my phone, I locate Gina Fleming's contact information on the Fir and Tide website and email her inquiring about a potential job. I don't expect to hear back from her on a Sunday, but she responds immediately, inviting me for an interview at two o'clock this afternoon. Inhaling a deep breath, I confirm the appointment and access the website for Pacific Towers, my favorite of the three apartment buildings I've toured. I'm scrolling through their available units when a flushed and winded Bennie plops down in the chair opposite me.

I set down my phone. "Well? How did it go?"

"They made me an offer I can't refuse." He takes in a deep breath and exhales it slowly. "There's only one problem. They want to close right away. They need to have some work done before school starts for their two young children in August."

"I'm afraid to ask. How soon is right away?"

"They want to get in by the end of next week. I'll grant them early access, and we'll close at the end of the month."

My jaw hits the table. "But I haven't found an apartment yet. And my boss informed me last night that he's closing The Lantern, so I no longer have a job. I realize that's not your problem, but . . ." I bury my face in my hands. "This is a nightmare."

"You don't have to cooperate since I'm breaking our lease. But I'll make it worth your while if you do. I'll reimburse you for this month's rent and throw in an extra month for good measure. I have a spare room. You can live with me until you find something. I'll borrow a friend's truck and help you move. This is a terrific offer, Savannah. I can't turn these people away."

First Doug and now Bennie. Everyone is so eager to get rid of me, they are paying me off. But I can see how much this means to him. If he's this desperate for money, who am I to stand in his way?

"I understand, Bennie. And I'm willing to cooperate. If I haven't found an apartment by Friday, I may have to take you up on your offer of a spare room."

He extends a hand across the table. "Deal. Thank you, Savannah. This means a lot."

An uneasy feeling settles over me. Life as I know it is officially over. I can either sink or swim. I say a silent prayer Gina throws me a life raft.

After leaving the coffee shop, I go for a long walk before returning home to shower and dress for my meeting. I can't help but be nervous. Despite being overly qualified for the position, I haven't been on a job interview in thirty years, and there's nowhere else in town I want to work. If I don't get this job, I don't know what I'll do.

I spend extra time on my appearance. After a steamy shower, I tame my golden curls into a wavy mane and search my wardrobe for professional attire. I settle on a short-sleeved black-knit swing dress and black ballet flats.

Even though the brunch rush has ended, a large crowd lingers at Fir and Tide. A hostess escorts me through the bustling kitchen to the manager's well-appointed office that features two-way mirrors looking out over the kitchen and dining area.

Gina enters the room in a cloud of intoxicating perfume, the fresh scent of roses reminding me of my childhood at Marsh Point. She's stylishly dressed in head-to-toe white linen, a poor choice for working in a restaurant. She must not be a hands-on kind of manager.

Instead of going behind her desk, Gina takes the chair beside me. "First of all, let me say how sorry I am about The Lantern's closing. Doug and Margaret are good people, and I hate to see them leave town." She sits tall, crossing her trim, long legs. "But their loss is our gain, and I'm thrilled at the prospect of having you work for us. I understand you're the Pacific Northwest's premier expert on artisan cocktails. Our signature beverage menu needs some work. You would have full creative control."

I perk up. This might not be such a bad gig after all. "I'm intrigued."

"And I'm curious. How does someone who doesn't drink become a mixology master?"

I'm impressed. If Gina knows this little detail about me, she's done her homework. "I'm not a teetotaler, Gina. My mother was an alcoholic. I taste. I don't indulge."

"I didn't mean to offend you, Savannah. In your line of work, I can see where someone could easily become an alcoholic. I can also see where being a recovered alcoholic bartender could be problematic."

"I've never had a drinking problem. I don't plan to start now."

"Good." Gina opens an iPad on her lap. "Now that we've got that settled, let me tell you more about the job." She then launches into a discussion of shifts, salaries, and personal time off.

While the position sounds ideal to me, there is little room for upward mobility. Josh Hardy, the current head bartender, is originally from Fairhaven and has a young family to support. He's not going anywhere anytime soon.

"Will I have an opportunity to perform?"

The puzzlement that crosses Gina's face is short-lived. "Oh, right. You're a singer. Our entertainment is booked out for months, but we can probably arrange for you to open for a main act on an off night."

While this is the answer I expected, it's not the one I had hoped for.

Gina gives me a dazzling smile. "Well? What do you think? Are you interested?"

"Honestly, I'm not sure."

Her smile fades. "Are you considering offers from other establishments?"

"No. *If* I stay in Fairhaven, Fir and Tide is the only place I'd like to work. I'm considering going home to South Carolina to visit my family." I'm surprised when the words spill from my lips. Am I actually considering returning to the Lowcountry?

"I see," Gina says in a disappointed tone. "Well, think about it. Let me know if you have any questions."

"I will." I stand to go. "Thanks for taking the time to meet with me. I appreciate the offer, and I'll let you know one way or another in a couple of days."

ON MONDAY MORNING, I take a second tour of the available apartments in my first-choice building. But a nagging doubt prevents me from placing a one-bedroom unit—the only one I can afford—on a twenty-four-hour hold. Living in a high-rise doesn't excite me. And nothing is charming about the white walls and beige carpet. A single sliding glass door leading to a tiny balcony provides the only access to fresh air. I will miss watching the sunset over Bellingham Bay from my porch, even if my current view is only a glimpse.

I spend the afternoon sorting through my possessions, making one large pile to donate to charity and another to take to the dump.

That evening, to dispel lingering doubts about accepting the job at Fir and Tide, I decide to experience the upscale restaurant as a customer. I change into a black halter top with white jeans and walk the short distance to the restaurant. While there is a forty-five-minute wait for a table, the bar is first come, first served. And I don't have to wait long for the customer at the end nearest the dance floor to vacate his stool.

Memories flood me as the young female bartender hustles to fill multiple orders simultaneously. I was once that efficient at the height of my career when The Lantern was the most popular hangout in Fairhaven. Just watching the bartender now exhausts me. I'm pushing fifty. Am I too old for such physical labor? Maybe I should look for a restaurant with a slower pace.

When the bartender finally notices me, she tosses a cocktail napkin like a Frisbee on the bar in front of me. "What can I get you?"

"I'd like a mocktail. Do you have a recommendation?"

"Caribbean Sunrise is my favorite," she says, pulling a glass from the shelf without waiting for me to approve her suggestion. She dumps a scoop of ice in the glass, then fills it with bright orange liquid from a store-and-pour container.

She slides the glass across the bar to me. "Would you like to order dinner?"

"Sure." Glancing at the menu, I say, "I'll have the kale salad."

I take a tentative sip of the drink and pucker my lips at the syrupy sweetness. I just paid fifteen bucks for a mixture of orange and pineapple juices. Gina was right. They definitely need to revamp their cocktail menu.

The kale salad is delicious, though, and I dig in. An exotic woman serenades the audience with her astonishing vocals as I eat. She's approximately the same age as the bartender. Both are around thirty, as are all the other servers and hostesses in sight. I'm too old to work here, and my dream of becoming a singing star died when I ran away from home.

I pay my tab and leave the restaurant feeling certain this job isn't for me. As I head toward home, I have a creepy feeling someone is following me, but when I turn around, no one is there. I dismiss the uneasiness. My uncertain future has me on edge.

I stroll down the quaint, familiar streets. I will miss charming Fairhaven, but I try to look on the bright side. I'm not broke or destitute. However, come Friday, I will be homeless. I have a long bucket list of cities and towns in the country I'd like to visit. I'll pack up my belongings and embark on an adventure. I'll establish new roots if I discover a place that feels like home. If not, I'll continue to South Carolina. I don't have to stay in the Lowcountry forever. Just long enough to catch up with my family and determine my next steps.

SEVEN
HARPER

I can hardly wait to tell Mollie I've decided to accept the management position. But her response is less than enthusiastic when I arrive at the shop on Tuesday morning. "Now, all we have to do is convince Will."

I stop dead in my tracks, just inside the door. "But I thought you said he wouldn't be a problem."

"He just needs to get to know you better." Mollie pulls out her phone. "I'll text him now to tell him you're definitely interested in the job," she says, her thumbs flying across her phone's screen.

I continue through the store to the checkout area, dumping my purse and lunch box on the counter. Mollie joins me at the counter a minute later. "He texted back already. He wants to interview you, but he's tied up with projects until Friday."

My jaw goes slack. "He wants to *interview* me? You might as well start looking for someone else. When Will grills me, he'll realize I have zero retail experience and know nothing about running a women's boutique."

"No worries. We have three days. By the time I'm finished prepping you, you'll be an expert."

I sweep an arm at the racks of sale items. "How do you plan to do that during our clearance sale?"

"We'll make the time. There's honestly not that much to know." Her phone pings, and she reads the text out loud. "He just confirmed the appointment. You're all set for Friday afternoon at three."

"I hope you know what you're doing," I say skeptically.

"Trust me, Harper. Everything will work out fine."

Pocketing her phone, Mollie strides to the front of the shop and unlocks the door for the stream of customers lined up for first dibs on clearance items.

For the next three days, Mollie uses every spare moment to instruct me on quarterly buying trips to the Atlanta market, inventory management, and finances—ensuring secure credit card transactions, making bank deposits, reconciling daily sales, and handling the cash register.

I'm a nervous wreck come Friday morning. I spill coffee on the checkout counter, and as I'm wiping it up, Mollie places a hand on my arm. "Calm down, Harper. You're going to do great. Will is an easygoing guy. Just be yourself. You have loads of wonderful ideas. Tell him your plans for rearranging the merchandise, sprucing up the shop, and implementing social media marketing. He'll be impressed."

"Ideas can't make up for lack of experience, Mollie."

"Well, the clearance sale was your brilliant idea." She gestures at the nearly empty racks. "And we've gotten rid of almost all the old merchandise."

I expel a deep breath of air. "I wish I had your confidence."

We're slammed with customers all morning, and staying busy takes the edge off my nerves. I tell myself it's not the end of the world if I don't get the promotion. I'll continue as sales assistant under the new manager that Will hires. But I need the job. It's my excuse for staying in Water's Edge until I connect with my birth mother.

Mollie has taken a late lunch at two o'clock when Will's sister Carrie enters the shop. I rush to the front to greet her. I'd texted her earlier in the week about the sale and was disappointed when she never responded.

"Hey, Carrie! Welcome to Tracy's Threads. I was hoping you got my message about the sale."

"I got it. Honestly, I hadn't planned to come. But on a whim, I decided to stop in on my way to the grocery store." She pauses to check the price of a pink silk top. "Now I wish I hadn't. Even on sale, I'm not sure I can afford these prices."

"Don't worry. We have prices for every budget. That particular blouse is new merchandise anyway. And it's on the upper end of our price spectrum." Taking her by the elbow, I lead her to the sale racks. Eying her pear-shaped figure, I assess her size and pull several summer dresses for her to try. "What do you think of these?"

Carrie's upper lip twitches. "Not my style."

I'm not sure this woman even knows her style. "Just try them on for fun. You might decide you like them." When she hesitates, I get the impression she's embarrassed. "Don't be shy, Carrie. Mollie has gone to lunch, and we're the only ones here." I grab another armful of clothes and usher her to the dressing rooms.

Carrie casts a wistful glance at the front door. "Maybe I'll come back another time."

"Don't do that. You're already here." I gently prod her inside. "Let me know if you find something you like or need another size."

While she's in the dressing room, I buzz about the shop, tidying things up in preparation for Will's visit.

Carrie is quiet for so long that I start to worry about her. "Are you okay in there, Carrie? Do you need anything?"

She holds back the curtain and steps tentatively out of the dressing room. "This is nice."

I spin her around, admiring the periwinkle dress with capped sleeves and A-line skirt. "It's way better than nice. The dress fits you perfectly. You look lovely."

"How much is it?" she asks.

I peek at the price on the tag dangling from the dress's label. Her face falls when I tell her the amount, and I quickly add, "But we can take an extra ten percent off."

"Are you sure?"

I smile. "I'm positive." As manager-in-training, Mollie has given me the authority to make further reductions to make a sale.

Moving to the three-way mirror, she tilts her head one way and another as she studies her reflection. "I wonder what my husband will think. I hope he's not mad at me for blowing our budget."

I join her in front of the mirror. "When he sees you in this dress, his eyes will pop out of his head. And it sounds like you're long overdue a little pampering."

I watch Carrie fidget with the dress's neckline and twist her honey hair into a knot. The other Darby sister, Ashton, the architect, seems more self-assured and assertive—more like me. Then again, I had a powerhouse attorney as a role model. Victoria carried herself with confidence and dignity. She had the respect of everyone she knew, and she never backed down from conflict.

Carrie turns away from the mirror. "You're right, Harper. I'm tired of pinching pennies. A woman is allowed to splurge a little now and then."

I clap my hands together. "That's the spirit."

Returning to the dressing room, Carrie tries on a half dozen other outfits before deciding on three.

As I'm processing the credit card charge, Carrie asks, "How long will the sale last? I want to bring my daughter in to shop for college."

"Until everything is gone. But I wouldn't wait. As you can see, things are flying out the door," I say, gesturing at the dwindling sales racks.

She scribbles her name on the charge form. "Then we'll come back in the morning. Will you be here?"

"Sure thing! I can't wait to meet your daughter. Maybe we can grab lunch together after you shop. I'd love to talk to her about Chapel Hill," I say, handing her the brown paper shopping bag.

"That would mean a lot to Sarah. She won't admit it, but attending such a big school intimidates her. Especially being from such a small town."

Will enters the store as Carrie is leaving. He appears surprised to see her. "Hey, sis. I didn't know you shopped at Tracy's."

"I don't usually." Carrie holds up the shopping bag. "But Harper texted me about the sale, and she's an excellent salesperson. You should give her a raise." Carrie waves at me one final time. "I'll see you tomorrow, Harper."

Will watches his sister drive away in her minivan before turning to me. "My sister is a tough nut, and you get bonus points for making her crack a smile."

"Why do you think she's a tough nut? She seems pleasant enough to me."

Will shrugs. "Maybe she only hates her family."

I wonder if Carrie will hate me too when she finds out I'm family. Since I'm pretty sure I'm not her daughter, I must be her niece, which makes Ashton my birth mother. Maybe I can use Carrie to get to know Ashton better.

Will and I are still standing by the front door when Mollie bustles in. "I'm sorry I'm late. I meant to be back in time for your interview at three, but I got tied up on the phone with my mom about this wedding. I've only been engaged a few days, and she's already driving me up the wall. I'll hold down the fort while you two talk." She herds us to the back of the store. "Why don't you go into the stockroom for privacy?"

Will extends an arm toward the stockroom. "After you," he says and follows me inside, sitting behind the desk with me opposite him.

"I'm sorry it's so crowded in here," I say about the boxes stacked high around us. "We're waiting until the sale ends before putting out the new merchandise."

"No worries." He leans back in the chair. "So, tell me about yourself, Harper. Why should I promote you to the manager position?"

"I'll be honest with you, I don't have any retail experience. I've worked as a paralegal since graduating college. I always assumed I'd go to law school. I just never got around to it. It was more my mom's dream than mine."

"What does your mom think about you working here?"

"She would roll over in her grave," I say in a deadpan tone.

Will's expression softens. "I'm sorry, Harper. Mollie didn't tell me about your mother. I know a little about what you must be feeling. I lost my first wife in a boating accident last summer. I assume you already know that since this was her boutique."

"I do. And I'm sorry about Tracy." I sit back in the chair and cross my legs. "My mom died suddenly in early April from a brain aneurysm. I didn't realize until after she was gone how much I'd been living my life to please her." I squirm beneath the intense scrutiny of his piercing blue eyes as I relate my fabricated tale of how I ended up working here. But he seems to buy my explanation.

"Good for you for trying something new. Mollie tells me you have ideas for improving the shop."

"I have a few," I say, and outline my ideas for sprucing up the storefront and updating the brand.

"How much will this cost me?" he asks, a smirk tugging at his lip.

"If I do the work myself, only the price of a bucket of paint and roller brushes. As for the new brand, I took a few graphic design classes in college, and I have some ideas for a logo."

"Wonderful. I appreciate your enthusiasm and resourcefulness.

I'm a building contractor. Give me a shout if you need help with anything."

I jump to my feet. "Does this mean I've got the job?"

He pushes back from the desk. "It's all yours. You'll need to start looking for an assistant right away."

I bounce on my toes. "Thank you so much for giving me this opportunity. I promise I won't let you down."

Will comes around the desk and claps me on the shoulder. "Congratulations, Harper. I have faith in you." He starts toward the door and turns back around. "Oh. I almost forgot. Julia wants to know if you can babysit next Thursday night. I told her I'd ask, but I'm sure you have things you'd rather be doing than babysitting."

"Actually, I'd love to. I haven't been in town long enough to develop a social life."

He wags his finger at me. "You need to remedy that. A pretty girl like you will have her choice of young men."

My cheeks burn. "That's nice of you to say, but I'm not in the market for romance." What I don't say is, *I'm searching for family.*

EIGHT
SAVANNAH

Doug and Margaret invite me to their house for a farewell dinner on Thursday night. We reminisce for hours about the wonderful times we've shared. It's almost midnight when I bid them a tearful goodbye and promise to visit them in the Florida Keys as soon as they get settled.

Before daybreak on Friday morning, I load my clothes and a few cherished household items into my Land Rover and leave Fairhaven for the last time. I bought the SUV new in 2001, but I've put less than fifty thousand miles on it. I serviced the engine and replaced the dry-rotted tires to prepare for my trip. With luck, she'll get me where I'm going, wherever that may be.

Except for Montana and Maine, most of my bucket list destinations are in the southern part of the country, which made planning my itinerary easy. Because I've been to Oregon and the wine country countless times, I drive straight through to Carmel, only stopping for food and gas. I fall instantly in love with Big Sur, but unfortunately, the cost of living in California is too high.

The Grand Canyon profoundly moves me. As I look out over the vast, rugged terrain, I have a spiritual reckoning, as though a higher being is promising a new life for me somewhere.

As I continue to Santa Fe, I sense a magnetic pull to the East Coast. My heart knows I'm headed to the Lowcountry, even though I haven't yet wrapped my mind around the idea of going home after thirty years.

During the long stretches of driving, I think about my childhood. The memories are dim, most tainted by my parents' neglect and abuse. But the closeness I shared with my siblings envelops me like a cocoon, urging me onward. Do my brothers and sisters resent me for running out on them, for leaving them to cope with our dysfunctional parents? Will they accept me back into the fold? Or will they turn me away at the door like the stranger I am?

After spending the night in Santa Fe, I continue to Texas, stopping in San Antonio and Houston to eat lunch and stretch my legs. I'm eager to get to New Orleans, and when I arrive, I'm charmed by the historic French Quarter. Various jobs are available in most renowned establishments, but I don't feel safe in the city. When did our country become so crime-ridden? I've had my head in the sand, living a sheltered life in the Pacific Northwest.

After spending only one night in New Orleans, I head to Nashville early the following day. Arriving around three o'clock, I check into the Renaissance Hotel and take off on foot to explore Lower Broadway. All my life, I've wanted to visit Honky Tonk Highway, and I can hardly believe I'm here. The bars aren't as crowded in the afternoon as at night, but the music is as vibrant. I wander from place to place, hitting the major players like Tootsies Orchid Lounge, Redneck Riviera, and Kid Rock's Big Honky Tonk. I peruse the memorabilia adorning the walls and generously tip the live entertainment.

Around eight o'clock, when I grow tired and hungry, I choose a smaller, less popular Western-style saloon to rest my legs and eat dinner. The tables are empty, and only a few people are seated at the bar listening to a female vocalist belt out Reba McEntire tunes.

"She's outstanding," I comment to the bartender about the female vocalist.

Nodding, the bartender's white-blonde bun dances around on top of her head. "She's amazing. Then again, you have to be to get a gig in Nashville, even in a small place like the Rustic Ranch. What can I get you to drink?"

I glance down at the drink's menu and back up at her. "I don't suppose you have a cup of hot tea?"

Her red lips part in a broad smile. "I could use a cup of tea myself. Let me see if I can locate a couple of teabags."

She disappears behind swinging saloon doors and returns five minutes later with two mugs of steaming water, the tea bag tags dangling over the sides. "I hope you like chamomile. It's all I could find."

"Chamomile is perfect." I bounce the bag in the water several times before setting it in the saucer beside the cup.

"Is this your first trip to Nashville?"

"Why? Do I look like an amateur?"

She laughs out loud. "Maybe a little. Welcome to Nashville. I'm Wynonna. And before you ask, I was *not* named after Wynonna Judd."

In my estimation, the woman is in her late fifties, about the same age as Wynonna Judd. "You're too young to be named after her."

Her green eyes light up. "Exactly. Most people I meet don't realize that. You know your country music stars."

I hold my hands wide. "What can I say? I'm a wannabe like everyone else."

She narrows her green eyes. "Something tells me you can sing better than most wannabes who come in here."

I give my shoulder a casual shrug. "I can hold my own on karaoke night. I'm Savannah, by the way. I'm also a bartender. Or I was back in Fairhaven."

"Nice to meet you, Savannah. Where is Fairhaven?"

"In the Pacific Northwest. It's the historic district, a neighbor-hood really, of Bellingham."

Wynonna gives her head a slow shake. "Never heard of it. Can I get you some dinner? We're known for our burgers." She hands me a menu. "The blue cheeseburger is my personal favorite, but the Cowboy Burger is our most popular."

I read the description for the Cowboy Burger. Grass-fed ground beef mixed with barbeque sauce and topped with melted cheese and crispy fried onion rings on a pretzel bun. "The Cowboy Burger sounds like a mouthful." I look up from the menu. "I'll take your suggestion and have the blue cheeseburger."

"Excellent choice." Taking the menu, she disappears into the back and returns with a small plate of chips and guacamole. "On the house. We're known for our guacamole."

I sink a chip into the dip and stuff it in my mouth. "I can see why. This is delicious."

Wynonna props a hip against the counter and folds her arms. "What're you doing in Nashville? Are you here for an audition?"

I laugh. "I'm flattered, but I'm way too old for auditions. I'm actually on my way home to visit my family in South Carolina."

"Are you moving back home or just visiting?" Her hand shoots out. "You don't have to answer that. I'm being nosy. But I'm a good listener. Something tells me you need to talk."

"Because everyone who eats dinner alone at a bar needs to talk." When she blushes, I add, "I'm a bartender, remember? I know the drill." I drag another chip through the guacamole. "The truth is, I've been estranged from my family for a very long time. I'm not sure I'll even be welcome."

"I bet they'll be thrilled to see you," she says with a sympathetic smile.

"How long I stay depends on whether or not I can find a job. You're about the same age as me," I say, even though she's at least ten years older than me. "Do you think we're too old to be bartending?"

"I'm actually the manager. I'm filling in for my regular bartender, who is out sick. But to answer your question, a lot depends on the individual. The job can be physically taxing, but some people thrive on that, regardless of age."

The sound of someone calling Wynonna's name comes from beyond the saloon doors, and she retrieves my burger from the kitchen. I remove the bun and examine the burger's toppings—grilled onions, semi-melted blue cheese, lettuce, and tomato.

"This looks delicious." I take a bite and moan my approval. "Amazing."

"I'm glad you like it." Wynona moves to the other end of the bar to refill a customer's beer. When she returns, she asks, "So, how long have you been bartending?"

"Thirty years," I say, dipping a french fry in a puddle of ketchup.

Her eyes widen. "At the same place."

"Yep. Mariner's Lantern, known by locals as The Lantern." I point a french fry at her. "And therein lies my problem. Thirty years of hard work and dedication with nothing to show for it except one measly listing on my resume. I can mix a mean drink, but so can practically everyone else."

Wynonna rears her head back in shocked disbelief. "That is definitely *not* true. I've interviewed plenty of bartenders who claim to be mixology specialists, but their drinks are so bad I wouldn't serve them to my drunkest customers."

I laugh out loud. "That's bad. Some of my drunk customers would drink turpentine if I served it to them," I say, which leads to a brief conversation about our most unruly customers.

My shoulders sag as I turn my attention back to my burger. "Whether I like it or not, I'm stuck being a bartender. I've only worked this one job. I have no other skills."

"You're looking at it all wrong, Savannah. Over thirty years, surely you did more than tend bar."

"True. I've waited tables. I cooked for a few days when our chef was out with the flu. And whenever the owners went on vacation, they left me in charge."

"See! You can put all of the above on your resume. Maybe you should consider looking for a management position."

I hesitate while I consider this. "Who knows? Maybe I will."

"I have a feeling you'd make an excellent manager. If you're like me, you would appreciate only having to answer to the owners. I get to do a little of everything, but mostly, I make sure things run smoothly," she says and excuses herself to check on her other customers.

I think about her suggestion while I finish eating. I may look for a management position. I'm not limited to the food service industry, but I enjoy establishments with frequent repeat customers, like The Lantern and The Turtle's Nest in Water's Edge. I wonder if The Nest is still open.

Curious to see how much Water's Edge has changed in my absence, I gobble down the rest of my burger and summon Wynonna for my tab. I thank her for her advice and walk back to my hotel. I want to get a good night's sleep ahead of my big day tomorrow. After thirty years, I'm finally going home.

NINE
HARPER

Carrie's daughter, Sarah, is gorgeous with baby blue eyes, a pert nose, and a tight body the college boys will swoon over. She's dazzling in every garment she tries on, from cutoff shorts to cocktail dresses, but respecting her mother's tight budget, she shops wisely, only picking a few versatile pieces.

Mollie minds the shop while I sneak away with mother and daughter for a quick lunch at Custom Crust. Seated at a table on the small patio, I tell Sarah about my experiences at Chapel Hill. Her bubbly personality is infectious, and despite her concerns about rush, I have no doubt she'll be invited into the sorority of her choice. Despite the twelve years separating us in age, I feel a special bond with this young woman. She doesn't know it yet, but she is either my half sister or my cousin. I'm betting my money on cousin.

When we part in front of the cafe afterwards, Sarah and I promise to keep in touch and have lunch again before she leaves for college in early August. As I walk back to the boutique, I wonder if I will have learned my birth mother's identity by then.

When business is slow on Saturday afternoon, we close an hour early so Mollie can head off overnight to Charleston with her fiancé, and I can begin preparing the shop for painting on Sunday. After a trip to Coastal Hardware for paint and supplies, I spend several hours removing the clothes from the wall racks, piling them on every available surface, and draping them with old sheets to protect them from paint splatters.

It's almost nine o'clock by the time I get home. I feel like a loser staying home alone on a Saturday night. So, with little to eat in my refrigerator, I decide to treat myself to a seafood dinner. Although Clam and Claw is packed, I score a seat at the bar. I order hush-puppies, steamed shrimp, and a glass of sauvignon blanc. But I feel even more lonely surrounded by couples and groups of friends chatting and laughing. Scarfing down my food, I pay my tab and leave.

Outside in the sultry night air, I'm greeted by loud funk music from The Turtle's Nest next door. On a whim, I go in for an after-dinner drink. How can I make new friends if I don't venture outside my comfort zone? The tavern is standing-room only. As I fight to the bar, no one notices or cares that I'm flying solo.

I order an expresso martini and watch the activity on the dance floor. When I sense a presence to my left, I glance sideways at the young man with an innocent face and rosy cheeks.

"You're new in town," he says loud enough to be heard over the music.

"How did you know?" I palm my forehead. "Duh. I forgot everyone knows everyone else in this town."

His pale blue eyes twinkle with mischief. "You're exaggerating. Five thousand people live in Water's Edge. It's impossible to know everyone. Unless, of course, you're a police officer like me. I've pulled nearly every citizen old enough to have a license for speeding down Main Street at least once."

I angle my body toward him. "Wow! Who knew Water's Edge had such a speeding problem?"

"A very serious problem. Someone is going to get killed one of these days."

"But not under your watch," I say with a smirk.

He puffs out his chest. "Not if I can help it."

"Then it's good that I live and work on Main Street. Since I walk everywhere, I don't have to worry about getting a speeding ticket."

He wags his finger at me. "Just make sure you don't drive too fast on the way to the grocery store."

When another song comes on the jukebox, he takes my empty glass and sets it down on a nearby table. "Dance with me," he says, leading me onto the dance floor before I can object.

He's an excellent dancer, light on his feet as he swings me around until I'm giddy and dizzy. When the music transitions to a slow song, he pulls me into his arms and presses his lips to mine. His feathery kiss sends a jolt of longing down my legs to my feet, curling my toes.

The kiss ends, but his lips remain near mine. "I've never kissed a total stranger before. But I couldn't help myself. I've wanted to do that since I first saw you."

"We haven't officially met yet." Pushing him away, I extend my hand. "I'm Harper Boone."

"And I'm Cody Porter. Now that it's official—"

A louder song comes on, drowning him out.

I tap my finger on my ear. "I can't hear you."

Taking me by the hand, he leads me away from the dance floor. Cupping his hands, he leans over and yells in my ear. "Will you go on a picnic with me tomorrow?"

I shake my head. "I'm sorry, I can't. I'm remodeling the showroom where I work."

"Cool! And where do you work?"

"At Tracy's Threads. I'm taking over as manager when Mollie leaves."

He gives a curt nod of understanding. "Right. I heard she's getting married."

I gesture at the door. "I should go. I have an early start tomorrow. I hope I see you around sometime."

He winks at me. "I'll make sure of it."

———

I'm pleased with the colors I've selected for the store's new brand. The pale taupe for the main walls and dusty rose for the alcoves that house the clothing racks are both soft and sophisticated. I set to work before eight on Sunday morning. I've nearly finished one main wall around ten when there's a knock on the front door. Setting down my roller, I hurry to the front, surprised to see Cody peering at me through the glass.

I crack the door open. "What're you doing here?"

"I figured you might need some help, so I brought the picnic to you." He holds up two shopping bags, one from Coastal Hardware and the other from Fancy Pantry. "I grabbed some sandwiches and picked up an extra roller and paint pan."

I look down at the bags and back up at him. "That's incredibly thoughtful. Are you sure you want to spend your Sunday painting?"

"Positive. I'm a home improvement kind of guy."

I open the door wider and step out of his way. "In that case, come on in." As I follow him into the shop, I update him on my progress. "You have your choice. You can pick up where I left off on the main walls or begin work on the nooks."

"Hmm . . .," he says, then purses his lips. "I'll continue with the main walls," he says as he hands me the bag with the extra supplies.

We work close together at the back of the store, chatting while we paint. When he asks how I came to live in Water's Edge, I repeat my white lie about detouring through town for coffee on my way to Hilton Head on vacation.

"Wow. That was bold of you to make such a spontaneous move," he says, dragging his paint roller down the wall.

"Not really. I've been yearning for a lifestyle change for some time. The opportunity fell into my lap, and I was in an adventurous mood." I tell him about my previous career as a paralegal and my mother's recent death.

"I'm sorry about your mom. Is your father still alive?"

"Nope. He died from cancer when I was a little girl."

"Mine too. I was ten when my dad was killed." He pours more paint into the pan. "He's the reason I became a police officer."

"Really? How so?"

"He was the victim of a random bank robbery."

My head jerks up. "That's awful. What happened?"

"He was a loan officer at Palmetto Bank at the time. A gang of robbers entered the bank and took hostages. My father was a hero. He saved several lives, but he was shot in the process. We have very little crime in Water's Edge. That's one of the worst things that's ever happened here. But I consider it my duty to maintain law and order. That's why I make it a point to know everyone who lives here personally."

"I feel safer knowing you're looking out for us," I say and laugh out loud. "OMG! What a cringy thing to say."

"I was flattered," he says with a chuckle. "Do you have any siblings?"

Good question, I think, but I tell him I'm an only child. "And now I'm an orphan. What about you? Do you have brothers and sisters?"

"I have an older sister and a much younger half sister. My mother remarried a few years after my father's death. My stepfather, Ken, is a good man. He's been an excellent surrogate dad to me."

"I'm glad for you."

We work for a while in silence, each of us lost in our thoughts. I wonder what my life would've been like if I'd had a stepfather. I never knew Victoria to even go on a date with another man. She was happily married to her work. I relish the idea of having a father figure in my life. Is my biological father still alive? Were he and my birth mother in love? Did he even know about me?

Around one o'clock, we break for lunch and spread Cody's picnic—turkey sandwiches, potato chips, and fresh fruit—out on the checkout counter.

"So, is there a special guy in your life?" Cody asks, sinking his teeth into a sandwich half.

I pop a handful of blueberries into my mouth. "I don't do relationships."

He wrinkles his nose. "What does that mean?"

"Commitment doesn't come easy to me. Don't ask me why. It's just the way I'm wired, I guess."

"Maybe you haven't found the right guy yet."

"Maybe." Eager to change the subject, I sweep an arm at the small section of unpainted wall. "We're on the homestretch. If not for you, I would've been here until midnight."

He lowers his gaze. "What about the floors?"

I look down at the worn hardwoods. "What about them? Refinishing them isn't in the budget."

"I understand. But you can revive them by buffing off the top layer of finish. You can rent a buffer at Coastal Hardware," he says, stuffing the last of his sandwich in his mouth.

I play-punch his arm. "How do you know so much about refinishing floors?"

"I've seen every episode of *This Old House*. Six months ago, I bought a small fixer-upper in the historic section of town. I enjoy working on projects."

"I'm impressed."

"Impressed enough to go on a date with me?" he asks, a smirk tugging at his lips.

I hesitate as I decide how to respond. "How about I buy you dinner to thank you for helping me paint?"

"I accept."

"It's not a date, Cody," I warn. "I'm not looking for anything but friendship."

"Friendship is a good place to start," he says, wadding up his sandwich wrapper and tossing it into the trash.

I laugh out loud. "Whatever." He can think what he wants, but I have no intention of getting romantically involved with him. I'll have to be careful though. I typically date jerks. It makes it easier when I dump them. Cody seems genuinely nice, and I wouldn't want him to get hurt.

Once the painting is complete, we rent a floor buffer from Coastal Hardware and spend a couple of hours cleaning and buffing the floors. We wrestle the pine wardrobe from the storage room to the back of the shop and load it up with folded knit tops and sweaters. After returning the clothes to the racks, we stand back to admire our work.

"It looks amazing," I say. "I can't wait for Will to see it."

Cody taps his chin as he inspects the showroom. "You need somewhere for your customers to sit. Especially if you have older women who can't stand for long periods. Here would be a good place for a couple of comfortable chairs," he says, gesturing to the space in front of the wardrobe.

"I have a pair of taupe suede chairs I brought from Raleigh that are too big for my apartment. I could bring those over. I drive a 4Runner. Maybe I could fit them one at a time."

"No worries. I have a pickup truck. I'll grab a friend one day after work and move them over for you."

"That would be great if you're sure you don't mind?"

He smiles down at me. "I don't mind a bit." I think he's going to kiss me again, and I'm disappointed when he doesn't.

TEN
SAVANNAH

M any of the original businesses occupy the same buildings on Main Street from when I was a little girl. But there are many new upscale boutiques and eateries as well. I'm curious about the changes on the waterfront, but I'm too eager to get home to take the time to drive by.

The moss-draped trees on Pelican's Way bring tears to my eyes, but when my childhood home comes into view, I stop at the head of the driveway as memories from my last night here come crashing back like waves pounding the sand. The ice storm, a rarity along the South Carolina coast. My mother's unforgivable betrayal. Driving away in my hand-me-down Toyota Camry with only a single backpack stuffed with clothes. I was in no shape, mentally or physically, to be behind the wheel that morning. I'd just given birth, and the roads were covered in ice. I drove to Birmingham, Alabama, checked into a roadside motel, and spent the next five days nursing my broken heart.

Sucking in an unsteady breath, I wipe my wet eyes and continue down the driveway. Two cars are parked in front of the house—a blue convertible sports car and a silver pickup truck— but no one answers when I ring the bell. Discovering the knob locked, I venture around the side of the house toward the marsh. When I hear my name, I stop dead in my tracks and press myself up against the side of the house.

"Savannah wasn't difficult to find, Ashton. Your previous investigator has been bleeding you dry all these years. You should sue him. You might be able to recover some of the fees you paid him."

"I'm not worried about the money, Carter. Where is my sister?"

My breath hitches, and I clamp my hand over my mouth. My sister has been looking for me. I'd assumed she'd forgotten all about me. Is the investigator that Carter is referring to the one who was following me that night after I left Fir and Tide?

"She's been living in Washington State in the popular historic district of Bellingham known as Fairhaven."

"Has she been there all this time?" Ashton asks.

"As best we can tell. Unfortunately, she's no longer there."

"What do you mean? Where did she go?" Ashton asks in dismay.

The man lets out an audible sigh. "My investigator had a break in another case he was working on. He was gone for a couple of days. When he returned to Fairhaven, Savannah had left town. He made some inquiries. Her landlord sold the house she was renting, and her boss at the tavern where she bartends had to close due to the economic downturn. We're tracking her down now. We think she may be heading this way."

"Really? That would be amazing."

Ashton's excitement makes me feel less guilty about my unexpected homecoming.

"My guy is hot on her trail," the man says. "I'll let you know what we find out."

My mind races as I consider my next move. When he leaves, the investigator will see my car with Washington State license plates. I should make my presence known now.

Pushing off the side of the house, I approach the veranda. "You can call off your search. I'm here."

Astonishment, followed closely by elation, crosses my sister's face, assuring me I did the right thing in coming home.

"Savannah? Is it really you?" With outstretched arms, Ashton comes down off the porch to greet me. "I don't believe it. You're here. And as beautiful as ever," she says, engulfing me in a hug.

As I inhale her scent, happy memories from my childhood flood me. As the oldest, Ashton was a mother to my siblings and me. She was the one I ran to when I fell off my bike and the one I cried out to when I woke from nightmares. We never would've survived childhood without her, and everything went south when she left for college. My life might've turned out differently if she'd stayed, but I don't blame her for escaping this house of horrors.

When I glance up at the veranda, the investigator has vanished, granting us privacy for our reunion.

"Let me look at you." When she holds me at arm's length, I see her cheeks are wet with tears. "You look amazing. Washington has been good to you. Are you home for a visit, or are you planning to stay?"

"That *is* a good question. Truth be told, I'm at a crossroads. My future is a blank slate. I figured I'd start by burying the hatchet with some ghosts in my closet."

"Well, you're welcome to stay here as long as you'd like. Marsh Point belongs to me now. Mama left it to me in her will." Ashton frowns. "Wait. Do you even know she died?"

I nod. "I keep up with you through Facebook. I know you recently renovated the house. I can't wait to see what you've done. The photographs from Will's wedding are part of the reason for my trip home."

"You know about us, but we know nothing about you." She loops her arm through mine. "I have so many questions, but I'll let you freshen up first. I'll help you bring in your stuff."

I get whiplash from looking back and forth as she leads me

down the center hallway, through the house, to the front door. The rooms are mostly the same, but the decor has changed dramatically. My sister has elegant tastes. She's chosen her furnishings with care. The fresh look will make being in this house more tolerable.

In the driveway, I say, "Don't freak out when you see my packed car. I promise I'm not moving in. As your investigator told you, I lost my home and my job in Washington."

Ashton's lips part in a broad smile. Aside from a few lines around her eyes, my sister hasn't changed much. "I'm sorry for you, but happy for me. Be forewarned, I will make it my mission to convince you to stay in Water's Edge."

"No promises, but I'm open to the possibility." From the back of my Land Rover, I remove a small rolling suitcase and a tote bag. Ashton takes the tote bag from me, and I wheel the suitcase back inside and up the sweeping staircase.

"When we renovated, I reconfigured the upstairs and added two more bedrooms," Ashton explains. "I converted my bedroom and the bath you and I used to share into a suite for me. We took the walls down to the studs, but I tried not to change too much in your room. I wanted you to feel at home if . . . when you came back."

We walk down the upstairs hallway and stop at the middle bedroom. From the doorway, the room looks like the day I left. The walls are the same sunny yellow, and the cherished patchwork quilt my grandmother made for me adorns the four-poster queen-size bed I slept in for the first seventeen years of my life. The only noticeable difference is the wooden shutters that have replaced the sheer curtains in the windows. I'm too choked up to tell my sister how deeply touched I am.

Ashton stands behind me, peering over my shoulder. "Your room shares a Jack and Jill bath with the one next door, but you can stay in the primary suite if you prefer. All traces of Mama are gone. You'll have your own bath and access to the second-floor veranda."

There's no way I'm going near that room, let alone sleep in it. "No, this is perfect. Thank you." Taking the tote from her, I enter the room and park my suitcase beside the bed.

Ashton lingers in the doorway. "My housekeeper, Mia, is a superb cook. She left a seafood au gratin casserole for dinner. I'll leave you to get settled. I'll be downstairs if you need anything."

Opening my suitcase on the bed, I move my hanging clothes to the closet and take my cosmetic bag to the bathroom. Stripping off my clothes, I step into the walk-in shower and relish the warm water, pounding my travel-weary muscles. As I wash my hair, I study the marble tile lining the floor and walls. My sister has an excellent eye for detail.

I dry my hair and dress in gray knee-length knit shorts and a matching top. Throwing open the wooden shutters, I stare out at the landscape. Low branches from a live oak in the back corner of the lot sprawl across the yard toward the small white sandy beach. I can almost see our wooden hull Chris-Craft tied to the dock with the American flag on the stern, flapping in the breeze. I learned to waterski behind that boat. Dad used to load us kids up on Sunday afternoons and go to town for ice cream. Our mother never joined us on these outings. She was usually sequestered in her room with a bottle of booze.

Leaving my room, as I hurry down the hall toward the steps, I imagine hearing my mother calling out from her bed for one of us kids to bring her the newspaper or a cup of coffee. Eileen's ghost lives on. She may be physically gone, but new walls and fresh paint have not rid this house of memories.

Closing the door to her room, I continue downstairs to the kitchen, where I find Ashton opening a bottle of champagne. "If ever there was a time to celebrate," she says, holding out a glass of bubbly to me.

I shake my head. "No thanks." But when Ashton's smile fades,

I take the glass from her. "I don't usually drink, but you're right. Our reunion is cause for celebration."

The smile returns to Ashton's face as she lifts her glass to mine. "Honestly, I don't drink much either. And neither does Will. For obvious reasons, we've always been careful not to overindulge."

"What about Carrie?" I ask, sipping the bubbly.

"I'm not sure. We're not close."

I lower my glass. "That surprises me. I figured with you both living in town, you'd spend a lot of time together."

Ashton leans against the counter, her arms folded over her chest and the wine flute dangling from her fingertips. "I stayed in Boston a few years after I got my degree. When I moved home, Carrie had grown bitter in my absence. She married a much older man and doesn't seem very happy. Mama leaving Marsh Point to me didn't help."

"What'd she leave Carrie?"

"Her silver tea service."

My skin prickles, and I rub my arm. "Ouch. And Will?"

"The boat slip at the end of the dock."

I shake my head in confusion. "I don't understand."

"I didn't either for a long time. Will kept his boat at the end of the dock but rarely came inside the house. He and Carrie rarely visited Mama."

"But Saint Ashton remained loyal to the bitter end."

Ashton winces at my snarky tone. "Someone had to. Mama knew I'd hired an investigator to look for you. She frequently asked if there had been any word on the investigation. Mama was well aware of the damage she caused our family. I believe she left the house in my care for all of us. Will and his girls lived here for a while after his wife's boating accident."

"Right. I read about that on your Facebook page. Where does he live now?"

Ashton gestures with her flute toward the front of the house. "Across the street. He bought and renovated the Sullivan property." Opening the refrigerator, she rummages around at the contents. "By the way, Mama left you her record collection. The boxes are in your closet."

I don't respond. I have no interest in anything that belonged to my mother, not even her extensive music collection, which includes rare titles from the sixties and seventies.

Ashton removes a block of packaged white cheese. "Are you hungry? Do you want some cheese and crackers?"

"I'd rather walk the property."

"Great idea!" Dropping the cheese back in the drawer, she closes the refrigerator and tops off her champagne. When she goes to pour more for me, I place my hand over the flute. "One glass is enough for me."

We exit the house through the french doors and cross the veranda to the lawn. As we stroll down the dock, Ashton says, "We have so much to discuss. Where do we start? Are you still singing?"

I hunch a shoulder nonchalantly. "I was. A few nights a week at the tavern where I work. I never published anything, but I'm still writing songs. Two of the boxes in my car are sheet music."

"I'd love to hear you sing again. Are you a waitress?"

"Bartender," I say.

Ashton cuts her eyes at me. "Interesting choice for someone who doesn't drink."

"When I first arrived in Fairhaven, Doug was the only one who would give me a job. I started bussing tables and worked myself up to waiting tables and then bartending. For thirty years, The Lantern was my home. Doug and Margaret were my family. And our customers were our guests. Most of our customers drank responsibly, but I had a few regulars who abused alcohol." I think of Donny and Glenn. "Watching them drink themselves to an early grave reminded me of Mama. Fortunately, I think I escaped the addictive gene."

Ashton doesn't respond, making me wonder if she's ever

suffered from addiction. "I'm sorry. I didn't mean to bring all that up."

"No worries. What happened to The Lantern? Why'd it close?"

"A glitzy new upscale hotspot across the street put them out of business."

"Oh. I'm sorry to hear that," Ashton says, lowering herself to the edge of the dock.

I sit down beside her with my feet hanging over the side. The years slip away, and we are teenagers again, talking about boys and sharing secrets. I tell my sister about the men I've dated but never wanted to marry, and she speaks about her failed marriage and the current love in her life. I remember Sully from high school. He was one of Ashton's two closest friends, but her dreamy expression tells me she now feels more than friendship for him. Good for her. I'm glad she found happiness.

I summon the nerve to ask her the one question I most want an answer for. "Did you not want children, or were you unable to have them?"

"I raised my children early," Ashton says, meaning my siblings and me. "Will's daughters, although technically my nieces, are like my grandchildren."

Dusk has fallen by the time we mosey back up to the house. Over dinner, she describes in detail some of the million-dollar homes she's designed. She's proud of her work, as she should be.

Afterwards, we settle into the rockers with mugs of lavender tea, and it's nearly midnight when Ashton stands and stretches. "We should get some sleep. Unfortunately, I have a busy day tomorrow. Will you be okay here by yourself?"

I wave off her concern. "I'll be fine. I'm exhausted from my trip. I'll probably sleep until noon."

She pulls me to my feet and draws me in for a hug. "I still can't believe you're home. I can't wait to tell the rest of the family. They will be thrilled. Would you like me to invite everyone over for dinner tomorrow?"

I bark out an emphatic *No* and immediately apologize. "It's not that I don't want to see them, but I'm feeling a little overwhelmed, and I'd like to ease into the situation."

"You know what's best for you, Savannah. But I wouldn't wait too long. With them living across the street, Will and his family are always in and out of here. And we share a housekeeper. Mia works for Will on Thursdays, but she'll be here Friday morning."

"I understand. Just give me tomorrow to settle in. Meeting with them one-on-one might be best."

After locking up the house, Ashton and I climb the stairs together like we did countless times in our youth. As we pass by my mother's room, I tell myself she's dead and can no longer hurt me. But an eerie feeling overcomes me as I hug my sister goodnight and retire to my room.

ELEVEN
HARPER

I'm disappointed when I don't hear from Cody on Monday or Tuesday. Even worse, I'm angry at myself for feeling let down. I can't afford the distraction of a love interest right now. I need to focus on my new job and finding my birth mother. But thoughts of him keep creeping into my mind, and I'm more excited than I should be when a text from him pops up on my phone's screen on Wednesday afternoon.

I snatch up the phone and read his message. *Are you free after work? I found someone to help move your chairs.*

Great! I'll meet you at my apartment at six fifteen. I text and drop a pin with the address of my apartment building.

Cody and his muscular coworker Chad are waiting when I arrive in the parking lot behind my building. They move the chairs from my apartment to Tracy's Threads in no time.

"You guys are the best," I say as I admire the new additions to the shop. "Can I treat you to dinner at The Nest to repay you? I already owe Cody for helping me paint." Taking them both to dinner would spare me from being alone with Cody. Not that I don't *want* to be alone with Cody. I'm *afraid* to be alone with him.

Cody's arm shoots up. "I'm in." But Chad shakes his head. "Thanks, but I need to get home to my wife."

Cody sends an elbow to Chad's ribs. "That works in my favor. I'm hungry enough to eat two dinners."

I roll my eyes at Chad. "Something tells me I'm going to regret this."

"I promise you won't," Cody says. "We'll have fun. We can drop Chad off at the station if you're ready to go now."

I sling my purse over my shoulder. "Ready as I'll ever be."

The drive to police headquarters takes less than five minutes. "He seems like a nice guy," I remark to Cody after Chad gets out of the car.

Cody glances over at me from the driver's seat. "He's a really nice person. As is his wife. I think you'd like her."

Alarm bells go off in my head. His comment is something a guy would say to his girlfriend. I could easily fall for him. I need to be careful not to let that happen.

The Nest is hopping, and the waiting time for a table is forty-five minutes. Luckily, two seats at the bar open up soon after we arrive. We order beers and burgers, and while we eat, Cody entertains me with stories from his more interesting cases. The enraged husband who chain-sawed his wife's beloved antique dining room table in half after he caught her sleeping with the appliance repairman. The wife who slashed her husband's tires when he refused to take her on a trip to Bermuda. And the group of teenage vandals who have been wreaking havoc on the town by destroying property and stealing automobiles.

I push my plate away and prop my elbows on the bar. "I don't understand. The other day, you told me Water's Edge had little crime."

"Very little *serious* crime. These are the typical cases you expect to find in a small town." His expression becomes somber. "Although the teenage delinquents are getting out of hand. And there was that whole mess last year with Will Darby."

The little hairs on the back of my neck stand to attention. "What about Will Darby?"

Letting out a deep sigh, Cody sits back in his chair and tells me about the boating accident that claimed Will's wife's life and his in-laws framing him for her murder to seek custody of his daughters. "Julia saved him, but that's a story for another day."

While I'm dying to know more about Will and Julia and his custody case, I refrain from asking too many questions for fear I'll appear overly interested in the Darby family.

Cody moves on to another case. He keeps me in stitches, and before I realize it, we've drank two more rounds of drinks. I enjoy his company and his good-natured sense of humor. His sparkling eyes, baby face, and dimpled smile make me swoon.

"I shouldn't have had that last drink," Cody admits when we finally leave the tavern around ten.

"I'm feeling a little tipsy myself. I can easily walk home. Do you live nearby?"

"A few blocks past your apartment. Like you, I usually walk to work, but I drove my truck today to move the chairs."

We start toward Main Street on foot. "So, tell me, Harper, what is the one thing you love to do the most?"

"Sing," I say and launch into the first lyrics of Patsy Cline's "Crazy."

Cody stops walking but motions for me to continue singing. I don't hold back, the alcohol having lessened my inhibitions. I hook an arm around a street sign and belt out the rest of the song at the top of my lungs.

"That was truly unbelievable," Cody says when I finish, his eyes glistening with unshed tears. "You have star-quality talent. Surely, I'm not the first to tell you that."

I start walking, and Cody steps in line beside me. "Singing was my passion growing up. My voice coach in high school encouraged me to seek fame, but my mother refused to allow it."

"That's a shame. Why did she prevent you from following your passion?"

"Because she wanted me to follow hers," I say in a tone that warns him not to press me for details.

We talk about our favorite country artists on the way to my apartment. Cody doesn't ask to come inside but gives me another kiss that once again curls my toes.

"You feel the chemistry, right?" he asks in a throaty whisper.

I press my finger to his lips. "I admit you're a good kisser. But I've warned you. I'm not good at relationships. The guys I date usually end up getting hurt."

"I'm willing to take my chances."

His man-boy charm is eating away at my resolve, and I'm not sure how long I'll be able to resist him. "I'm not looking for a relationship right now, Cody. I'm going through some stuff. I just lost my mother, and I'm trying to figure out my life."

"I respect that, and I'm a patient man. I'm willing to accept friendship while you sort through your issues."

I've never felt this way about a guy before, and I'm not sure I can be just friends with him. "You deserve better than me, Cody."

His face grows serious. "Let me be the judge of that." He runs a finger down my cheek. "I'm a good listener, Harper. I'm available whenever you need to talk."

"I'll remember that. Thanks again for helping me move the furniture," I say and disappear inside my apartment before I throw myself at him in the hallway.

———

CARRIE IS WAITING outside the boutique when I unlock the front door at ten on Thursday morning. "Good morning, Carrie. Come on in." I open the door wider. "If you're back for more sale items, we still have a few things left. But our new stuff is fabulous.

You might find them pricey, but if you buy one item a month, the hit to your wallet isn't as bad."

A flush creeps up Carrie's neck to her cheeks. "My husband was not happy when he saw the charges on the credit card for the sale items."

I frown. "I'm sorry to hear that. Unfortunately, we don't accept returns on sale merchandise."

"I understand. But that's not why I'm here. After twenty-nine years of marriage, I've concluded that I need my own spending money." She gestures at the sign in the window. "I'd like to apply for the sales assistant position. Sarah will soon leave for college, and Noah is busy with sports. I have nothing but time on my hands. I don't have a résumé. I've never worked a day in my life. But I efficiently manage my household and my children's busy social lives. And I'm extremely neat and organized."

I'm at a loss for words. Hiring her would enable me to get closer to the Darby family. But she lacks both experience and fashion sense as far as I can tell. I'm grateful when Will bursts through the door, saving me from having to respond.

He stops dead in his tracks. "Whoa. This place looks fabulous. I thought I was in the wrong store for a minute." He circles the shop, inspecting the changes. "Excellent job, Harper."

"Thanks," I say, bursting with a pride I never experienced as a paralegal. Giving the shop a facelift was easy and fun. I didn't consider it work at all.

Will notices his sister for the first time. "Morning, Carrie. Fancy finding you shopping at Tracy's twice in one month. You're becoming quite the fashionista."

Carrie lifts her chin high. "I'm not shopping this time, Will. I'm here to apply for the sales assistant job." She repeats her speech about wanting to earn spending money and the skills she's acquired managing a busy household.

Will glances over at me. "What do you think?"

I shrug. "Since you're here, I'll let you decide."

Will returns his attention to Carrie. "Are you ready to give up your freedom? Having a full-time job will be a departure from your accustomed schedule."

"I realize it'll be an adjustment, but I've given this considerable thought and want to do this. Honestly, I should've gotten a job years ago. I need something just for me that I don't have to share with my husband or kids. I promise I won't let you down," she says with pleading in her slate-blue eyes.

Will smiles softly at his sister. "Then I say we give her a chance."

"Fine by me," I say in a cheerful tone.

Carrie presses her hands together. "Thank you both. You won't regret it. When can I start?" she asks me.

"How about the first of next week? Saturday is Mollie's last day, and Mondays are usually slow, which will give us time to review some things."

"Then I'll see you on Monday. Thank you both for the opportunity." Carrie gives us both a quick hug before hurrying out the door.

Will watches her go. "I hope this is okay with you. She seemed almost desperate. I hated to tell her no. Working in a fun environment and being accountable to someone else might be just what she needs."

"She'll do great," I say with feigned enthusiasm.

"But if she doesn't, let me know and I'll handle it."

"Deal." If she doesn't work out, I'll let Will be the one to fire his sister. I don't want her holding that over my head when she discovers I'm her niece. Or her *daughter*. The thought gives me chill bumps. What if Carrie is my mother? Our relationship could go south pretty darn fast if she wants nothing to do with the child she put up for adoption.

I busy myself behind the counter while Will takes a final spin around the shop.

"I mean it, Harper. The place looks great. Tracy would've

approved. If you decide you don't like managing the boutique, I'll hire you to consult with my clients on interior decor."

I laugh. "I'll keep that in mind. Do you actually have a staffer who does that?"

"Not yet. But I'm considering it. With all the choices available these days, my clients need guidance when selecting paint colors, tile, and appliances."

"Sounds like a fun job."

"Sounds like a migraine headache to me," he says with a chuckle. "I stopped by to make certain you're still available to babysit tonight."

"I'm looking forward to it. What time?"

"Seven o'clock. We shouldn't be out late."

"No worries. I don't have a curfew," I tease.

TWELVE
SAVANNAH

Nightmares plague my sleep, bringing back memories of traumatic events I'd long since buried in the back of my mind. I wake multiple times to the unmistakable cries of a newborn. I finally fall into a deep sleep around daybreak. When I wake again around noon, still disturbed by last night's dreams, I have to summon the courage to leave my room and walk past my mother's closed door. In the kitchen, as the Keurig brews a stream of coffee into a large mug, I have an eerie feeling someone is watching me. And that someone is my mother's ghost. Coming to Marsh Point was a mistake.

Dressing in white jeans and a yellow top, I drive to town, where I'm thrilled to find my favorite hangout is still in business on the waterfront. I immediately feel at home when I step inside The Nest. The mounted sea turtles bring back fond memories, and the worn wooden floors and bar remind me of The Lantern back in Fairhaven.

Patrons linger over late lunches, but plenty of seats are available at the bar.

The harried bartender slides a laminated menu in front of me. "I'll be with you in a minute," she says, but a long time passes before she returns to take my order. "I'm sorry. We're slammed today."

"No worries. Looks like you could use some help."

"For real!" she says, blowing a stray strand of blonde hair off her forehead. "We've been short-staffed for months. If you know anyone looking for a job, please send them our way."

"I'll keep that in mind. What positions are available?"

"All of them from dishwasher on up," the bartender says as she pulls a draft beer for another customer.

"Are you looking for a manager?"

"I wish! Our manager is part of the problem. She's the owner's daughter, fresh out of college, and she has no clue what she's doing." The waitress removes her order pad from her apron pocket. "What can I get you?"

"The mixed green salad with summer berries and grilled chicken, please."

She scrawls my order on her pad. "And to drink?"

"I'll have sweet tea."

"Coming right up," she says, hurrying to place my order.

Maybe I should work here while I'm figuring out my next move. The restaurant has plenty of business, which means lots of tips. On the other hand, I have enough drama in my life without dealing with management problems.

When I leave The Nest, I drive across the Merriweather Bridge to Sandy Island. I park in a public lot and walk down to the beach, leaving my sandals beside the boardwalk. The landscape has changed in my absence. Many of the cottages I remember have been torn down or destroyed by hurricanes. In their place are gaudy McMansions several stories high that take up entire lots.

I walk on the beach for over an hour before returning to town. I'm passing through the historic district when I notice a sign advertising a carriage house for rent at a stately home I've always admired. I tuck this into my memory bank for later if I stay in Water's Edge for a while.

Back at Marsh Point, I stretch out on my bed and fall into a deep sleep. I wake at five thirty to the sound of rain pounding the copper roof and to voices downstairs.

I tip-toe out of my room and peer over the railing at the top of the stairs. Anger surges through me at the sight of my family gathered in the hallway. I specifically told Ashton I didn't want a welcome-home party.

Curiosity gets the best of me, and I study each in turn. Will was just a boy when I last saw him. He's taller than he appears in his social media photos, handsome with light brown hair and electric blue eyes I remember so well. Aside from a few wrinkles around her eyes and mouth, Carrie is still the same shorter, rounder version of our older sister. Dad has changed the most. He's now an old man with leathered skin, thinning gray hair, and stooped shoulders. Also included in the group are May May and Will's wife, the dark-haired beauty standing beside him.

Carrie looks up at me, and we lock eyes. I was closest to her when we were growing up. Not only was she my best friend, she was also my protector. She always knew what I was thinking and feeling. A thousand unspoken words pass between us as we stare at each other. Even from a distance, I can see the hurt in her eyes. She resents me for leaving and for staying away for so long.

I return to my bedroom and begin throwing my stuff into my suitcase.

Carrie appears in the doorway, out of breath from racing up the stairs. "You can't leave town already. You just got here."

"Coming home was a mistake. I specifically asked Ashton not to invite the family over for dinner." I zip up my suitcase. "But it's not just that. I can't be in this house."

When I go into the bathroom for my toiletries, Carrie follows me. "You're welcome to stay with me. You'd have to sleep on the sofa, but we can make it work."

I rake my toiletries off the counter into my cosmetics bag. "That's kind of you, but I need my space."

"But where will you go?" she asks with a tight voice, on the verge of tears.

"I'll figure something out. Maybe I'll stay at Myrtle's," I say about the town's iconic bed and breakfast.

Leaving the bathroom, I drop my cosmetic case into my tote bag and toss in my reading glasses and mystery novel from the bedside table.

Carrie pulls me in for a hug. "I can't believe you're home. Please don't leave until we've had some time together."

Pushing her away, I draw an *X* over my heart. "I promise I won't. I'm sorry I can't stay for dinner. Seeing everyone at once is too much for me."

"I understand." She swipes at her eyes as she crosses the room to the door. "We need to get you out of here. Everyone's waiting for you in the hallway downstairs. I'll herd them into the kitchen so you can escape through the front door. I'll text you when the coast is clear. But first, I need your number."

I call out my number, and she enters it into her phone. I blow her a kiss. "Thanks, Carrie. I owe you one."

After she's gone, I toss my tote over my shoulder and wheel my suitcase to the top of the stairs to wait for her text. When my phone pings, I pick up my suitcase by the handle and hurry down the stairs and out the front door.

The rain is coming down in torrents, and even with the wipers on full speed, I can barely see the road as I drive slowly back to town. I'm nearing Myrtle's when I pass the sign announcing the carriage house for rent. I pull to the curb and stare at the main house, its lights casting a warm glow in the windows and welcoming guests on such a nasty night. Should I inquire about the rental details? Why would I sign a lease when I'm unsure how long I'm staying in town? It doesn't hurt to ask. Maybe the owner will consider a month-to-month lease.

I turn into the circular driveway and park in front of the columned porch. I sprint the short distance to the porch, but I'm not wearing a raincoat, and my clothes are quickly drenched. When I ring the bell, a dog barks from within, followed by the click of heels on hardwood floors. The door swings open to reveal a striking older woman.

"Yes? May I help you?"

"Sorry to disturb you, ma'am. I'm here about the carriage house for rent?"

She narrows her gray eyes. "You look familiar. Have we met?"

"I'm not sure. My name is Savannah Darby. I'm originally from Water's Edge but haven't been home in a long time."

Recognition crosses her face. "Of course! Savannah! Bless your heart. Come inside and get out of this dreadful weather," she says, pulling me into the foyer.

I look down at the marble floor, where a puddle forms at my feet. "If this is a bad time, I can come back tomorrow."

She waves at the floor in a dismissive gesture. "Don't worry. Biscuit will take care of it," she says, looking down at the golden retriever lapping up the rainwater. "Let me grab a towel for you."

Her slim figure glides up the curved staircase. Her silver hair is cut in a sleek bob, and she's elegantly dressed in pale gray linen slacks and a white silk blouse. She's attractive and fit for a woman who's at least in her seventies, probably early eighties.

I survey my surroundings while I wait for her return. The house is magazine-worthy, with priceless antiques and traditional furnishings. To the right is a dining room with a mahogany table and crystal chandelier, while on the left is a paneled cozy den.

When Biscuit whimpers, I drop to my knees and nuzzle her gray muzzle. "You're an old girl, aren't you?"

"Going on thirteen," the dog's owner says as she floats back down the stairs. She hands me a fluffy white towel and a terrycloth robe. "Why don't you change out of your wet clothes. We'll put them in the dryer while we talk about the carriage house."

Abandoning my sodden sandals beside the front door, I follow her into the powder room.

"Take your time. I'll be in the kitchen when you're through," she says, closing the door on her way out.

I peel off my wet clothes, dry my body, and slip into the robe. Emerging with my wet bundle of clothing, I plod on bare feet down a short hallway to a large farmhouse-style kitchen where the woman is filling a Keurig reservoir with water.

"The dryer's in there," she says, gesturing to the adjacent laundry room. "Tea or coffee?"

"Tea would be great."

After putting my clothes in the dryer, I watch her from the doorway as she dunks teabags in cups of steaming water. I'm supposed to know this woman, but from where? Church? Was she one of my teachers? My mother didn't have many friends. This society woman wasn't her type anyway.

Entering the kitchen, I ask, "I'm sorry, I don't remember. I was young when I left home. How do we know each other?"

She laughs. "Don't worry, sweetheart. We never really knew each other. But you may remember my late husband, Dr Paul Richardson."

The mention of our family doctor makes my knees go weak, and I drop to a nearby stool. Her husband was at Marsh Point that night. I can still see his handsome, sun-weathered face between my legs, encouraging me to push harder as I delivered my baby.

Mrs. Richardson joins me at the island, placing a warm mug before me. "Your case was the only time Paul breached a patient's confidentiality agreement. I begged him not to go out in the ice storm that night. But he was determined to get to you. When he returned just after midnight, he reported the new mama and baby girl were doing well. Then, two days later, when he went back to check on you and the baby, you were both gone. Your mother told him you had given the baby up for adoption and run away. He suspected she was lying. You seemed so overjoyed about the birth of your baby."

She hesitates, waiting for me to respond. But I'm too choked up to speak.

Mrs. Richardson sips her tea. "So, about the carriage house . . ."

My heart sinks when she tells me the low rent price. There must be something wrong with the house. Does it have roaches? I can handle an outdated kitchen, but I refuse to live in a dirty house.

Before I can question the amount, she tells me there's a condition on the rental. "How do you feel about dogs?" she asks.

I smile down at Biscuit, curled in a ball at her owner's feet. "I love dogs. I've never owned one, but I often took care of my former boss's labs when he traveled."

"Good! My children and grandchildren are scattered all over the country. They lead busy lives, and it's easier for me to visit them than for them to come here. Biscuit is getting on in her years. She's fine staying in the house alone, but she needs to be walked and fed twice daily."

"So, dog sitting makes up for the rest of the rent?"

"Exactly. I'm usually only gone a few days a month."

"I'll be honest with you, Mrs. Richardson, I'm not sure how long I'll be in town. I'm planning on staying for a while. Maybe even permanently. But that could change. Would you consider a month-to-month lease?"

"Please, call me Muriel. And month-to-month works fine. I've never had a tenant rent the carriage house, so this is all new to me. If you decide to move out, I ask that you give me fair notice so I can make other arrangements for Biscuit."

"Absolutely! You have my word."

"Can I offer you some dinner? I took some chicken and rice soup out of the freezer earlier. I don't usually eat soup during the summer, but this lousy weather calls for it."

I'm still full from my late lunch, but I won't be able to buy groceries until morning. "Soups sounds great."

While we eat, Muriel humors me with stories about her eight grandchildren. I'm grateful she doesn't ask any personal questions. She must sense I'm troubled. Why else would I be looking for a place to rent when I have three siblings who live in town?

The rain has slowed by the time we finish eating. While she rinses the dishes, I change back into my clothes and retrieve my shoes from the foyer. We walk across the rain-drenched small garden to the one-story carriage house.

As she fumbles with the lock on the double-arched paned doors, Muriel says, "I've done my best to maintain the house. On the rare occasion they visit me, my children prefer to stay here over the main house." She pushes the door open, and we step inside.

The interior is a casual version of the main house, with warm oriental rugs and cozy furnishings. A multipurpose room offers a seating area with a large adjacent kitchen featuring an enormous island that doubles as a table, with four barstools at one end. Flanking the main living area are two bedrooms, each with its own bath.

"This is perfect, Muriel. I'd love to be your tenant if you'll have me."

"I'm thrilled to have you, sweetheart. I have a hunch we're going to be good friends. When would you like to move in?"

"Is now too soon?" I ask with a sheepish grin.

"Now is fine. We can worry about the paperwork tomorrow." On the walk back to the main house, we discuss keys, parking, and trash collection. When we part at the screened back porch, I continue to the front of the house for my car. I can hardly believe my luck. I have a place to live for now, and tomorrow, I will apply for the bartending job at The Nest. I'll reunite with my other family members one at a time and take the rest of my life as it comes.

THIRTEEN
HARPER

I develop an instant girl crush on Will's wife, Julia. She's several years younger than her new husband, not much older than me. Her boy-short hair complements her striking features, and she carries herself with a badass confidence that makes me admire and fear her. She tells me their plans have changed. "Our hosts came down with bad summer colds and had to cancel the party."

"We're going across the street to my sister's house instead," Will says as he slips on a heavy-duty yellow rain slicker, the kind commercial fishermen wear.

"Ashton has a surprise for us. I'm praying she and her boyfriend, Sully, got engaged." Julia steeples her hands under her chin with her eyes cast heavenward.

Will's smile tells me he's hoping for a proposal as well. "The kids have requested pizza for dinner. Order two larges so we'll have leftovers." He removes two twenties from his wallet and hands them to me.

Julia rolls her eyes. "You mean so that *you* can have the leftovers. My husband has the eating habits of a child. Some men never grow up."

I laugh as I take the twenties from him. "Any requests for toppings?"

"Nope. I'll eat anything." Will helps his wife into her red rain slicker, and they venture out into the pouring rain.

I turn to Will's daughters, Sophie and Caroline, ages three and five. "Well, girls? What should we do?"

"Let's go to our playroom," Caroline says, and Sophie shouts, "Yes! Let's play."

Taking me by the hands, the girls drag me out of the kitchen and down a wide hallway toward the back of the house. I peek into the rooms as we go. Will's recently renovated house is a spectacular mix of traditional and contemporary decor.

Their playroom is a comfortable room with sectional sofas and a wide-screen television mounted above the mantel on the brick fireplace. Julia's son, Buddy, is working on a Lego project at the table by a window overlooking Catawba Sound.

He looks up when we enter the room. He has the same chestnut brown hair and doe eyes as his mom.

"Hi, Buddy. I'm Harper."

"Hi." He waves at me and returns his attention to his Legos.

I plop down on the sofa with the girls on either side.

Caroline moves close, practically sitting on top of me. "Can I play with your hair?" Before I can object, she tugs my hair free of its ponytail and rakes her fingers through my tangled locks. "Your hair is curly like Sophie's. But much whiter."

Sophie runs a hand over her golden mop of unruly corkscrews. "Mine used to be long like yours until Daddy cut it."

"Why'd he make you cut it?" I ask.

"He didn't *make* her cut it," Caroline says. "He did it himself. He got the brush caught in her hair and had to cut it out with scissors."

My jaw drops. "Seriously?"

"Yep," Caroline says with a nod. "That was right after Mama died when he was still mean and angry."

My head rears back. "How old are you again?"

Caroline's hand shoots up, fingers splayed. "Five. Going on six."

I laugh. "You mean five going on fifteen?"

Sophie bobs her head. "That's what Daddy says."

"Guess what, Harper." Caroline cups her hands around her mouth and whispers in my ear, "Daddy and Julia are trying to have a baby."

I furrow my brow. "How do you know this?"

With a sheepish grin, Caroline says, "I overheard them talking in their room. I was listening in the hallway."

"That was a private conversation, Caroline. I don't think they would want you sharing their personal information with just anyone."

Caroline hunches her shoulders up to her ears. "You're not just anyone. You're our babysitter."

I wonder how many other babysitters she's told this to. Poor kid is in for a big letdown if Will and Julia can't conceive. "Let's play a game," I suggest.

"I'd rather read instead," Caroline says, gathering a stack of books.

I assume she expects me to read to them, and she surprises me when she starts reading out loud to Sophie and me. The going is slow, and I have to help her with some words, but she's advanced for someone her age.

We're on the third book when Buddy announces he's starving.

"Me too!" Caroline and Sophie say in unison.

"Then let's order." I pick up my phone from the coffee table. "What's your preference, Domino's or Papa Johns?"

Caroline scrambles off the sofa to her feet. "We have to get Sal's. They have the best pizza in town. The menu is in the kitchen."

Forty-five minutes later, the four of us are sitting down at the farm table in the kitchen with our pizza when Julia and Will return.

"That was fast," I say. "I expected you to stay longer."

Will sheds his dripping raincoat, tossing it at the coat rack in the corner. "Ashton's little surprise turned out to be a bombshell. After thirty years, our missing sister has come home."

My eyes widen. *His sister? There's a third Darby daughter?* "What do you mean by missing? Was she abducted?"

He shakes his head. "She ran away. In the middle of an ice storm. Everyone worried she'd gotten in a wreck or fell into harm's way, but her body was never found."

"Why did she run away?" I hold up my hand. "Forget I asked that. It's none of my business."

Will drops down to the chair next to Caroline. "She was going through some personal stuff at the time."

I glance over at Julia, whose expression is dazed as she waits for the teakettle to boil. "Where has she been all this time?" I stare down at my plate. "Sorry, I'm prying again."

Will transfers a slice of pizza from the box to a paper plate. "I don't blame you for being curious. Apparently, she's been living in the Pacific Northwest."

My appetite vanishes, and I push my pizza plate away. "That's crazy. I can't imagine what it was like for you to see her after all this time."

Will hangs his head. "Unfortunately, we didn't get to see her. Ashton meant well. She was thrilled about Savannah's return and wanted to share her excitement with the rest of the family. But Savannah explicitly asked her not to throw her a welcome-home party."

Tea mug in hand, Julia leans back against the counter. "She felt overwhelmed and snuck out the front door while we were all in the kitchen. I hope she hasn't left town again."

The walls close in on me, and I suddenly find it difficult to breathe. I stand abruptly. "I should go."

Setting down her mug, Julia hurries over to me. "Do you feel all right? You're very pale. Was it the pizza? Did you eat a bad pepperoni?"

"I'm fine. I'm just tired."

"Let me pay you so you can go home and get some sleep," Will says, tugging his wallet from his pants pocket.

I wave off his money. "This one's on the house. You weren't gone long anyway." Forcing a smile, I tousle each of the kid's hair. "Bye, kiddos. I hope to see you again soon."

Putting on my raincoat, I make a dash for my car. Will's words replay in my head as I drive slowly through the torrential downpour to town.

After thirty years, our missing sister has come home. She ran away. In the middle of an ice storm. She was going through some personal stuff at the time.

Having a baby definitely counts as personal stuff. Ice storms happen in wintertime. And I was born in January. *Thirty* years ago. I pound the steering wheel. *This is it. I'm sure of it. Savannah Darby is my mother.*

Not wanting to be alone, I continue past my apartment building through the flooded streets of downtown to The Nest. Only a few tables are occupied, and no one is seated at the bar. No one in their right mind is out on a night like tonight.

From my previous visits to The Nest, I've come to know the bartender by name. Amber gives me a funny look when I order a decaf coffee. "I'll have to brew some. It'll take a few minutes."

"Never mind. I'll have a cognac. Hennessy, please."

My mother, my adoptive mother, Victoria, often had a snifter of Hennessy after dinner when she was pondering a crucial legal case. She claimed it helped her make difficult decisions. Maybe it'll help me sleep. Although, after what I just learned, I may not sleep for days.

Amber pours two fingers into a glass and sets it before me. "Rough night?"

"You could say that." I hand her my credit card. "I'd like to pay. I'm going to move to a booth."

"Sure thing, honey." She processes the charge and hands me a slip to sign. "I didn't mean to drive you away."

"It's not you. I'm just lousy company right now."

I take my drink to the far corner booth and sit down with my back to the door. The golden liquid burns my throat and spreads warmth through my body, but it offers little insight into my situation. I wish Victoria were here to explain all this to me. But she was never planning to tell me about my adoption. If I hadn't found that envelope, I would've lived out my life thinking she was my biological mother.

I'm glad to see Cody's smiling face when he slides into the booth opposite me. "Hey there." Noticing my gloomy expression, he drops his smile. "What's wrong?"

I burst into tears, and he moves to my side of the booth, drawing me close while I cry. When I finally pull myself together, I tell him I came to Water's Edge after learning I had been adopted, and that I suspected one of the Darby sisters is my birth mother. I conclude with Savannah's sudden return home.

Cody listens patiently until I finish. "I understand why you're so upset. You're dealing with a lot. But what happened tonight is a good thing. It makes sense that Savannah is your birth mother."

"But what if she leaves town again before I have a chance to know her?"

He kisses my hair. "Then it's a good thing your new best friend is a cop who can track her down."

From behind the bar, Amber makes the last call for drinks. "We're closing early because of the weather."

Craning my neck to see behind us, I realize we're the only two people left in the tavern. "I guess we should go."

Cody removes his arm from around me. "Do you need a ride home? I'm not sure you should be alone right now."

"I drove. But you're right. I could use the company. Do you want to follow me to my apartment?"

"Sure thing," he says, and we walk to the parking lot together.

I collect myself during the short drive home, and by the time I let us into my apartment, I'm feeling more encouraged about the situation. "What can I get you to drink?" I ask Cody as I turn on the lamps in the living room. "Coffee? Tea? Beer?"

"Decaf coffee would be great," he says, following me into the kitchen while I put a pot on to brew.

"I'm sorry I got so upset, Cody. Everything hit me at once. But you're right. This new development is a good thing. Savannah has to be my mother. Now I need to figure out how to approach her. Assuming she hasn't left town again. If she has, you need to find her for me before she gets too far away."

"I will. But I'd be willing to bet she's still here. I can understand how her family crowding her might freak her out. She's been gone for thirty years. I imagine it took a lot of courage for her to come home. Why would she leave again after only one day?"

"I hope you're right." The coffee maker finishes brewing, and I fill two mugs. "Cream or sugar?"

"Black is fine," he says, taking one of the mugs. "Keep in mind, Water's Edge is a small town. Word about her return will spread like wildfire."

"True. And my customers love to gossip. I also hired Savannah's sister Carrie as my sales associate. She starts on Monday."

"Perfect. You can keep tabs on Savannah through her sister." Cody sips his coffee. "Have you considered sending your DNA to 23andMe?"

"I ordered the kit, but I haven't sent it in yet. What's the point when I know my mother is one of the Darby sisters?"

"I'm playing devil's advocate, but what if Marsh Point was merely the pickup destination for the adoptive parents? Someone in the Darby family may have brokered the adoption for another birth mother."

I fall back against the counter. "That seems far-fetched, but I can't eliminate the possibility."

"If your biological mother *or* your biological father is looking for you, either may have already sent their DNA to the website."

"Good point, Cody. I'll send in the kit first thing tomorrow."

"Doesn't hurt to cover all your bases. You never know what you might turn up."

"You're right." We discuss other possible scenarios while we finish our coffee, but we don't discuss the one that gives me the most pause. What if my mother, Savannah, or whoever she is, doesn't want to know me?

FOURTEEN
SAVANNAH

I wake early on Friday after a dreamless and restful night's sleep. I take in my new surroundings—the bamboo double bed, tropical print fabric on the drapes, and marble fireplace with gas logs. I got lucky in renting this carriage house. Now all I need is a job.

I relish in the soft sheets and fluffy duvet for a few more minutes before forcing myself to get up and dressed. I brew coffee and wander outside to the small patio off the kitchen. After last night's rain, the air is fresh and fragrant with the citrusy scent of blooms on a nearby magnolia tree.

Finishing my coffee, I begin unloading my car and unpacking my belongings in my new home. Around nine o'clock, I venture up to the main house with my checkbook and knock on the back door.

Muriel, seated at the kitchen island with the newspaper, motions for me to come in.

"Morning." I wave my checkbook at her. "I'm here to pay the rent and sign the lease."

She slides off her stool to her feet. "And eat some breakfast, I hope. I was getting ready to make an omelet. Can I offer you one?"

"Thanks, but I don't want to impose more than I already have."

She places a hand on her hip. "No imposition at all. Take pity on an old woman and keep her company."

I laugh out loud. "You're not old. But I could use the company as well. And I'm starving. I worked up an appetite, unpacking and getting settled. Can I help you with anything?"

"I've got this. Why don't you fill out the lease while I make breakfast?" Crossing the room to a small built-in desk, she rummages through stacks of mail and file folders until she locates the stapled papers. I found this standard lease document on the internet. It should do the trick."

While Muriel works at the stove, I fill out the form and write my check for the rent.

"Here you go." She sets a plate with an omelet, two strips of crispy bacon, and a fluffy buttermilk biscuit on the island in front of me.

"This looks amazing, Muriel. You're going to spoil me."

"I love having someone around to cook for." She sits down next to me with her plate. "So, what's on your agenda today?"

"On the top of my list is seeing the manager at The Nest about a job."

Spreading a napkin in her lap, Muriel says, "Good for you. Are you a waitress?"

"No, bartender." I take a bite of the cheesy omelet. "Delicious. Do you eat such a hearty breakfast every morning?"

Muriel smiles. "Heavens no. Only when I have company. I'm a creature of habit. I usually eat a bowl of oatmeal with fresh berries."

"Then we're kindred spirits because I eat oatmeal every day."

Muriel breaks a small piece off her biscuit. "Is bartending as challenging as it appears to be?"

I nod. "Both physically and mentally. I should have a degree in psychology after listening to people's problems all these years.

Sometimes, they're looking for advice. But most of the time, they need for someone to listen." I add a slab of butter to my biscuit. "On another note, where should I go for groceries?"

"You have a couple of options. Harris Teeter is in the shopping center near Mariner's Landing. But I buy most of my groceries at Fancy Pantry. The cost is about the same, and their produce is fresher." Muriel sips her orange juice. "Oh! I almost forgot." She tugs a slip of paper out of her pocket. "I jotted down the dates I'll be gone this summer. The first isn't until July, which should give you plenty of time to get to know Biscuit."

I take the paper from her. "I'll add these to my calendar. If you like, I can start walking her some mornings now."

"That's an excellent idea."

After helping Muriel with the dishes, I return to the carriage house to shower and dress for what I hope will be a job interview.

The door is locked when I arrive at The Nest, but peering through the window, I spot Amber behind the bar preparing for her shift. I knock on the window, and she comes from behind the bar to unlock the door.

"Sorry. We don't open for another"—she glances at her watch —"thirty minutes."

"I'm here about the bartending job."

"Praise, Lord! Hallelujah!" She opens the door and steps out of the way. "Get in here. You picked a good time to come. Our manager, the owner's daughter I told you about, will be making a rare appearance momentarily."

I follow Amber to the bar and sit on the end stool. "Tell me more about the job and your clientele."

"One thing's for sure, we are never bored," she chuckles. "We're busy most of the time. We occasionally get tourists, but most of our customers are locals who appreciate the service and tip well."

I reach for the drink's menu. The few selections are uninspired.

Amber notices me looking over the menu. "It needs some work. I keep meaning to update it, but I haven't had time."

"I have some experience with mixology." I set down the menu. "A lot of experience. My old boss called me a master."

"Cool! Tell me more," Amber says, leaning against the counter.

"I'm a fanatic about using fresh juices and herbs. My drinks may be too fussy for your clientele though."

Amber shrugs. "Maybe not. We could float a few specials to gauge interest." Her gaze shifts as a white convertible sports car screeches to a halt at the front door. "Brace yourself. Here comes trouble."

An attractive young woman with shiny black hair gets out of the car and lets herself into the restaurant, not bothering to lock the door behind her. She's wearing white jeans and wedges. The periwinkle silk fabric on her halter top barely covers her small breasts. She's dripping with gold—bangle bracelets adorning both arms and chains dangling from her neck. She looks more like a pampered sorority girl than the manager of a dive restaurant.

When Amber introduces me, I stand to greet her. "Nice to meet you, Taylor."

"Savannah would like to speak to you about a bartending job," Amber explains.

Taylor breezes past me on a cloud of floral perfume. "I don't have much time. I'm going out of town with friends for the weekend. Can you come back on Monday?"

Amber's death glare stops her dead in her tracks. "Make time, Taylor. We're desperate for more help."

Taylor lets out a huff. "Whatever. Do you have any experience?"

"Plenty. You can check my reference." I hand Taylor a folded piece of paper containing Doug's contact information.

She unfolds the paper. "Who's Doug?"

"My former boss. I worked for him for the past thirty years, doing everything from bussing tables to managing the tavern when he was out of town."

"Whoa. You worked for him longer than I've been alive." She hands me back the paper. "You're hired. I'll get the forms for you to fill out." She continues behind the bar and disappears into the kitchen.

"That was easy," I say, slipping the paper with Doug's name on it into my purse.

"Taylor is a figurehead. The staff runs the place. I prefer more supervision, but we do an okay job on our own."

Taylor emerges from the back, her arms loaded with frozen food boxes." She stops in front of me. "Your forms are on top. Fill them out and leave them on my desk in the office. Welcome aboard . . . uh . . ." She scrunches up her face. "What did you say your name was again?"

"Savannah Darby," I say, removing the employment forms from the top box. "Thanks for this opportunity."

"Just don't screw anything up," Taylor says and walks to the door, struggling to open it under the weight of the boxes.

As we watch Taylor load the boxes in her trunk, Amber says, "Can you believe her? I guarantee she didn't pay for that food. Her daddy would be furious if he found out."

A woman with a thick auburn ponytail emerges from the kitchen, and Amber waves her over. "Morning, Sheila! Come meet our new bartender, Savannah Darby. Sheila is our head waitress."

"Well, bless your heart. Aren't you a godsend?" Sheila's forehead lines deepen. "Your name sounds familiar. Did we go to high school together?"

"Probably. I grew up here." I hold my breath, waiting for her to remember I was the classmate who got knocked up.

Sheila's face lights up. "I remember you. You're the pretty girl all the boys chased after. You're one of those who went off to college and never came back."

"Something like that," I mutter.

Amber fiddles with her messy bun. "So, you're a bartender. Despite your fancy college degree, life hasn't treated you any better than me."

I hold her gaze. "Life has given me exactly what I've asked of it."

Sheila laughs. "I like that. We're going to get along just fine," she says, offering me a high five.

I wait until Sheila leaves before returning my attention to Amber. "When should I start work?"

"As soon as possible. I realize it's short notice, but is there any chance you can start this afternoon? With happy hour from four till seven, we're always mobbed until midnight on Fridays."

I owe my family members a visit, but I'd rather spread those reunions out over a few days. "Sure! I can work tonight. I have some errands to run. Do you mind if I come in around three?"

"Three is perfect. See you then."

I gather up the forms. "I'll fill these out at home and bring them in later."

When I leave The Nest, I drive two blocks to Fancy Pantry. In addition to typical grocery store items, the upscale gourmet market offers prepared dinners and salads I can eat on the fly or take to work. I load up my cart and head to the checkout.

I'm waiting in line when a loud, squeaky voice behind me makes my skin crawl. "Well, Savannah Darby, as I live and breathe. I heard you were back in town. And aren't you as pretty as ever."

She heard I was back in town. Word of my return has spread already?

She pats her chest. "I'm Flora Fields. I was Flora Greene."

Who could forget a name like Flora? For the life of me, I can't place her face. "I'm sorry. It's been a long time."

"Of course, you wouldn't remember me. I was the chubby girl two grades below you. I had a huge girl crush on you. You were the prettiest thing ever in your cheerleading outfit."

Relief washes over me. She had a crush on me, yet she doesn't remember the pregnancy. "That's kind of you to say. That was a long time ago."

"I hear you've been living on the West Coast. Is Washington State as pretty as everyone claims?"

Don't these people have anything better to talk about than me? "It truly is. You should visit sometime."

The woman in the line ahead of me moves away, and I proceed through the checkout. After paying for my groceries, I wave goodbye to Flora. "Nice to see you again."

I'm encouraged she remembered me as Savannah Darby, the pretty cheerleader, not the girl who had a baby and ran away. My second chance at living in Water's Edge may turn out better than my first.

FIFTEEN
HARPER

Before work on Friday morning, I spit my saliva into the test tube and sealed the specimen pouch. Walking three blocks to the post office, I snap a selfie as I drop my 23andMe package into the mailbox, sending the pic to Cody.

As I exit the post office, his words from last night come back to me. *What if Marsh Point was merely the pickup destination for the adoptive parents? Someone in the Darby family may have brokered the adoption for another birth mother."*

I pause on the sidewalk in front of the building, wondering if I should beg a postal worker to fetch my package out of the bin. Not knowing my biological mother's identity might be better than finding out she's a random person who lives in a faraway state.

My phone vibrates with a text from Cody. *Good for you. You can handle the truth, whatever it may be. I'm here for you if you need to talk.* I read the text three times. How does he always seem to know what I'm thinking?

I pocket my phone and continue to work.

Saturday is Mollie's last day at Tracy's Threads. She'll be moving to Charleston on Wednesday. I'll miss her. She's my only girlfriend in town, and we've grown close these past few weeks. Some of her childhood girlfriends and bridesmaids have organized a going away party tonight at The Nest. I'm in no mood to socialize, but I shouldn't pass up this opportunity to make new friends.

Our reservation is for eight o'clock, which leaves me time for a strenuous workout on my Peloton before showering and dressing for the party. After careful consideration, I choose a mid-thigh-length floral dress with a halter neck and a fan of spaghetti straps down the back. I slip my feet into gold wedges and walk the short distance to The Nest.

I'm the last to arrive, and I find myself seated between Kayla and Heather, two of Mollie's closest friends who frequent the shop. I've never met any of the remaining eight young women, but the champagne flows like water, and I'm soon giggling and chatting with them like we're old friends. The customers are rowdy, the music is loud, and I find myself having fun for the first time since Victoria died.

When our waitress delivers our fourth—or maybe the fifth—round of drinks, Kayla asks Sheila, "Who's the gorgeous new bartender?"

"That's Savannah Darby." Sheila's eyes travel to the bar. "She's pretty, isn't she? We went to high school together. All the boys were in love with her."

I shift to see the woman moving fluidly behind the bar as she fills drink orders. She has a slim build and average height. Her wavy golden hair is pulled back in a high ponytail, and her green eyes are mesmerizing. I see nothing of myself in her face, yet something about her is oddly familiar.

I'm so spellbound by Savannah that I miss the discussion at the table about moving on to another bar until Heather nudges me. "What about you, Harper? Are you in?"

I tear my eyes away from Savanah. "Sorry, what? My mind was elsewhere."

Heather laughs. "Clearly. We're moving the party next door. Are you coming with us?"

"Y'all go ahead without me. I'm meeting a friend here later." I add my credit card to the pile in the center of the table and wait for Sheila to process the charges.

When the others vacate the table, I stand awkwardly until a seat opens at the bar. Savannah is filling a line of shot glasses with tequila when she notices me.

"What can I get you?" She finishes with the tequila and looks more closely at me. She tilts her head slightly as though she recognizes me. Then she shrugs as though deciding she doesn't.

"I'll have a glass of the house rosé," I say, not because I want more alcohol but because I need an excuse to remain at the bar.

"Coming right up." She delivers the tray of tequila shots to a waitress and returns with my wine. "Would you like to open a tab?"

I smile at her. "Please."

I watch in awe as she pulls taps, shakes martinis, and pours wine. Thirty minutes later, I'm still watching her like a lovesick teenager, my untouched glass of rosé before me, when someone taps me on my shoulder.

I crane my neck to see Cody standing behind me. "Oh. Hey."

He wedges himself in between me and the guy sitting next to me. "What's up?"

I give a slight nod at the bartender. "That's her. Savannah."

Cody glances at Savannah and then does a double take. "Whoa. That's so strange. How is it possible she looks nothing and everything like you?"

"I've been trying to figure that out myself. I have a button nose, hers has that little crease. Her eyes are olive and almond-shaped, mine are blue and round. I wish I had her killer dimples."

"You may not be the spitting image of her, but you look enough like her to be her daughter."

Propping my elbows on the bar, I cup my chin and stare at

Savannah with a dreamy expression. "She's amazing. I can't believe we're flesh and blood. All my life, I've wondered why I look nothing like my adoptive mother. It's both unsettling and comforting to see yourself in another person."

Cody tugs on one of my curls. "Stop staring. She's going to think you're a weirdo. Let's go dance."

I reluctantly tear my gaze away from Savannah and hear Lynyrd Skynyrd's "Sweet Home Alabama" playing. "Okay. But only because I like this song," I say.

By the time we reach the dance floor, the song has ended, and a slow one has begun. When I try to escape, Cody hooks an arm around me and pulls me close. "I know what you mean about genetics. My sister and I are clones of our father. Every time I look in the mirror, I think of him."

His dejected tone makes my heart hurt for him. "Are you and your sister very close?"

His warm smile tells me how much he loves his sister. "We're pretty tight. Lucky for me, Melissa lives in town. Neither of us is close with our mother and stepfather. They are always busy with our half sister, Becky."

"I wonder if Savannah has other children. Maybe I have a half sibling." Feeling claustrophobic, I push him away. "I need some air. Wanna take a walk on the boardwalk?"

"Sure. Do you want me to pay your tab?"

My eyes widen. "And miss a chance to talk to Savannah? No way! I'll meet you out front."

I fight through the crowd to the bar and flag Savannah down. "I need to pay for my wine, please."

"Sure thing," she says, taking my credit card from me.

While she's processing the charge, the words, "Do you like to sing?" slip from my lips.

Savannah's head jerks up, and a quizzical expression crosses her face. "I do. I write songs too. Why do you ask?"

I hunch a shoulder. "The jukebox songs are tired. I was

thinking some live entertainment would liven things up around here."

She flashes me a dimpled smile. "I agree wholeheartedly. I'll pass your request along to management."

"Cool!" As I turn away from her, a sense of loss overcomes me. How can I leave when I just found her?

Cody is waiting outside on the sidewalk when I emerge. He offers his arm, and we stroll toward the boardwalk.

"Savannah likes to sing. And she writes songs. Do you think musical talent is hereditary?"

"I'm not sure," Cody says. "Maybe. How do you know she likes to sing?"

"I asked her. I suggested they have live music. I'm dying to know her better. I need to figure out how to approach her. I could order two glasses of champagne and say, 'Let's celebrate. I'm your daughter.'"

He looks at me as though I've lost my mind.

I lean into him. "I'm just joking, Cody. I would never do that."

"I hope not. I would suggest a casual approach. Take your time. She took a job at The Nest, which means she's planning to stay in Water's Edge. Word about the mysterious Savannah Darby's sudden return and rumors about her past will spread. With luck, we'll learn more about why she ran away."

I stare down at the ground as we walk. "I guess you're right. I should give her a little more time to adjust to being home. I don't want to overwhelm her." We reach the water and lean against the railing, staring at the full moon. "You're different than I expected, Cody."

"Really? How so?"

"Whenever I've told other guys I wanna be friends, they can't handle it. They always want more. I appreciate you respecting my wishes. And I'm grateful for your friendship. I need someone to lean on right now."

"Glad to be of service." With a twinkle in his baby blues, he asks, "How many other guys are we talking about?"

"Too many to count. I told you I have commitment issues."

He rests a hand on my shoulder. "Now that I've gotten to know you better, I feel comfortable saying this. In my humble opinion, Harper Boone, the person you have trouble committing to is yourself."

SIXTEEN
SAVANNAH

A text message from my sister is waiting for me at the end of my shift on Saturday night. *Brunch tomorrow at the Sandy Island Club. Eleven o'clock.* It's more of a summons than an invitation. After running out on the family on Thursday night, I wouldn't dare turn her down. I know how eager she is to see me. And I'm grateful she gave me a few days before reaching out. With only two years in age separating us, Carrie and I have always shared a close relationship. Our family's dysfunction made that bond even more profound. Of all my family members, I'm most looking forward to my reunion with her.

Arriving ten minutes late to the Sandy Island Club, I find Carrie at a table on the edge of the terrace overlooking the ocean. With temperatures in the nineties, I prefer eating inside the air-conditioned grill room. I assume Carrie chose the terrace for privacy. We have much to discuss. Not all of it will be pleasant.

Carrie rises from her chair and hugs me tight. "I can't believe you're home. Not a day has gone by that I haven't thought of you."

I hold her at arm's length. "I've thought of you often as well, Carebear. I've missed our late-night talks." As teenagers, we often stayed up until the wee hours, confessing our secrets and sharing our hopes and dreams for the future.

"Me too." She gestures at the empty chair. "I hope you brought your appetite. The food here is delicious."

"Better than when we were children, I hope."

Carrie laughs out loud. "How could it get any worse?"

Our parents often brought us here when our mother was sober enough to dine out. The food was awful, but we enjoyed hanging out with our friends.

I take a seat opposite her. The limbs of a giant magnolia tree towering over us prevent us from burning to a crisp in the midday sun. Even under the tree's shade, the air feels heavy with humidity, and sweat soon streams down my back.

I spread the linen napkin on my lap. "Forgive me for saying this. We are practically strangers to each other. But you don't strike me as the country club type."

"Tom and I aren't members. Whenever I come here, which isn't very often, I use Dad's membership." Carrie presses a finger to her lips. "Don't tell him. So far, he hasn't figured it out."

I draw a zipper across my lips. "Mum's the word."

Our server arrives within minutes, filling our coffee cups and taking orders—a southwest omelet for Carrie and eggs benedict for me.

"So." Carrie places her folded hands on the table. "We have a lot of ground to cover. Where shall we start?"

"Let's save the beginning for last," I suggest, and Carrie nods. "That's probably best."

We talk through our entrees, dessert, and several cups of coffee, filling each other in on the past thirty years. More than once, I gaze at the white clapboard home down the beach in the distance. I don't realize I've grown silent when Carrie places a hand over mine. "Do you think about him often?"

I jerk my head toward her. "Think about who?"

"Pritchard. You keep looking at his parents' house."

"I'd forgotten how magnificent the house is. But no, I never think about Pritchard. Why would I? That part of my life ended decades ago."

"You had his baby, Savannah. A child binds you together for life."

I slip my hand out from under hers. "I realize we agreed to save this discussion for last, but I'm not really up to talking about it today."

A pall of sadness falls over her face. "I'm sorry, Savannah, but I've waited thirty years to talk about it, and I won't wait another day. I've done something I need to tell you about. I've kept this to myself all this time. I can't hold it inside another second," Carrie says and bursts into tears.

I lean close to my sister, aware of the other diners watching us. "Carrie, what on earth? Are you okay?"

She shakes her head as the tears stream down her cheek.

I need to get her out of here. The last thing I want is more rumors being spread about me. Fortunately, Carrie has already settled the bill. "Let's go for a walk on the beach."

She sucks in a sob. "Okay."

Leaving the table, we go down the terrace steps and cross the lawn. We take off our sandals and follow the meandering path through the dunes to the beach.

"Let's go this way," I say, guiding her north in the direction opposite the St. Clair home.

I give her a minute to collect herself. But instead of calming down, her sobbing grows louder. "For heaven's sake, Carrie. Whatever it is can't be that bad. Just tell me."

Her chin hits her chest, and she's unable to talk from hiccupping. Drawing her near, I reminisce about a joyful memory from our childhood, a ritual born out of necessity to comfort each other during our mother's drunken outbursts. "I remember like it happened yesterday. We're out on the boat with Daddy. Ashton is in the passenger seat next to him, and Will is wedged between you and me on the back bench seat. It's the Fourth of July, and we're anchored near the bridge, waiting for the fireworks to start. Our picnic dinner includes fried chicken, potato salad, and deviled eggs. With festive cupcakes for dessert."

When my sister's sobs finally subside, we drop down to the beach together, and she rests her head on my shoulder. "I'm so ashamed, Angel."

I smile at the nickname. As a child, my sisters called me Angel because of my halo of golden curls.

Carrie goes on, "I live with the guilt every single day. It's eaten out my insides. I'm a hollow person. And it's affected my relationships with everyone in our family."

"You're scaring me, Carrie. Just say it. Whatever it is happened over thirty years ago. It doesn't matter anymore."

"Yes, it does. It totally matters." Inhaling deeply, she draws herself to her full seated height. "Okay. Here goes." She takes another breath. "I don't know how much you remember about that night. You were in so much pain. I'd supported you during the pregnancy, held you all those nights you cried yourself to sleep. Knowing how much you wanted this baby made witnessing her birth all the more miraculous. Your labor went on forever. When she finally arrived, you could barely keep your eyes open. Just before you fell asleep, you asked me to be her godmother."

I smile. "I remember."

"I wanted to stay with you that night, but Mama made me sleep in my room. She brought me a glass of milk. I think she put one of her sleeping pills in it. I slept until eleven o'clock the following morning. By then, you and the baby were both gone."

A searing pain cuts my chest as the most defining moment of my life comes back to me. "I woke during the night and went in search of my baby. She was nowhere in the house. When I went to Mama's room, she was surprisingly sober. She told me the baby was gone, that she'd arranged for a private adoption. She must have sedated you. Otherwise, you would've heard the screaming fight that followed. I'd just given birth and I was delirious from exhaustion, but I knew if I didn't get away from Mama, I would strangle her with my bare hands."

Carrie's face contorts with anguish. "Mama tried to convince me that you'd willingly given the baby up and run away from home. But I didn't believe her. What she did was illegal. She abducted your baby."

I shake my head. "Not technically."

Carrie furrows her brow. "What do you mean?"

"When I was in labor, Mama made me sign some papers. She claimed they were consent forms for Dr. Richardson to deliver the baby."

"I don't remember that. I would never have let you sign anything. Where was I?"

"I'm not sure. You weren't in the room at the time. You kept trying to reach Pritchard, but the phone lines were down because of the storm."

A look of disbelief crosses Carrie's face. "Whoa. She actually had the papers in hand. Which means she'd been planning the adoption the whole time. She found out you and Pritchard were going to elope, and she was determined to stop you. If not for the ice storm, she would've figured out another way to take the baby from you."

I look away from my sister, staring out at the calm ocean. "Our parents were so wrong about Pritchard and me. They were convinced we were too young to get married, but we loved each other enough to make it work."

"If I hadn't intervened, things might have turned out different," Carrie says as a single tear spills over her lid and rolls down her cheek.

"What do you mean? What did you do?"

Carrie's shoulders slump as she lets out a loud sigh. "Pritchard appeared not long after I woke up. He was distraught when he learned you'd delivered the baby. He didn't believe Mama when she told him you'd put the baby up for adoption and left town to start a new life without him. He called her a lying drunk and threatened to get the police involved. He sat on the front stoop in the cold for hours, refusing to leave the house."

Dropping my gaze, I absently draw a heart in the sand with mine and Pritchard's initials. Pritchard had been a freshman at Alabama at the time, still home on Christmas break. The baby wasn't due for another ten days. We were to leave for Tuscaloosa together the following weekend. I'd already lined up an obstetrician to deliver the baby.

"What happened after that?" I ask, my voice barely audible.

"Mama insisted that lie to him. I wasn't thinking straight. I'd grown close to Pritchard during your pregnancy and loved him like a brother."

"What'd you say to him, Carrie?"

"I told him you had betrayed him. That you'd given away your baby and run away to start a new life. That he was better off without you. That you didn't love me or Pritchard or anyone else in our family." Carrie's eyes travel south in the direction of the St. Clair house. "I broke his heart that day."

"You did him a favor. You spared him a lot of heartache in the end. Did anyone ever try to find me?"

"Not at first. Mama believed you'd eventually come home. But I knew better. Once you made up your mind, you seldom changed it. After a few days, she notified the police, but since they considered you a runaway, they didn't try very hard to find you. For the longest time, I was sure you'd been killed in a car accident, that your car and body were mangled beyond recognition. The roads were covered in ice pellets. How *did* you manage to escape in your little Toyota?"

I grimace, thinking back on that harrowing drive. "I was terrified. The car slipped several times on my way through town. I'm lucky I didn't land in a ditch. But the roads outside of town were much better. Once I got on the interstate, it was smooth sailing."

Carrie and I sit for a long time in silence, lost in our thoughts. When I finally check my watch, I'm surprised it's already past three o'clock. I scramble to my feet. "I need to go. I'm due at work at four. I took a job bartending at The Nest."

As we walk back down the beach toward the club, Carrie says, "Do you hate me?"

I loop my arm through hers. "Of course not, Carebear. Mama did this, not you. I'm only sorry you've carried the burden of guilt all these years."

"I thought confessing would make me feel better. But reliving that awful time in our lives has only made me feel worse."

"That's why I try not to think about what happened. There's nothing either of us can do to change the past." I stop when we reach the pathway. "Something has always bothered me about that night. Where was Dad while I was in labor?"

"In the house. But he refused to go near your room. He said he couldn't bear to hear your cries of pain." Carrie kicks at the sand. "But there's something that's always bothered *me* about that night. Yours were the only tracks in the driveway when I woke up. The storm was still raging when Dr. Richardson left around midnight. So his tire tracks were covered up by ice."

I gesture for her to continue. "Your point is . . ."

"There were no other tracks in the driveway besides yours, which means no one came for the baby that night."

I furrow my brow. "Unless they came earlier. Right after the doctor left. Then their tire tracks would've also been covered."

"Maybe. But highly unlikely. They would've waited until morning when the storm cleared."

I glance at my watch again. "I don't have much time, Carrie. What are you getting at?"

"Where was the baby? She was not in the house. Neither was Dad."

I suck in a breath as though the wind has been knocked out of me. "If he'd left the house with the baby, you would've seen his tracks."

My sister nods. "Exactly."

"I don't know what to think about any of this. I need to let it process. But I've got to get to work." Turning my back on her, I take the lead down the path toward the club. When we reach the parking lot, I pull my sister in for a hug. "Thank you for brunch. I'm sorry my teenage drama so greatly impacted your life. I've made a lot of mistakes, Carebear. Not reaching out to you sooner is among the biggest."

Carrie's body goes slack in my arms. "I've waited a very long time to hear you say that."

SEVENTEEN
HARPER

I ponder my conversation with Cody throughout the remainder of the weekend. As much as I hate to admit it, he's right. The person I most have trouble committing to is myself. And I blame Victoria. I desperately needed her approval, and she never gave it to me. Because nothing I ever did was good enough. Because I was too busy trying to make her happy, I neglected my own needs and desires. I gave up on more than a singing career. I completely disregarded my creative side, the essence of who I am. How can I make a man happy when I'm emotionally unfulfilled? But I've been given a second chance, a fresh start. Things will be different this time around. I have a new role model I can more easily identify with. *If* Savannah will have me in her life. This brings us to the question of why she gave me up for adoption.

Carrie arrives fifteen minutes late for her first day at work on Monday. Her sullen mood warns me not to reprimand her. Everyone has off days. I see no need to worry unless she makes a habit of it.

I put her to work in the stockroom unpacking and tagging new merchandise. We've been open for about an hour when three attractive women enter the store. To the best of my recollection, none of them have shopped at Tracy's during my short time here.

I call out to them, "Welcome to Tracy's Threads. Let me know if you have questions."

They ignore me, continuing their conversation as they flip through the clothing racks. They're talking loud enough for me to hear them at the checkout station, and I can't help but eavesdrop.

The platinum blonde says, "I don't remember Savannah at all. She was two grades below us."

The striking brunette says, "I don't know how you could forget her. She was gorgeous and carried herself confidently and had a voice like an angel."

The redhead huffs out, "Unforgettable is right. I remember her proudly strutting through the hallway with her big belly as though being a pregnant teenager was an accomplishment. Why didn't her parents send her away to have the baby?"

The blonde lowers her voice, but I can still hear her. "I heard her mother made her put the baby up for adoption."

I'm about to say something to these tactless women in Savannah's defense when Carrie comes out of the storeroom. "Good morning, ladies. Are you looking for anything in particular?"

The three women drop their smiles, and the redhead says, "Carrie! So good to see you. Are you working here now?"

Carrie gives her head a curt nod. "Today's my first day."

The blonde's lips part in a sheepish grin. "I guess you heard us talking about Savannah."

"I heard you," Carrie says with a cold stare.

The brunette moves closer to Carrie. "I'm sure you're aware of the rumors circulating about Savannah. You can set the three of us straight, and we'll spread the word to others. What *did* happen to her baby?"

"That's none of your business," Carrie snaps.

The redhead ignores her. "Some say the baby died in childbirth, and your daddy buried it in the backyard."

"Others are even claiming your mother killed the baby. Which wouldn't be that far-fetched. After all, she was crazy." The blonde circles her finger near her temple.

The brunette barks out a laugh. "Their mother wasn't crazy, Eva. She was a drunk."

Anger surges through me, and I come from behind the counter. "I've had enough of this conversation." I swing open the door. "Please take your catty selves elsewhere."

The three women exit the shop in single file, huffing and puffing, promising never to shop at Tracy's Threads again.

Tears fill Carrie's eyes as she watches them leave. "Savannah's my sister."

"I know. I was babysitting for Will's children the night of Ashton's failed surprise welcome-home party. What did happen to her baby?"

Carrie hesitates as though on the verge of telling me. "It's Savannah's story to tell, not mine," she finally says, swiping at her eyes.

"I understand." My heart goes out to Carrie. She's obviously struggling. "I don't know about you, but I could use a coffee. I retrieve a twenty-dollar bill from my purse. "Do you mind running down to Corner Coffee? My treat. I'll have a chai latte."

She takes the money from me. "Thank you. I'll be back in a flash."

Carrie has no sooner disappeared down the street than Cody bursts through the front door. "Have you heard the rumors? Everyone in town is talking about Savannah's sudden return this morning."

"I'm aware. I just kicked three women out of the store for gossiping about her. Poor Carrie was near tears. I sent her out for coffee. This is too much for me. I need to sit down." I stumble on weak legs to the back of the store.

Cody follows me, plopping down in the taupe suede chair opposite me. "What did you hear that upset you?"

"Just their speculations." I repeat the overheard conversation. "Did you know Savannah's mother was an alcoholic?"

"That's public knowledge, Harper. I forgot you're new in town. I should've told you. But yes, Eileen Darby was a nasty drunk. She's rumored to have mistreated her four children."

I cover my face with my hands. "I wish I hadn't heard that part."

"There's a lot you need to know about the Darby family. Whenever you're ready, I'm happy to fill you in. There is good news. Apparently, Savannah and her baby daddy were very much in love."

My hands slide down my face. "Really?"

"That's what some are saying. Apparently, they were planning to elope."

I warn myself to take this with a grain of salt. I'm not sure who to trust with all the rumors going around. "Then maybe it is true. Maybe Savannah's mother put the baby up for adoption without her permission."

"Maybe. What kind of sick person would do such a thing?"

"An alcoholic. You just said yourself that she was a nasty drunk. Do you know who my father is?"

"I haven't heard any names mentioned," Cody says. "I can easily find out if you want me to do some digging."

I hesitate, considering how much I can handle at once. "Not yet. And if you find out, please don't tell me. For now, knowing they were in love is enough." Getting to my feet, I pace back and forth in front of the chairs. "Isn't it ironic that Savannah decided to return home after thirty years, just as I discover she's my biological mother?"

"I would call it fate like it was meant to be." His tender tone makes my heart melt. Cody is a genuinely nice guy who seems to understand me. More than anyone I've dated before.

I sit back down in my chair. "I'd like to repay you for your kindness. Can you come for dinner one night this week?" My hand shoots out. "Don't expect home cooking. By dinner, I mean prepared food from Fancy Pantry and a bag salad."

He smiles. "Sounds perfect. We have several officers out on vacation this week. I'm working overtime tonight and tomorrow. How does Wednesday sound?"

"Wednesday is great."

"I should get back to work," he says, pushing himself out of the chair as though he dreads leaving.

I walk him to the door and watch through the window as he gets in his patrol car and speeds away. While the timing is all wrong for a romantic relationship, when it comes to Cody, I can't help myself. I find everything about him irresistible. Overall, I'm happier in Water's Edge than in Raleigh. And discovering my creative side is boosting my confidence.

I'm still standing at the window, contemplating my life, when Carrie returns with our coffees.

She hands me my latte and change. "I'm sorry, Harper. I've gotten off to a bad start. I promise to do better going forward."

I pat her shoulder. "Don't worry about it. You have a lot going on with your family."

She stares down at her coffee. "That's no excuse. This job means a lot to me. I don't want to blow it."

"All I ask is for you to be transparent. Tell me if you need time off or are having a bad day."

Carrie smiles. "Deal."

"We both could use a distraction. And I have a project that will keep our minds occupied."

We work in companionable silence for the next few hours, rearranging merchandise to accommodate the new items Carrie tagged earlier. She has a good eye and suggests small changes that render dramatic results.

Business is slow, which is not unusual for a Monday, and only a handful of customers enter the shop that afternoon, one of them being Carrie's sister Ashton around four o'clock. When Carrie goes to wait on her, I hover nearby, not to eavesdrop on them, but in case she needs me for backup.

"I'm looking for a dress to wear to a wedding next Saturday," Ashton explains. "One of Sully's nieces is getting married in Charleston."

"That sounds like fun. You've come at the right time. We just put out a bunch of new things," Carrie says, showing her sister to a rack of cocktail attire.

Ashton flips through the dresses, choosing several to try on. She turns her nose up when Carrie suggests a tiered silk floral dress, but Carrie insists. "Just try it on. The blues and pinks will look lovely with your coloring."

Ashton holds the dress up to her body in front of the mirror. "It's too froufrou. I'll look like a lollipop. But I'll try it on to satisfy you."

I secretly agree with Ashton. The layers are too much for her, and my jaw drops when she emerges from the dressing room. She's tall enough to carry the layers, and the colors soften her complexion.

Ashton twirls around in front of the mirror. "I never would've picked it for myself, but I love it. I won't even waste time trying the other dresses on. You're good at this, Carrie."

"I'm glad you found something."

Ashton changes back into her street clothes and meets Carrie at the checkout counter. I stand behind Carrie to guide her through her first credit card charge.

"Have you seen Savannah?" Ashton asks, taking the receipt from Carrie.

"We had brunch yesterday."

"Oh? How did that go?" Ashton asks with a hint of jealousy.

"Better than I expected. We talked for hours." Carrie places a plastic cover over the hanging dress and hands it across the counter to her sister.

"Did she tell you how long she's staying in town?"

Carrie joins her sister at the front of the checkout counter. "Indefinitely, I think. She's renting a carriage house in the historic district and bartending at The Nest."

"Good for her. I've texted her several times, but she's ignoring me. I guess she'll reach out when she's ready."

"She will. But she needs her space right now. Coming home and facing so many memories is hard on her."

When the sisters head toward the door, I remain at the counter to give them privacy. I sense friction between Ashton and Carrie. With an alcoholic mother, their family dynamics must be complicated. I can't imagine the dysfunction the Darby siblings experienced as children. While I want to know everything about Savannah, I'd happily leave that part out.

EIGHTEEN
SAVANNAH

I'm working my first lunch shift on Monday when I look up from my mixology project to find Will seated at the bar. Even if I hadn't seen pictures of him on Ashton's social media posts, I would recognize those piercing blue eyes anywhere.

His name is soft on my lips. "Will."

"Hey, Savannah. I didn't realize you were working here. I come in often for lunch, but I can leave if I make you uncomfortable."

"Please don't. I'm sorry I ran out of Marsh Point the other night. Seeing everyone at once was too much."

"I understand. Ashton feels terrible about what happened." He smiles. "She can't help herself. Even after all these years, she's still taking care of us. She would've made an excellent mother. It's a shame she never had children. Give her a chance. She truly wants to do right by you. She's been a good friend and ally this past year."

"I was too hard on her. I'll text her soon." I tug my order pad and pen out of my apron pocket. "What can I get you? Since you're a regular, I assume you already know what you want."

"I have several favorites, but today, I'm in the mood for the Asian sesame salad with grilled shrimp. And water is fine to drink."

I scribble the order on the pad and tear off the paper. "Got it. I'll be right back."

When I deliver the order to the chef, I pause to collect myself. This surge of emotions is unexpected. We weren't close because of the six years of age separating us. As the baby, we doted on him. He was the innocent one, the sibling who most needed protecting from our deranged mother.

Feeling calmer, I return to the front. I fix Will a glass of iced water, assure him his order will be ready soon, and focus again on drink mixing.

"What're you working on there?" Will asks, watching me.

"I'm revamping the drinks menu. This particular concoction is honey lavender lemonade." I add a sprig of lavender to the drink and slide it across the bar to him. "Tell me what you think."

He sips the drink and smacks his lips. "Very tasty. I love the freshness. What's in it?"

"A mix of vodka, lemon juice, homemade lavender-infused honey syrup, and a splash of soda water."

He takes another sip. "I assume you don't want it back now that my germs are on the glass."

I chuckle. "No, you can have it."

At almost two o'clock only a few lunch stragglers remain in the restaurant. Sensing the two young men sitting several seats away watching me, I make a funny face at them.

Will sees me and yells at them. "Hey! Didn't your mama teach you not to stare?"

"Chill, man," says one guy.

"We're just checking out the sexy new bartender," says the other.

Will appears as though he's going to lay into them when I shake my head. "Don't, Will. They're not worth it," I say, although I admit it's nice to have a man defend my honor. A man who isn't interested in getting in my pants. A man who is my grown-up little brother.

Will gives the guys one last menacing scowl. "I'll let them off the hook. But only because I don't want to cause trouble for you."

I hunch a shoulder. "In case you haven't heard, I'm the primary source of gossip for the rumor mill. Today's popular opinion claims I killed my baby and ran away to avoid murder charges. Yesterday, everyone was certain I went insane after the baby was stillborn, and I've been in the nuthouse for the past thirty years."

I go to the kitchen for Will's salad. When I return, the rude customers next to him are paying Amber for their orders.

Once they're gone, Will says, "I understand what you're going through, Savannah. I've been the subject of town gossip, not once but twice. And it's not a good feeling."

"That surprises me. I know so little about you, only the happy times Ashton has posted on social media."

"I won't bore you," Will grumbles as he stabs a shrimp with his fork and stuffs it into his mouth.

"You won't be boring me. I want to know. I *need* to know what I've missed."

He takes another bite of salad and wipes his mouth with his napkin. "When I was fifteen, my best friend died in a freak accident. All my schoolmates and their parents blamed me."

My hand flies to my neck. "Please tell me you're not talking about Bert."

Dropping his gaze, he nods. "Unfortunately. We were at a party. Bert had been drinking. I had not. I tried to get him to go home when he started making a fool of himself. We wrestled, and he collided with a rotten porch railing on the second-story balcony. He broke his neck when he fell."

I clamp my hand over my mouth. "That's awful. Poor Bert."

"The police charged me with manslaughter, but because I was underage, the case never went to trial."

"I'm so sorry, Will. I can't imagine what that must have been like for you. When was the second time?"

"I'll give you the abbreviated version of a complex story. My first wife, Tracy, tragically passed away in a boating accident last summer. Following her death, her parents wrongfully accused me of murder to gain custody of my girls. After Labor Day, I met Julia, who had recently moved to town. Our children brought us together, and we forged a friendship. This friendship eventually blossomed into a romantic relationship. A local journalist found out about us. He falsely claimed Julia and I were having an affair at the time of Tracy's death and that we conspired to kill her. The town turned against me."

"I saw the photographs of Julia from your wedding. She's lovely."

His expression softens. "She's the best. I hope you get to meet her soon." He lifts his hand. "No pressure. Whenever you're ready," he says and returns to his salad.

I smile as I move on to my next mixology experiment, a modified Bee's Knees with the same lavender-infused honey syrup. My brother seems like a good guy. Maybe we can have a relationship.

When he finishes eating, he pushes his plate away. "I have a confession to make, Savannah. I idolized you when we were growing up. You were seriously cool, a total badass with your killer vocals and mad guitar skills."

My heart flutters. "That's sweet of you to say."

"Despite the differences in our age, we might've been close if not for Carrie."

"What did Carrie have to do with it?" I ask, stirring the drink with a cocktail straw.

"She refused to let anyone close to you. She wanted you all to herself."

In hindsight, I realize he's probably right. Carrie was possessive of me to the point of being obsessive.

"I'm not judging her," Will says. "Thanks to Mom, none of us were normal. She screwed us all up."

"That's for sure." I slide the Bee's Knees to him. "Try this one."

Will takes a sip and pushes the glass back to me. "Meh. I much prefer the other one."

I dump the drink in the sink and place the glass in the dishwasher. "Where were you during the ice storm? The night I gave birth to my baby?"

"I spent the night with Bert. We were excited about the storm, although we were hoping for snow and disappointed when we got ice. I remember his mother taking us shopping. We loaded up on junk food from the grocery store and movies from Blockbuster." The faraway look on Will's face is replaced by sadness. "I was heartbroken when I found out you had run away. For the longest time, I slept with the framed photograph you gave me that Christmas. Remember? The one of us double water-skiing the previous summer?"

I smile. "I remember. Do you recall anything strange about the days following the storm? Did Mom or Dad do anything out of the ordinary?"

Will peers at me from under his furrowed brow. "Are you kidding me? They never did anything ordinary."

I give him an exasperated look. "You know what I mean, Will."

He folds his arms over his chest. "That's one of those dark places in my memory I prefer not to think about. Carrie cried all the time. Mom and Dad fought more than usual. The police were in and out, although they never had any good news to report. Whenever I was home, I stayed in my room as much as possible." He leans across the counter and lowers his voice. "Have you ever tried to find your child?"

"Nope," I say in a clipped tone that warns off further discussion.

Will appears wounded. "I'm sorry, Savannah. I didn't mean to bring up a touchy subject."

"And I didn't mean to snap at you." I take his plate to the back, and when I return, his credit card is waiting on the bar. I process the charge, and he signs the slip.

He stands to go. "I'm glad you're back, Savannah. We can't make up for thirty years of lost time, but maybe we can start over. I'd like for us to be friends."

"I'd like that as well." I come from behind the bar to hug him. "I never meant to cause anyone pain, Will."

"I know that, Savannah." He draws me away so he can see my face. "Since you're working here, I assume you plan to stay in town. Have you found a suitable place to live?"

"Yes! I'm renting Muriel Richardson's carriage house."

He drops his hands from my shoulders. "Nice! Muriel is a dear lady. I've done renovations on both the main and carriage houses. She keeps her property in excellent shape. And she is a wonderful cook. Ask her if you can sample her rosemary Parmesan wafers. They are the best things I've ever eaten."

"I've noticed she spends a lot of time in her kitchen and loves cooking for other people. I've only been there a few days, and I've already eaten two meals with her."

"You're in a good spot. Let me know if you need anything." He glances at the door. "All right then. I need to get back to work. I hope to see you again soon," he says, kissing my cheek in parting.

With my fingers pressed to my cheek, I watch him leave The Nest and drive away in his pickup truck.

During the remainder of my shift, I replay our conversation on auto-rewind, and my thoughts continue to weigh heavily on me during my walk home later that evening. I'm so distracted, Muriel startles me when she calls out from her back-screened porch.

I press my hand against my racing heart. "Muriel! I didn't see you sitting there."

"I'm sorry if I frightened you. Would you like to join me for some tea?" she asks, holding up her mug.

I move closer to the porch. "Depends. Do you happen to have any rosemary Parmesan wafers on hand?"

Muriel laughs out loud. "You've been talking to your brother. Will is a dear man."

"Funny. He used that exact word to describe you." I climb the porch steps and sit in a rocker beside her.

"Coincidentally, I made a fresh batch of wafers this morning." Muriel rises out of her chair. "And I have about every flavor of tea imaginable. What strikes your fancy?"

"I'm fine with whatever you're having."

"Licorice. I'll be back in a flash." She hurries inside.

While I wait for her return, I study her manicured garden, a square of boxwoods forming a border around colorful perennials in all shapes and sizes.

Muriel appears on the porch with a tray. "Here we go." She sets the tea tray on the small table between our chairs. "Now, tell me what's on your mind that has you so distracted."

I lift a mug and take a sip of the honey ginger tea. "Will asked if I've ever tried to find my child. I didn't mean to snap at him. But it's a sore subject. I think of her every single day. What do you think, Muriel? Am I a bad person because I've never tried to find her?"

"Everyone handles things differently, Savannah. There is no good or bad, right or wrong, in this difficult situation."

I stare down at my tea. "I never would've considered it when she was a child. But she's an adult now, thirty years old last January. Still, I'm not sure it's my place to interfere in her life. What if her parents never told her she was adopted? A revelation like that could be devastating."

"Or, depending upon her circumstances, it could be a blessing. She may have lost her parents. Or she may not get along with them. Or maybe she knows she's adopted and is curious about her birth parents."

I take a rosemary Parmesan wafer off the tray and pop it into my mouth. The combination of flavors delights my palette, and I let out a satisfied groan. Helping myself to another wafer,

I say, "I have no idea how I would even go about looking for her."

"You could start with one of those genetic matching websites." Muriel shifts in her chair to face me. "What are you afraid of, Savannah?"

"Of getting hurt. Not only did I lose my child, I lost the love of my life. The pain was unbearable, and I vowed never to let myself be vulnerable like that again. It's why I never let myself get close to another man. And why I never wanted more children."

"In making these sacrifices, you denied yourself the opportunity to find love again. To be the wonderful mother I know you would've been. But it's not too late, sweet girl."

"I don't know why I'm telling you this. I've never admitted it to anyone before."

"Sometimes talking to a stranger is easier."

I roll my head on the back of the chair to look at her. "That's true. But some people are better listeners and less judgmental than others."

NINETEEN
HARPER

I make the mistake of telling Carrie I've invited a friend over for dinner. After grilling me for much of the afternoon, she assumes, correctly, that I'm hoping my dinner guest will become more than a friend. She insists I cook for him instead of serving prepared food from the Fancy Pantry, curling her lip in distaste at the mention of the gourmet grocery store.

I chuckle. "Gee, Carrie. What do you have against the Fancy Pantry?"

"It's entirely too expensive for what they offer. I can cook a better meal for half the price. We'll find an easy recipe for you," she says and clicks on the recipe organizer app on her phone.

I peer over her shoulder as she scrolls through recipes in the casserole category. We discuss several options at length before deciding on a simple version of chicken Parmesan.

"The recipe calls for store-bought marinara, which will cut your cooking time in half. Buy a bag of Caesar salad and a loaf of crusty French bread, and you have a meal. You can't go wrong. Everyone likes chicken Parmesan." She taps on her phone's screen. "There. I emailed you the recipe."

"I'm impressed by your organizational skills."

She waves her phone at me. "There's no reason to be unorganized when you have so many tools at your fingertips."

After work on Wednesday, I stop by the market for the ingredients on the way home. I'm surprised at how easy the dish is to prepare. The recipe instructs me to sauté the breaded chicken, add several layers of provolone cheese, and pour in the marinara, sprinkling Parmesan cheese over the top. Within a few minutes, the casserole is ready for the oven. I dump the salad in a wooden bowl and arrange the wedge of Drunken Goat cheese I bought for an appetizer with some crackers on a small plate, covering both with plastic wrap. After changing into a casual black knit dress that clings to my curves, I light a few candles and turn on soft jazz music. I'm opening a bottle of red wine when the doorbell rings promptly at seven o'clock.

I smile when I see Cody holding a bouquet of summer wildflowers and wearing that dimpled grin that makes my stomach somersault. He's handsome in slim-fit khaki jeans and a blue striped polo shirt. I get a whiff of his sandalwood cologne when he kisses my cheek.

Cody hands me the flowers and enters the apartment. "It smells amazing in here. But I thought you said you weren't cooking."

"I found a dish I was dying to try," I say casually, as though experimenting with recipes is a hobby. "I hope you like chicken Parmesan."

"I love chicken Parma."

"What do you want to drink?" I ask, heading to the kitchen with the flowers. "I just opened a bottle of red wine. But I also have beer and vodka."

Cody joins me in the kitchen. "Wine sounds great."

He pours the wine while I locate a handblown cobalt vase that belonged to my mother and fill it with water. Adding the flowers, I place the vase on the small kitchen table I've set with linens and more candles.

"I hope you're not starving. The chicken Parma needs a few more minutes in the oven."

He rubs his belly. "I *am* starving. But I'll survive a few more minutes."

"Lucky for you, I have snacks." I remove the plastic wrap from the cheese and crackers. We take the appetizer to the living room and sit on the sofa.

Cody loads a cracker with cheese. "Have you seen Savannah again?"

"Unfortunately, no. Have you?"

Cody sits back on the sofa with his wine. "Yes! I went to The Nest for lunch yesterday. By the way, she took your advice about live music. They are having karaoke on Friday night."

"Cool! Not exactly live, but it's a start."

His smile fades. "I feel sorry for her though. The rumors are getting more vicious by the day. I ate at the bar. Amber served me, not Savannah. But I watched her. She seems sad. People openly talk about her as though she's not even there." Cody pauses for a sip of wine. "I find it strange no one is talking about the father of her baby."

"*My* father, Cody. Not *the* father." I get up from the sofa and walk over to the window.

Cody comes to stand beside me. "I'm sorry, Harper. I didn't mean to touch on a sore nerve. Say the word, and I'll find out who he is."

"No, Cody. I told you. I'm not ready for that. Stop playing detective. This is my life, not some investigation."

He appears wounded. "I understand. I'm only trying to help." Placing an arm around me, he pulls me in for a half hug.

"I know. And I appreciate your friendship. I have two choices. I can either tell Savannah my suspicions about her being my birth mother, or I wait to get the results from my DNA test and hope there's a match. I'll probably let the situation play itself out. Whatever happens, happens."

"That's a good plan of action. What if I hear mention of your father's name? Do you want me to tell you or keep it to myself?"

"Keep it to yourself." I wriggle free of his arm. "If it turns out Savannah was assaulted, I'm not sure I can handle knowing my father is a rapist."

"She wasn't raped, Harper. We already know she was in love with your father."

"We don't know that for sure. We *heard* it, along with a bunch of other crazy rumors. I'm not listening to gossip. I want proof. All the more reason for you not to tell me if you hear my father's name."

He throws his hands up, his wine sloshing in his glass but not spilling over. "Okay. I get it."

Irritation prickles my skin, and I excuse myself to check on the casserole. Over dinner, we avoid the topic of my birth parents, and Cody entertains me with funny stories of our town's more eccentric citizens. He insists on doing the dinner dishes while I scoop ice cream onto warmed creamy slices of pound cake—Carrie's contribution to the dinner.

After dessert, we stand at the window, watching dusk settle and lights twinkle across town. Cody fingers a lock of hair off my cheek. "If I didn't know better, I'd think you were trying to seduce me with a romantic dinner—candles, home cooking, and sultry music. What happened to just wanting to be friends?"

I turn toward him. "I'm finding *this* irresistible," I say, touching the tip of my finger to his dimple. "And no matter how hard I try, I can't stop thinking about what a good kisser you are."

"What about your commitment problem?"

"Who said anything about committing? Besides, I'll never find the right guy if I don't keep trying."

He tilts his head to the side. "Does that mean I'm a candidate for the position?"

"Maybe. But there's more to it than that. As you pointed out, my lack of commitment to myself is part of the problem. And I'm working on that. Now that my mother is gone, I have no one to answer to, and I'm learning to live my life for me." I place my hands around his neck. "And right now, I would very much like for you to kiss me."

"It would be my pleasure," he says and kisses me with an intensity that warms my belly. Taking him by the hand, I lead him into the bedroom.

"Are you sure about this?" he asks with desire in his blue eyes.

"Positive," I respond in a throaty whisper.

Cody is an experienced lover, and our passion is equal parts hot and tender. It's well past midnight by the time we exhaust ourselves and fall asleep in each other's arms.

I wake at seven on Thursday morning to find him gone. But he left a warm coffee beside my bed and a note inviting me to attend karaoke with him at The Nest on Friday night.

Smiling, I nestle beneath the covers, my body exquisitely sore from sex. It's too soon to know if Cody is my soul mate, but he's come closer to being the right guy than anyone I've ever dated.

TWENTY
SAVANNAH

I do my best to tune out the gossipmongers. But it isn't easy when they don't bother lowering their voices, and the nasty things they say about my family cut deeply.

I focus my attention on my work. I finalize the new drinks menu and suggest the chef try a few appetizers that were popular with our patrons at The Lantern. Using my own money, I rent a karaoke machine, hire a local deejay, and organize the first event for Friday night. The customers seem excited. I hope we have a good turnout. I'm trying to impress my new boss, but Taylor only breezes through a few times during the week without staying long enough to notice the changes.

During a lull in business on Wednesday afternoon, Amber catches me standing in the middle of the restaurant, assessing the decor.

"What are you plotting now?" she asks, standing beside me.

"Getting rid of all these turtles. The mounts have been hanging on the wall since I was a kid. The walls could use a fresh coat of paint."

"I agree to a certain extent. This place needs a facelift to bring it into the twenty-first century. But the turtles are our mascots. We aren't *The Nest* without them."

"I agree. But what if we depict the turtles in a different way? We could hire a local artist or photographer to paint or photograph scenes of sea turtles in their element."

"That's an interesting idea. Good luck convincing Taylor. She follows the 'If it ain't broke, don't fix it' motto. She could care less what the place looks like as long as we're making money."

When I wake up early on Thursday morning, Ashton is the first person to enter my mind. Hoping to catch her before she leaves for work, I throw on some clothes and drive out to Marsh Point. When I clang the knocker, she comes to the door with a mug of coffee in hand.

"Savannah! This is a surprise."

"Hey, Ashton. I've been meaning to text you. But I decided it was best to apologize in person. I'm sorry I ran out on you the other night. You went to the trouble to organize the welcome-home party, and I acted like a brat."

"I'm the one who owes you an apology. You specifically asked me not to tell the others, and I went against your wishes. I was beyond myself with excitement, and I wanted to tell the whole world."

I smile at her. "And I appreciate your enthusiasm."

She lifts her mug. "Would you like some coffee? I was getting ready to have a second cup."

"I would love some." I enter the house and follow her to the kitchen. "Don't let me hold you up if you need to leave for work."

"You're fine. I have plenty of time. My first meeting isn't until ten." She drops a pod into the Keurig and presses the button to brew. "I understand you've seen Carrie and Will."

I drop my purse on the counter. "Carrie and I had brunch on Sunday, and I ran into Will at The Nest. Coincidentally, I took a job there as a bartender."

"Will told me. He says you're renting the Richardson's guesthouse. You are always welcome here if that doesn't work out."

I shake my head. "Too many memories. But thanks for the offer."

"I'm just glad you're staying in town." She hands me the coffee. "Cream or sugar?"

"Black is fine," I say, sipping the coffee.

Ashton opens a bakery box on the counter. "Would you like a croissant? They are still warm from the oven at Custom Crust. Mia dropped them off on her way to Will's this morning."

My stomach rumbles at the sight of the flaky pastry. "Sure. They look delicious."

We take our croissants and coffee to the table on the veranda. The morning is glorious, with the salty scent of the ocean filling the air and the marsh grass swaying beneath a gentle breeze.

"What a lovely way to start the day. If not for Mama's ghost haunting the house, I'd take you up on your offer to live here," I say, only half teasing.

"The door is open any time. Renovating the house helped Will get over the worst of his memories. Maybe if you spent more time here," she says, her voice trailing off.

"I can spend more time at Marsh Point without living here. I'm set in my ways. I like having my own place."

"I understand that," Ashton says.

I bite the end of the croissant. The pastry, so light and buttery, dissolves in my mouth. "I'm trying to make sense of the awful things people are saying about our family. What was Mama like in her later years?"

"She'd mellowed a lot. She still drank too much and was a total recluse, hardly ever leaving the house. But she wasn't the angry shrew she'd been during our youth. I spent a lot of time with her. She could be quite pleasant."

"I find that hard to believe," I mutter. "Did she ever talk about what happened? Did she ever say why she took my child away from me?"

Ashton lowers her gaze to her plate. "Many times. Mama felt enormous guilt about what happened. She blamed Pritchard's mother."

My brow shoots up. "What do you mean? How so?"

Ashton steeples her fingers on the table. "She didn't think you were good enough for her son."

"That's crazy. Our family has as much money and prestige as the St. Clairs."

"Not in Isabelle's mind. She thought we were trailer park trash because of the way Mama behaved." Ashton leaves the table and walks over to the railing, looking out across the sound for a long minute before turning back toward me. "Did you know she threatened to cut Pritchard off without a dime?"

"Of course. Pritchard didn't think she was serious."

"She was serious, all right. She went ballistic when she found out you two were planning to elope. She confronted Mama. Isabelle actually came here to Marsh Point." Ashton points at the porch floor. "The adoption was her idea. She was never going to let her son marry you. She threatened Mama. Either Mama made you put the baby up for adoption or she was going to destroy your life."

Flashes of angry arguments with my mother come back to me. "Mama begged me to consider adoption, but there was no way I was giving up my baby. And so, she stole her from me."

"Mama saw no way out for you. Pritchard needed his parents' financial support to finish college."

The anger I've suppressed for three decades propels me to my feet. "That's the lamest excuse I've ever heard. Mama knew how much I loved Pritchard and our baby. *She* could've helped us until we got on our feet. *She* could've loaned us money or allowed us to live here. Instead, she gave away her grandchild, her own flesh and blood."

Ashton closes the distance between us. "She was a sick woman,

Savannah. Her judgment was severely impaired from the effects of the alcohol."

"Maybe so. But Dad was mentally competent, and he went along with her. And now you're making excuses for her." I throw up my hands. "I've had it with this family. I was better off on my own."

Spinning on my heels, I flee the porch, retrieving my purse from the kitchen on my way out. Waves of emotion crash over me during the drive home. Anger and remorse and sadness. Arriving back at the carriage house, I burst into tears at the sight of Muriel pruning rose bushes in her garden.

Hearing my sobs, she drops her pruning shears and rushes toward me. She engulfs me in a hug, and I collapse against her sweaty body. I don't remember my mother ever comforting me. Ashton was always the one who held me when I cried. This revelation makes me weep harder. My sister does not deserve the rotten treatment I've shown her since my return home.

When my tears finally subside, Muriel walks me inside to her kitchen and plants me on a stool at the island. As she fills two tumblers with ice and water, I tell her about my conversation with Ashton.

"I'm so sorry, Muriel. The last thing you need is a tenant with so much baggage. I don't blame you if you kick me out."

She hands me a tumbler and sits down next to me. "Not on your life, Savannah Darby. I believe the good Lord sent you to me for a reason." She slides a box of tissues across the counter to me. "Is what you learned from Ashton about Pritchard's mother a new revelation?"

I shake my head as I blow my nose. "Not really. What I didn't know I suspected. So what if Isabelle came up with the idea for the adoption? Mama still went along with it. Thinking about that awful time in my life is too painful. It's much easier to pretend it never happened."

"When you were in Washington. But now that you're home, you can no longer hide from the past."

My chin drops to my chest. "I guess not."

"However difficult it may be, the time has come for you to face reality, Savannah. Otherwise, you'll always be running from the truth, and that's no way to live. Take a few days to process everything. Wallow in self-pity, if it makes you feel better. Then bury the whole ugly mess in your graveyard of memories. Because no good will come from dwelling on what happened."

"I knew coming back to Water's Edge was a risk. Maybe I was hasty in taking a job and signing a lease."

"Maybe. But it's too soon for you to know for sure. You've made a huge lifestyle change. Give yourself more time to acclimate. The lease and job are the least of your concerns."

"I should let you get back to your yard work." I drain the rest of my water and take the empty tumbler to the sink. I press my cheek against hers on the way out. "Thank you for being so understanding."

"You're most welcome, sweetheart. I'm here for you anytime."

I walk with my head lowered back to the carriage house, where I spend the rest of the morning, until it's time for me to go to work, feeling sorry for myself.

TWENTY-ONE
HARPER

Cody and I share appetizers—fish tacos, garlic fries, and a California sushi roll—from the new specials menu while we wait for karaoke to begin. The vibe is lively. Many of the customers arrived at five for happy hour, and now, at almost nine o'clock, they are rowdy and eager for the entertainment to begin. In the back corner of the restaurant, a makeshift karaoke stage awaits. Lamar Clayton, a local deejay The Nest recruited to MC the event, waits nearby for the action to start.

"Do you know what you're gonna sing?" Cody asks, his mischievous smile reaching his dimples.

I give my head a vigorous shake. "No way. I'm not singing karaoke."

"Why not? You have the best voice in the house."

"Says you, who's only heard me sing once when I was goofing around."

"Once was enough. And if that was goofing around, I want to hear you sing when you're being serious. Removing his phone from his pocket, his fingers fly across the screen. "Here's a list of popular karaoke songs. What about . . ."—he scrolls down the list —"'I Wanna Dance with Somebody.'"

I nearly choke on a bite of sushi roll. "Whitney Houston? Are you kidding me? I can't remember the last time I sang to a live audience. There's no way I would attempt Whitney Houston. Besides, karaoke is for people who don't mind making fools of themselves. I am not one of those people."

I've never been to a karaoke event. I have no idea what to expect. But the talent of the young woman who begs to be first surprises me. She sings a Britney Spears song I despise, but her vocals do it justice, and the audience cheers her on.

When no one volunteers to go next, Lamar convinces a woman who can't hold a tune to try it. After her disastrous performance ends, Cody jumps to his feet, pulls me out of the booth, and marches me to the stage.

Lamar hands me a microphone and flashes me a grin. "What's your pleasure, young lady?"

I take the microphone from him. "'Because of You' by Kelly Clarkson," I say, one of my favorite songs from my youth.

The crowd applauds my choice. Even though I haven't performed the song in years, the lyrics flow effortlessly from me. I'm sixteen again, in command of the stage as I perform at my school's talent show. The restaurant goes wild when I finish, chanting my name and begging for another song.

"That was sensational," Lamar says. "Do you have one more in you?"

Feeling bold, I request that he play Whitney Houston's "One Moment in Time."

Confidence overcomes me, and I belt out the vocals with the carefree abandonment I haven't known in years. I'm out of breath, and my heart is pounding as I hand Lamar the microphone and escape the stage.

Cody beams with pride as he hugs me. Walking back to our booth, he says, "I knew you were good, but that was spectacular."

"Thanks," I say, sliding onto the bench seat and taking a long drink of white wine to calm my nerves.

"Thank you, Harper," Lamar says to the audience. "Amateur night quickly went pro. Is anyone brave enough to follow Harper's act?"

Someone in the crowd calls out in a singsong voice, "Sa-van-nah. Your turn."

My eyes dart about the restaurant, landing on Will seated at a table with Julia, Ashton, and Ashton's boyfriend, Sully.

"Calling Savannah Darby," Lamar says into the microphone.

Savannah's head jerks up from mixing cocktails. "Are you calling me?"

Lamar waves her over. "Your fans await."

Wiping her hands on her apron, Savannah comes from behind the bar. When she reaches Lamar, she whispers in his ear, and he plays the music for Aretha Franklin's "You Make Me Feel Like a Natural Woman."

Savannah holds the crowd spellbound with her powerful and haunting vocals. By the time she finishes, there is no dry eye in the room, including mine.

When she starts to leave the stage, Lamar grabs her by the arm. "How about a duet with Harper? What do you say, audience? Would you like to hear Harper and Savannah sing together?"

The crowd roars its approval. Fear clinches my gut, and I look over at Cody. "I can't do this. She's my birth mother. And we haven't even officially met yet."

He nods encouragement. "You've got this, Harper. I'll go with you," he says, walking me back to the stage.

"How about if we let the audience pick the song?" Lamar suggests.

Savannah and I both shake our heads. "Not fair," Savannah says.

"Then why don't each of you name a song, and we'll let them choose?" Lamar's green eyes shine. He's clearly enjoying himself.

I nominate "Shallow," and Savannah suggests "Perfect."

"Excellent choices," Lamar says. "Two lovely contemporary ballads. What's it going to be, audience? Hands up for 'Shallow.'"

Nearly everyone raises their hands.

"'Shallow' it is." Lamar produces a third microphone, and the music begins.

Savannah's glorious presence awes me. Standing so close to her sends a shiver down my spine. But when the music starts, she smiles at me, setting me at ease. Our voices are as one, blending harmoniously, creating a captivating melody that brings the crowd to their feet.

Amongst the thunder of applause, Savannah and I exit the stage together. When she turns to me, I'm so mesmerized by her that I long to reach out and stroke her cheek.

"You have a lovely voice," Savannah says. "I can't remember when I've had so much fun. We should do it again sometime."

"I would like that." The words are on my lips, and I'm about to tell her I believe she's my birth mother when someone in the audience catches her attention. The color drains from her face, and she utters a name that starts with a *P,* but I can't make out the rest. She excuses herself and goes in search of the person.

I turn around to face Cody, who lifts me off my feet. "You were amazing. But why do you look like you lost your best friend?"

I'm about to explain when he is also distracted by someone in the crowd. "Hold that thought. I'll be right back," he says, disappearing into the crowd.

As the next karaoke person screeches out the lyrics to a Taylor Swift tune, I return to our booth and gulp down the last of my wine.

With chin propped in hand, I'm staring down at the table when the screen on Cody's phone lights up with a text message from someone named Carl Payne. I glance around the room, and when I don't see Cody anywhere, I pick up the phone and read the text. *I asked around. It wasn't difficult to find out Savannah's baby's father was Pritchard St. Clair.*

I drop the phone on the table with a clatter. Is he the person whose name begins with a *P* that Savannah appeared shocked to see in the audience just now? Is this her first encounter with him since her return home? Why was Cody's friend or coworker making inquiries about my father when I specifically asked him not to?

Grabbing my purse, I flee the restaurant into the humid night air. Cody's truck is still in the parking lot. Through the back window, I see the silhouette of two people in the front seat, a man and a woman.

Fury rages through me as I take off on foot toward my apartment. What a jerk. He's out on a date with me. Meanwhile, he's making out with another girl in his truck. Cody is the one with commitment issues. Not me. My problem isn't committing. My problem is men in general. None of them can be trusted.

TWENTY-TWO
SAVANNAH

K araoke has ended, the crowd has thinned, and the noise level has dimmed by the time I get a chance to speak to my siblings. Approaching their table, I hook an arm around my sister's neck from behind and press my cheek to hers. "I'm sorry I'm such a pill."

Ashton squeezes my arm. "You're not a pill, Savannah. I understand you have a lot going on in your life. I have thick skin. You can take your frustration out on me anytime."

"You're the best." I kiss her cheek and straighten. I introduce myself to Will's wife, Julia, and play-punch Sully's bicep. "You old dog. I always suspected you had a crush on Ashton."

Sully's lips part in the same genuine smile I remember from our younger days. "Everyone did but Ashton," he says, winking at my sister.

"And you," I say, jabbing a finger in my brother's direction. "Thanks for throwing me under the bus."

Will laughs. "You set yourself up by hosting a karaoke event."

I sweep an arm at the remaining crowd. "And what a success it was. We brought in a lot of people. Practically the whole town was here. I've seen so many old friends tonight," I say, hoping someone at the table would mention seeing Pritchard. But no one does. He must have been a figment of my imagination.

"Hearing you sing again made my night," Sully says. "Your voice has matured. The soulful edge moved me. You probably don't remember, but I was your biggest fan back in the day. I was always front and center when you sang into your hairbrush from your makeshift stage on the fireplace hearth."

I laugh. "I remember!" My mind slips back in time as I imagine my friends gathered for my performances, making special requests and cheering me on. Did Pritchard ever attend one of my concerts? I don't remember.

Will brings me back to the present. "Coincidentally, Savannah, we were just discussing our plans for the Fourth of July next week. Ashton and I are organizing a picnic at Marsh Point, and we'd love for you to come."

Ashton chimes in, "We're just inviting a few friends."

I smile. Fourth of July holidays at Marsh Point were some of my few happy memories from childhood. "Does the town still host the professional fireworks display? I remember the view from Marsh Point was spectacular."

Ashton shows fingers crossed. "Weather permitting."

I glance at the bar, where a group of newcomers has inundated Amber. "Unfortunately, I have to get back to work. I'd much rather hang out with y'all. I'll look at the work schedule and let you know about the Fourth of July."

"You don't have to let us know," Ashton says. "Just come if you can. And bring a friend if you'd like."

———

HOURS LATER, I'm scrubbing the bar sink in preparation for closing when a familiar voice from decades past sends shivers down my spine. "Hello, Savannah."

My body stills as my gaze travels from his broad chest to his strikingly handsome face. He's filled out since I last saw him. He's a middle-aged man, his dark hair now streaked with gray. But he wears his years well, with only a few laugh lines around those beautiful sparkling sapphire eyes. "Hello, Pritchard. I thought I spotted you in the crowd earlier."

"I'd heard you were back in town. I had my speech prepared, but I panicked when I saw you in person." His shoulders slump as he drops down to a barstool. "Oh boy. I'm gonna need a drink for this. Can I have a splash of brandy?"

"You may." I remove a glass from the shelf and pour in two fingers of Remy Martin.

"Thanks." Bringing the glass to his lips, he takes an audible gulp. "I only have one question for you, Savannah. Why did you run away without talking to me first?"

My breath hitches as though he kicked me in the gut. "Your *one* question is a loaded one. I think I'll join you in having that drink." I retrieve a second glass and pour in a splash of brandy, sipping and savoring the burn. "I was in a frantic state of mind, Pritchard. I'd just given birth, and my mother had taken my baby from me. I was not thinking clearly. I was desperate to get away from her for fear I might cause her bodily harm."

Pritchard's fist comes down on the bar. "*Our* baby, Savannah! She was *our* baby. Your mother insisted you'd readily agreed to the adoption."

"That's not true, Pritchard. I was in labor when I signed the papers. Mama said the forms gave Dr. Richardson consent to deliver the baby. But the baby was gone. And it was my fault because I'd signed the papers."

"I suspected something like that had happened. I threatened to call the police, but then Carrie convinced me you'd run away to start a new life. You two were so close. I had no reason not to believe her. By the time your mother finally got the police involved, you were long gone." Pritchard's eyes flash with anger. "If only you'd trusted me, we could've worked things out, Savannah. We would've found *our* baby. We would've gone to the police or hired an investigator while the trail was still hot. But you chose to run away. You decided my future without consulting me."

"Your mother conspired with mine about the adoption. Isabelle threatened to destroy my life. She was going to cut you off, Pritchard. And you needed money to finish college. You had your heart set on moving to Nashville."

His brow hits his hairline. "That was *our* dream, Savannah. As your agent, I was going to make you a star. We would've figured out the money."

"Our mothers made my life a living hell during the pregnancy. They beat me so low that I lost sight of pursuing a music career. I was so confused, and with the baby gone, I figured you were better off without me. I gave you the freedom to become the person you were meant to be without a wife and kid tying you down."

"I've spent the last thirty years trapped in my own mind, haunted by thoughts of my child. What kind of freedom is that?"

An uncomfortable silence settles between us, and I'm still reeling from his last blow when he asks, "Did you find her?"

I look up, dazed. "Find who?"

Pritchard's face tightens. "Our daughter, Savannah. Who do you think I'm talking about?"

I shake my head. "I haven't been looking for her. I gave up my right to be part of her life."

His blue eyes darken with disapproval. "Well, my right to know her was taken from me. I've been looking for her for years. I submitted my DNA to all the genetic websites. I haven't found her yet, but I will. I won't give up on her like you did." He stands abruptly, dropping a twenty-dollar bill on the bar. "Having a family is all I ever truly wanted out of life. I married right out of college, but it only lasted a few years. I've never found anyone I loved as much as you. Turns out I was wrong about you. You're not at all the person I thought you were."

Turning his back on me, he takes several steps and stops. Over his shoulder, he says, "During my career, I've heard thousands of wannabe stars sing. None of their voices, except the young woman you sang karaoke with tonight, hold a candle to yours."

I smile, thinking about the performance. "She was pretty amazing," I say, but Pritchard has already left the tavern.

A sick feeling overcomes me as I finish closing up. I ruined my life. But I never meant to ruin Pritchard's.

The main house is dark when I arrive home. I wouldn't dare wake Muriel. She's leaving first thing in the morning to visit her daughter in New Hampshire for the Fourth of July holiday. Muriel's is not the advice I need now anyway. I crave the arms that comforted me during that difficult time all those years ago. But it's past midnight, too late to call Carrie now.

Pritchard's words replay in my head as I get ready for bed. *Turns out I was wrong about you. You're not at all the person I thought you were.*

I was once that person. But somewhere along the road, she got lost.

TWENTY-THREE
HARPER

I'm waiting for my order at Corner Coffee on Saturday morning when Cody steps in line behind me. "There you are, Harper. I've been looking all over for you. Why aren't you answering your phone?"

I turned off my phone when I went to bed last night to avoid his calls and texts. I continue to watch the barista make my latte as I flash my phone's black screen at him. "Because it's not turned on."

Cody's fingers graze my arm. "Why are you mad at me? And where did you disappear to last night? I looked everywhere for you."

My eyes still on the barista, I say, "Why would I be mad? We were on a date, and you snuck outside to make out with your girlfriend. No big deal."

"What're you talking about? What girlfriend?"

I turn to face him. "The one I saw you with. In your truck."

Recognition crosses his face. "That was my sister, Melissa." He glances around, ensuring no one is within earshot, and lowers his voice. "She found a lump in her breast. She was freaking out and was afraid to tell her husband. I was consoling her."

A pang of guilt stabs me in the chest. His worried face says it all. He's telling the truth and obviously cares very much for his sister. "I'm sorry, Cody. I hope everything will be okay."

"I hope so too. She has an appointment for a mammogram this morning."

When the barista calls my name, I retrieve my drink and wait for Cody to get his. We exit the coffee shop together and stand on the sidewalk out front. "When you went outside with your sister, you left your phone on the table. I couldn't help but see the text from Carl Payne. Who is he? And why was he asking around about the father of Savannah's baby when I specifically asked you not to?"

"Because your comment about your father possibly being a rapist got to me. News like that would be difficult for you to hear, and I wanted to be prepared so I could help you. However, as we suspected, the rumors are true. Your parents, Savannah and Pritchard St. Clair, were very much in love."

"Somehow, that makes me feel worse. Why did they give me up if they were so in love?" I say and start walking towards Tracy's Threads. I remember what one of those catty women said in the shop the other day. *I heard her mother put the baby up for adoption without Savannah's permission.*

Cody catches up with me. "I'm sure there's a logical explanation, Harper. You need to talk to Savannah. I think it's time to tell her you're her daughter."

"I'll tell Savannah when I'm good and ready," I snap, increasing my pace.

Cody walks faster to keep up with me. "You're still angry."

"I'm not angry, Cody. Just confused about a lot of things." We reach the shop, and I rummage through my purse for my keys. "I made a mistake. I honestly thought I could handle the commitment, but I'm not ready for a relationship. I need to figure this thing out with Savannah on my own."

Cody gives his head a bewildered shake. "Boy, you really do have commitment issues."

Heat rises to my cheeks. "And trust issues. How can I believe anything anyone tells me when my own mother lied to me all my life?" I jam the key in the lock and turn it. "I'll see you around, Cody," I say, locking the door behind me.

I spend a few minutes straightening the shop in preparation for opening. With Cody's words on constant replay in my mind, feeling overwhelmed, I take my coffee to the taupe suede chairs in the back.

What am I doing here? I enjoy shopping for and wearing pretty clothes, but managing the boutique has become a drag. I've seen the numbers. Even if I bought the boutique from Will, I'd have to expand our product lines to turn a profit. Renovating the store, making it cozier and more appealing, was rewarding. But now I'm bored. This is not who I am. The problem is, I don't know who I am. I feel utterly and completely lost. This is about more than my career. To better understand myself, I need to know who my people are—the ancestors on both sides with whom I share the same genetics. Did anyone on my family tree win the Pulitzer Prize? Do I come from a long line of doctors or politicians? Was my great-grandmother a well-renowned artist? These and so many more answers lie with Savannah Darby and Pritchard St. Clair.

I mope around the shop for the rest of the morning. I'm in the break room, toying with my salad, when I hear the sound of a dog barking in the showroom. I peek through a crack in the door to see Savannah talking to Carrie at the checkout counter. She's so close I can practically touch her. Sitting beside her is a beautiful golden retriever, its tail thumping the floor.

When they mention Pritchard's name, I press myself against the wall and eavesdrop on their conversation.

"He hates me, Carrie. I've never seen him so angry."

"Wait until he calms down. Then talk to him again. He'll understand everything once you explain."

"He's not likely to calm down anytime soon. He's harboring thirty years of hostility." There is a pause, and then Savannah continues. "He's been looking for her, Carrie. He sent his DNA into the genetic websites. He made me feel terrible because I haven't tried to find her."

"I admit that surprises me as well," Carrie says. "Why haven't you been searching for her?"

"Because I'm a coward," Savannah says with a loud sigh. "What if something tragic happened to her? For all we know, she could be dead. Or maybe she knows she was adopted and resents me for giving her up. Or maybe her parents never told her she was adopted. What if she has a loving family—caring parents and siblings she is close to? Who am I to show up on their doorstep and break up their beautiful lives?"

"Geez, Savannah, you're being melodramatic."

"No, I'm not, Carrie. Any of the above scenarios lead to more heartache for me. I'm terrified of finding her and losing her all over again." Savannah sniffles. "So, you see. I am a coward. I ran away from home, for crying out loud. And I stayed gone for thirty years because I didn't have the nerve to own up to . . ."

"Up to what, Savannah?" Carrie asks in a gentle tone.

"Betraying Pritchard."

"Come on, Savannah. Give yourself a break. You didn't betray him."

"Like hell, I didn't. I signed the papers. And I broke his heart. I'm a coward. No better than Mama. She chose to hide in a bottle of booze. I found a hiding place three thousand miles away."

Savannah's loud sob brings a tear to my eye, and I quietly pull the door shut. Returning to the table, I stare down at my salad without taking a bite. I wanted to find out more about my biological family, but in that brief conversation, I learned more than I can process. I replay the conversation in my head from the beginning.

She's afraid of losing me all over again. How did she lose me the first time? Is it possible her mother really did put me up for adoption without Savannah's permission? But wait. What papers did she sign? My adoption papers? Maybe she was coerced into signing them, into putting me up for adoption? Savannah's mother was an alcoholic. That must have drastically affected Savannah's childhood. Who can blame her for running away and staying gone for thirty years?

Is Savannah a coward? She doesn't seem like one. Maybe I'm a coward too. That would certainly explain a lot, like why I've accomplished nothing in my life. On second thought, that makes me an underachiever, not a coward. Come to think of it, Savannah is a bartender. She's an underachiever as well. We have something else in common. We are both running from ourselves.

TWENTY-FOUR
SAVANNAH

Returning from my walk, I feed Biscuit breakfast and brew a pot of coffee. Taking my coffee out to Muriel's porch, I settle into a rocker for my chat with Doug. I texted him earlier, letting him know I would soon be calling, and he answers on the first ring.

"Savannah! So great to hear from you. Margaret and I are just finishing up breakfast. I'll put you on speaker."

I groan inwardly. I wanted to speak to Doug alone.

Margaret says, "Hey, girlfriend. How are things in the Lowcountry?"

I smile to myself. It *is* good to hear my friend's voice. "Hot as hades. How are things in Florida?"

"Even hotter," she says, and we talk about their new lives in the Keys for a few minutes.

"You don't sound like yourself," Doug says. "Is something wrong?"

"You know me so well." I take a deep breath. "I think I made a mistake in coming home. I've never felt worse about myself. Do you think I'm a coward?"

The line goes silent, a pregnant pause hanging in the air, and I envision Doug and Margaret exchanging a look.

"So you *do* think I'm a coward."

"Don't put words in my mouth, sweetheart," Doug says. "I don't think you're a coward. There is no right or wrong way to handle a difficult situation. With that said, I think you've been in survival mode these past thirty years, and the time has come for you to start living again. Going home was a step in that direction. Have you made amends with your family?"

"With my siblings. But I'm not living at Marsh Point. I'm renting a carriage house," I say, my eyes on the dog sleeping at my feet.

"Good! Have you found a job?"

"Yes. I'm bartending at an iconic tavern much like The Lantern. The job fell into my lap. I figured I might as well be getting paid while I sort out my life."

"Sounds like things are progressing smoothly. What is it you're *not* telling us?" Margaret asks.

"Ugh! I can't hide anything from y'all, even across phone lines." I tell them about my conversation with Pritchard last night. "He was so cold. So hurt. So livid. I don't blame him. After what I did, I deserve it."

"He doesn't understand, Savannah. He wasn't in your shoes at the time," Doug says.

I white-knuckle the phone. "That's just it. I ran away without talking to him first. She was his baby, too, and I handled the situation with total disregard for his feelings."

"Is he married?" Margaret asks.

"He was once. Briefly. Why would you ask that?"

"Because I think you're still in love with him, and I hope you two have a second chance to be together."

I let out a humph. "Don't hold your breath."

I hear a scraping noise like a chair sliding across the floor, and Doug lowers his voice to almost a whisper. "Margaret stepped out of the room. She would not be happy knowing I'd mentioned this to you. She thinks it's none of my business. This is nothing new to you. I've told you before how I feel. You signing those adoption papers is beside the point. Your baby was stolen from you, and you need vindication for that crime. I don't know how you go about getting it. But searching for your child would be a good start."

I take a sip of coffee. "Maybe you're right. I'll think about it."

A rustling noise on the other end of the line is followed by Margaret saying, "I'm sorry, Savannah, but I've gotta run. I'm due at work. Let's talk again soon."

"Bye, Margaret." I wait a long minute, giving her a chance to leave the room. "Tell me the truth, Doug. How do you like working with her family?"

"Better than I expected," he says in a cheerful tone. "Her father is eager to retire. He's letting go of the reins sooner than I thought."

"That's great news for you. Do you have any openings? In case things here don't work out for me?"

"I will always create a spot for you. But give it a few more weeks before making such a big decision."

"I will. And thanks for the advice, Doug. I miss you," I blow a noisy kiss into the phone before hanging up.

No sooner have I ended the call than I receive a text from Amber. She isn't feeling well and asks if I can work the early shift today. I respond with a thumbs-up emoji and hurry to the carriage house to shower.

I arrive at The Nest to find Taylor sitting at the bar next to a heavyset man with a thick neck and broken capillaries covering his cheeks. When I go behind the bar, he gives me a suspicious look. "Who are you?"

I raise an eyebrow at him. "Savannah Darby. Who are you?"

"Rodney Daniel. I own this joint."

Taylor smacks the man's trophy beer gut with her hand. "Dad, this is Savannah, our new bartender."

I extend my hand to him. "Nice to meet you, Mr. Daniel." His hand is calloused and sweaty, and I resist the urge to wipe my hand on my black pants.

He turns to his daughter. "You never told me you hired another bartender. Did we need one?"

"Duh, Dad. That's why I hired her. Don't you trust me?"

Rodney looks at his daughter as though she hung the moon. Clearly, Taylor rules the roost in the Daniel family. "Of course, sweetheart. You know I do." His gaze shifts back to me. "My daughter was just filling me in on the changes she's been making around here. All the new drink and appetizer menu items and her idea for karaoke night, which was an enormous success."

The changes *she's* made? Those were my changes. I give Taylor an expectant look, waiting for her to correct him, but she glares back at me as though daring me to contradict her.

I busy myself preparing the bar for opening. Rodney leaves a few minutes later, and when Taylor passes me on her way to the kitchen, she doesn't say a word about what just transpired. She obviously intends to take the credit for making the changes at The Nest.

After stewing for a few minutes, I gather my nerve to read the lying brat the riot act. I find her in the office taking a stack of twenties out of a bank deposit bag.

"What're you doing?" I ask.

"Just borrowing a little spending money from petty cash." She zips up the deposit bag, stuffs it back in the safe, and slams the door, spinning the combination lock. "This is nothing for you to be concerned about, Savannah. Keep your mouth shut, and we'll get along just fine." Folding the wad of bills into her purse, she brushes me out of the way as she leaves the office.

We are slammed for much of the day on Saturday. The dreary weather—drizzle with overcast skies—keeps locals off the beach. They come for lunch and linger into the afternoon, drinking and watching the first segment of the Tour de France on the widescreen television behind the bar.

I look up around four o'clock to find Pritchard's mother staring death daggers at me. Isabelle St. Clair doesn't appear to have changed much in thirty years. Age has been kind to her. If anything, she has grown more striking. Her silver hair grazes her shoulders, and her skin is flawless, no doubt maintained by a highly skilled plastic surgeon. Even though I am approaching fifty, her haughty air and dignified manner still intimidate me, as though I was a teenager all over again.

"So the rumors are true. You're back in town," she says with upturned lip, as though she smelled something rotten.

I hold my arms by my sides. "As I live and breathe. Are you here on a social call, or would you like to look at the menu?"

"Neither. I'm here to warn you to stay away from my son. My husband is terminally ill, and Pritchard's focus needs to be on his family right now. He doesn't need you distracting him."

"You have nothing to worry about, Isabelle. Pritchard hates me."

Isabelle lifts her chin an inch. "Pritchard doesn't hate anyone. Although he should after what you did to him."

After what *I* did to him? Is this bitch for real? Quivering with fury, I open my mouth to tell her exactly what I think of her, but my tongue is tied, and no words come out. A man at the far end of the bar signals for another beer, providing my escape. When I return, Isabelle is gone. No wonder I ran away all those years ago when I had awful people like Isabelle Pritchard dictating my life.

TWENTY-FIVE
HARPER

A steady stream of customers enters the shop throughout the day, but I let Carrie handle most of them. After witnessing the exchange between Savannah and Carrie this morning, I'm in no mood to be cordial with strangers. Besides, Carrie is in her element. She has a knack for picking the right garment for our customers based on their coloring, personality, and body shape. She's a way better salesperson than me.

Because I only picked at my salad for lunch, I'm starving by the time we close at six o'clock. Avoiding facing an empty apartment, I cross the street to the Velvet Spoon and order two scoops of Tiramisu gelato in a cup. Ice cream has always been my go-to comfort food. Strolling over to the waterfront, I pause at the railing to look over Catawba Sound.

The drizzle has stopped, but the overcast skies remain. The dreary weather matches my mood, and I'm grateful for a break from the relentless Lowcountry heat. I'm watching two wave runners zoom about atop calm waters when I sense a presence behind me.

I angle my body to catch a glimpse of a handsome middle-aged man with dark hair, graying at the temples. "Can I help you?"

His face lights up. "I thought I recognized you from your karaoke duet with Savannah last night. Congratulations on your spectacular performance."

My eyes widen at his enthusiasm. "*Spectacular*? Wow. Thanks."

He laughs. "I'm not just blowing smoke. I'm actually an agent for some of today's top country music sensations, and I would label your talent as extraordinary. Are you a professional musician?"

I bark out a laugh. "Not hardly. But thank you for your kind words. I currently work in a clothing store." I drop my empty gelato cup in a nearby trash bin. "My high school voice coach encouraged me to pursue a music career, but my mother would have nothing of it."

"That's a shame." He tilts his head as he studies me more closely. "I assume you're over eighteen, old enough to make your own decisions now. Perhaps you should reconsider. Are you still in college?"

"I'm older than I look. I'm thirty, past my singing prime. Last night was the first time I've sung in front of an audience in years."

His bushy brow shoots up. "Really? If that was your rusty voice, I'd love to hear you sing after a tune-up." He removes his wallet from his back pocket and pulls out a business card. "I'm currently on leave from my job. My father has end-stage pancreatic cancer, and I came home from Nashville to be with my family. I'm not sure how long I'll be in town—another couple of weeks at least. Call me if you'd like to have coffee to discuss your music," he says, handing me the card.

My heart skips a beat at the name on the card. *Pritchard St. Clair.* I've been talking to the man I assume is my father without even realizing it. I look up at him, seeing him in a new light. I didn't know to look for it before, but the resemblance is undeniable. We have the same round face, high forehead, and deep blue eyes.

"You seriously don't think I'm too old to become a musician?"

"Not at all. I never consider age when I'm searching for talent. Savannah is the only woman I've ever met with a voice as exceptional as yours. Ironically, both your voices have the same rich timbre and resonance." He glances at his phone. "I've gotta go. I'm supposed to be at the market, picking up some items for my mother. She keeps me on a short leash these days. She just texted me, wanting to know where I am." He gestures at the parking lot the waterfront establishments share. "I parked over here. If you're headed that way, we can walk together."

"Sure," I say, eager to prolong the conversation.

"Do you play any musical instruments?" he asks as we stroll down the boardwalk toward the lot.

"A couple. But not in years," I say.

"Do you write songs?"

"No. Sorry. Is that a requirement to be in the music business?" I ask in a teasing tone.

"No, but it helps. Savannah is a brilliant songwriter. I wonder if she has any new material."

"Are you and Savannah close?" I ask, even though I already know the answer. They were once close enough to have a baby together.

He gives his head a grave shake. "We used to be. But not anymore."

At the parking lot, he points at a gray sporty Audi. "This is me. It was great meeting you . . . " A flush creeps up his neck. "I must be losing my touch. I didn't even ask for your name."

"I'm Harper Boone. And I'm sorry about your father. I lost my mother in April to a brain aneurysm."

Pritchard grimaces. "Gosh. That's awful. And so sudden. Is your father still alive?"

I shake my head. "He died when I was young. And I don't have any siblings. I'm all alone now."

"That's tough. I don't know what I'd do without my sister.

Even though she lives in Texas, my father's illness has brought us closer together." His phone rings. "This is my mother calling me. I should take it."

"I understand. Go!" I say, motioning him to his car.

After he drives away, I practically skip home to my apartment. I met my father, and he's fabulous. Pritchard St. Clair, agent to country music stars. I wonder which stars he represents. When I see him again, I'll be sure to ask.

I spend the evening lying on my sofa, thinking about my father. I don't even mind being alone on a Saturday night, and I'm no longer mad at Cody. If not for him, I wouldn't have recognized Pritchard's name when we met at the waterfront. I daydream about us, father and daughter, working together to build my music career. Not that I care about being a professional singer. I gave up on that dream a long time ago. This is about forging a relationship with my father. My real father. My adoptive father died so long ago that I barely remember him. I'm getting a second chance to have a daddy. I overheard from Carrie and Savannah's conversation this morning that Pritchard wants to find his daughter. He's looking for me. He sent his DNA to the genetic websites.

A thought occurs to me, and I sit bolt-upright on the sofa. Pritchard will be notified when our DNA matches. The 23andMe website said it could take two to three weeks to get results. Next Friday, which is almost a whole week away, will mark two weeks since I sent in my sample. Should I tell him my suspicions that I'm his daughter? Or wait and find out for sure we're a match?

Not wanting to appear too eager, I wait until Tuesday morning to text Pritchard about meeting for coffee to discuss career opportunities. I'm disappointed when he doesn't respond right away, and I check my phone multiple times throughout the day. When I still haven't heard from him by late afternoon, plausible scenarios enter my mind. Maybe his father died. Or perhaps he's no longer interested in representing me. Or maybe he somehow found out I'm his daughter.

I'm closing out the day's transactions when Will drops by to invite Carrie to a Fourth of July party at Marsh Point.

Carrie beams, thrilled to be included. "That sounds like fun. Have you invited a lot of people?"

"Just family and a few friends. Savannah may come if she doesn't have to work."

Carrie's smile fades. "What about Dad? Did you invite him?"

"No. For Savannah's sake, Ashton and I decided not to include him. I don't think Savannah has seen him yet, and they should have that reunion in private." Will turns his attention to me. "We'd love for you to come too, Harper. If you don't already have plans."

"Really? I would love that," I say, and then it dawns on me he may want me there to babysit.

As though reading my mind, Will says, "Don't worry. Our nanny will be there to look after the kids."

"I'd love to come either way. I'm looking forward to seeing the girls. What can I bring?"

"Just yourself. We're having the picnic catered. Marsh Point is the perfect spot to watch the town's professional fireworks show."

"Cool," I say, excited to have plans for the holiday.

Will turns away from the checkout counter, and Carrie walks with him to the front. I can't help but overhear when she says, "I realize what today is. Are you holding up okay?"

Will nods solemnly. "I can't believe Tracy's been gone a year. I don't want the Fourth to be a sad time for the girls, which is why Ashton and I decided to have this party. I want to commemorate the anniversary of Tracy's passing in a positive way."

Will and Carrie move out of earshot, and I'm curious about what they're saying as they hover near the door. My heart goes out to him. I can't imagine what it was like to lose his wife in a tragic boating accident during a horrific storm.

When Carrie returns to the counter, she asks, "Will you bring your young man to Will's party? I'm sure Will won't mind."

"No. Cody and I are taking a break. Things were moving too

quickly, and I'm not ready for a serious relationship." I lower my head to finish the close-out transactions, signaling the conversation has ended.

After Carrie leaves, I try on every dress in the store in my size. I finally choose a festive blue-and-white striped sleeveless shift. As I admire my reflection in the mirror, I consider my accessories—my natural espadrilles and maybe some fun earrings. Since we're closed tomorrow for the holiday, I'll spend an hour or two on the beach in the morning to add a little color to my bare shoulders.

The thought of seeing Savannah again excites me. With luck, I'll find some time alone with her. I would never break my news to her at a party, but if our conversation goes well, I may invite her to lunch.

TWENTY-SIX

SAVANNAH

Taylor makes several appearances on Monday and Tuesday before Wednesday's Fourth of July holiday. I sense she's up to something during her brief visits. On Tuesday afternoon, I follow her into the back and once again catch her taking money out of the safe.

When I mention it to Amber, she waves her hand in a dismissive gesture. "She's the owner's daughter. It's her money to do with what she wants."

I give Amber a funny look, but I hold my tongue. That's not how businesses operate. I'd be willing to bet Taylor's daddy doesn't know she's borrowing from the till.

On Wednesday morning, Taylor surprises the staff by announcing we're closing early for a private party tonight.

"Won't servers be needed to tend to the guests?" I ask.

"Nope. The hostess is bringing in her own caterers."

I don't argue. I'm thrilled to have the Fourth of July off.

I call Carrie during my next break. "Are you going to Marsh Point tonight? I was supposed to work, but I just found out we're closing early for a private party."

"I'm not sure," Carrie says. "My children have other plans, and

I can't convince Tom to go."

"Let's go, Carebear. We can ride together, so neither of us has to go alone."

Carrie doesn't hesitate. "I would love that. Shall I pick you up on my way?"

"That would be great. I'll ping you the address."

I'm waiting in front of Muriel's when Carrie arrives a few minutes before seven. When I slide into the passenger seat, I notice her attire—a sleeveless white dress with red and blue plastic beads dangling from her neck.

"Is this too casual?" I ask about my white jeans and red knit top. "I could run inside and change."

"Don't you dare. You look beautiful as always. Will didn't mention the attire. I assume this is one of those events where anything goes," she says as she pulls out of Muriel's driveway.

On the drive to Marsh Point, I ask my sister something that's been on my mind lately. "At the risk of bringing up a touchy subject, I'm curious why Mom left you her silver tea service."

Carrie grips the steering wheel tighter. "Mama often accused me of caring too much about social status and material objects. Especially during the early years of my marriage. It's easy to obsess about these things when you don't have them." She glances over at me. "Tom is a schoolteacher. We've had to scrimp so I could stay at home with the kids."

"There's certainly nothing wrong with that," I say, even though I've never supported anyone but myself.

Carrie returns her eyes to the road. "I'm not proud of the person I've become, Angel. I let the green-eyed monster get the best of me. But I've done a lot of soul-searching this past year, and I realize people matter more to me than houses and cars and jewelry. Working at Tracy's Threads has given me a new lease on life. For the first time in years, I feel productive. For the first time ever, I'm contributing to society."

I smile over at my sister. "Good for you!

"Speaking of material goods, I was furious when Mama left her jewelry to Ashton. But I no longer care. She can have it. I don't want any mementos from the woman who ruined our childhood."

"Nor do I. She left me her record collection. It's still in my closet at Marsh Point, where it will stay. If someone else wants it, they can have it."

"Leave it there! You may change your mind one day. Collecting rare albums was one of the few things Mama did well. Besides, vinyl records are making a comeback." Carrie puts on the blinker as she turns onto Pelican's Way.

"Are you happy with Tom? I realize that's a personal question, but we are sisters, after all. How much older is he than you?"

"Fifteen years. I've never admitted this to anyone, but I shouldn't have married him. I wasn't in love with him. I was trapped in my life at Marsh Point, and he provided a way out. I'm not talented like you or smart like Ashton. Being a homemaker is all I've ever wanted. I believed being a positive role model for my children would somehow right Mama's wrongs."

I squeeze Carrie's arm. "I hope to meet your children soon. I'm sure they are wonderful, like their mother."

Carrie swipes at her eyes. "Stop! You're making my mascara run."

"Sorry. But I meant what I said." I rummage through my clutch for a tissue and hand it to her.

Carrie inhales a deep breath to collect herself as she adds her car to the long line parked along the road leading to Marsh Point. "So much for only inviting a few friends," she says.

Marsh Point is a three-ring circus, and I immediately wish I hadn't come. As we approach the house, squeals of children splashing in the pool greet us. A bar is set up on the veranda, and an enormous tent covers much of the side yard between the house and the sound. Under the tent are clusters of round tables dressed in red gingham linens. A long food table, sporting enormous arrangements of blue hydrangeas, stretches the length of one side of the tent. A parquet dance floor and stage for the small country music ensemble are in the back corner. Boats in all shapes and sizes are tied up at the dock. I imagine many of those boat owners will leave the party after dinner and anchor in Catawba Sound to watch the fireworks.

Feeling like a fish out of water, I stick close to Carrie as we mingle with the other guests. Some are people I knew back when, but there are plenty of new faces. Either they don't remember, or they are being polite, but I'm relieved no one brings up my infamous past.

Carrie has gone inside to use the restroom when the young woman I sang a duet with on Friday night wanders up to me. "Hey there," she says. "Karaoke was fun. Are you planning another event anytime soon?"

"Probably. We've been getting a lot of requests for it. I enjoyed singing with you. You're quite talented. Tell me your name again."

She extends a hand. "I'm Harper Boone. I just moved to town from Raleigh."

I give the girl a once-over. She's adorable with white-blonde curls and a cameo complexion I would kill for. I can't quite put a finger on it, but there is something hauntingly familiar about her. "That's ironic. I just moved back to town myself. I've been gone for thirty years."

"I heard. I work with Carrie at Tracy's Threads and sometimes babysit Will's children." Harper's blue eyes widen as though struck with a thought. "Say, would you wanna grab lunch sometime? I'd love to talk music with you. I'm considering taking my singing to the next level, and I would appreciate any advice you can give me."

"Unfortunately, I have zero advice to offer you." When Harper's face falls, I add, "I've been working a lot of lunch shifts lately. Why don't you stop by sometime, and I'll tell you what I don't know about professional singing careers?"

She giggles. "Okay! Cool. I'll do that."

When Carrie returns, she says, "I see you two have met. Harper is my boss at Tracy's Threads."

"She just told me you two work together." I notice servers putting food trays in the chafing dishes on the table. "Are y'all hungry? Shall we get in line for dinner?"

We load up our plates with fried chicken, deviled eggs, and a variety of salads. Finding all the tables under the tent occupied, we go to the veranda to eat. Harper peppers me with questions about my music background, which leads to a lengthy discussion about songwriting and playing instruments.

The band waits until everyone has finished eating before stepping up their performance to liven the mood. During a break between songs, a tipsy Will takes the microphone from the lead singer. "Is everyone enjoying themselves?" he calls out to the crowd, who respond with cheers and finger-whistles. "Fireworks start at ten." He consults his watch. "That gives you an hour to drink up and be merry." A serious expression slides behind his smile. "I'm especially grateful to have all my siblings here tonight. Especially my sister, Savannah, who recently moved back to town. Savannah, where are you?"

My face warms as all eyes under the tent search for me.

Will spots me and grins. "There you are! Will you sing for us?"

I give my head a vigorous shake. "No way," I call out.

"Aww, come on." He sweeps an arm at his audience. "Who wants to hear Savannah sing?"

The crowd begins chanting my name, and Carrie gives me a gentle nudge forward. "He won't give up. You might as well give in."

I walk across the dance floor, and Will gives me a hand up to the stage. He whispers in my ear, "I have a special request. Will you sing 'Lullaby Blues'?"

I'm touched he remembers the song I wrote about us, four siblings comforting one another during the dark times of their dysfunctional family. I sang this song to him on rough nights when he couldn't sleep. I palm his cheek. "I'd be honored. Let's hope I remember it."

I take the microphone from him, securing it on the stand, and one of the band members offers me his guitar. Although I haven't sung "Lullaby Blues" in thirty years, the music and lyrics come easily to me. During my performance, my eyes remain on Will, who is standing in front of the stage. We are kids again, hiding in a darkened room from our mama.

The crowd cheers wildly and begs for more. But I'm deeply moved by memories and need a few minutes to collect myself. "Sorry, folks. That's all from me tonight." Returning the guitar to its owner, I remove the microphone from the stand and wave it at the crowd. "I'm going to pass the baton to Harper Boone. Harper, get yourself up here."

The sea of people parts, and Harper appears. "First stop on your singing career," I say to Harper as I make room for her onstage.

She laughs. "Gee, thanks."

Stepping off the stage, I find an empty seat at a nearby table to watch her performance. Harper huddles briefly with the band. They nod approvingly and play the first strands of Lee Greenwood's most famous song. Her vocals are flawless as she engages with the audience, letting them know how proud she is to be an American.

As the song ends, two little girls, miniature versions of Will, appear before me. They both have unruly curly hair—one girl's hair is the color of sand, and the other girl's is darker. The older daughter's smile reaches her electric blue eyes, much like her father's, while the younger daughter tucks her chin, her doe eyes peering at me from beneath her brow.

The older girl lifts her hand in a wave. "Hi! We're your nieces. I'm Caroline, and this is my sister, Sophie."

"Hello, Caroline and Sophie. I've been hoping to meet you. Can I hug you?"

They nod in unison, their untamed curls dancing around their faces. I hook an arm around their waists, pulling them onto my lap, one on each leg. They tilt their heads back in laughter as I smother their faces and necks with kisses.

"Sorry, I got a little carried away. You two are irresistible." I slide back in the chair with the girls still on my lap. "Are you excited about the fireworks?"

Caroline's face lights up. "Yes! I wanna go out in the boat to watch, but Daddy says we can't leave our guests."

"He's right. This is your party, and you have to be a good host. But I'll tell you a secret." Glancing around, I hold my finger to my lips. "The best place for viewing fireworks is at the end of the dock."

Caroline scrunches up her nose. "How do you know that?"

"Because I grew up at Marsh Point. When I was a little girl like you, I lived here with your daddy."

"Duh," Caroline says, palming her forehead. "You're Daddy's sister, like Aunt Ashton."

I tousle her curls. "Bingo."

When a lively song comes on, Caroline and Sophie scramble out of my lap. "Aunt Savannah, come dance with us!" Caroline says, dragging me onto the dance floor before I can protest.

I'm impressed with Caroline's moves. She has an excellent rhythm for someone so young. Although her dancing is awkward, Sophie manages to keep up with Caroline. I don't remember when I've had so much fun. As I flail my hands and shake my butt, I'm transported back to the pajama parties of my youth.

Several songs later, I shepherd the little girls off the dance floors. "I need a break. I'm an old lady."

"You're not *that* old, Aunt Savannah," Caroline says with a hand on hip.

I laugh out loud. "Gee. Now I feel even older."

"Look, Sophie!" Caroline points her sister toward a server handing out ice cream sandwiches. "Let's go get some ice cream!"

As though reluctant to leave, Sophie throws her arms around my legs. "Bye, Aunt Savannah."

I kneel beside her. "Goodbye, sweetheart. I had fun dancing with you. Maybe I'll catch you later for the fireworks."

This makes her smile, and she chases after her sister.

Noticing my siblings gathered around the bar, I mosey over to the veranda. "Great party! You two outdid yourselves," I say to Ashton and Will. "And Will, your daughters are adorable. Caroline's going to be a heartbreaker."

He rolls his eyes. "Don't I know it?"

I ask the bartender for a glass of ice water, and when I turn back around, I spot my father and May May heading toward us. "I thought Carrie said Dad wasn't coming."

Following my gaze, Will presses his lips thin. "We didn't invite them."

My eyes dart about, searching for an escape. But it's too late. They are already on the porch steps. May May reaches me first and envelops me in a hug. "Savannah, darling. I can't tell you how overjoyed I am to see you." When she pulls away, there are tears in her eyes.

I smile at her. "I'm happy to see you too, May May."

When Dad moves to hug me, my angry glare stops him in his tracks. He greets me with a nod instead. "Savannah, you're looking well. It's been a long time."

"Thirty years. Thirty-one come next January ninth. But who's counting?"

Dad appears wounded. "Let's not do this now."

"Why not? There's no time like the present." I close the distance between us. "You were here that afternoon. I remember watching you stack firewood in preparation for the ice storm. But I never saw you again after I went into labor. I don't blame you for not wanting to watch your daughter give birth. But where were you the morning after? When I realized my baby had been taken from me." From the corner of my eye, I glimpse our guesthouse in the far corner of the property beyond the pool. I gasp as reality hits home. "Of course! Why didn't I think of it before now? You were hiding out in the guesthouse with the baby, waiting for her adoptive parents to come get her." A wave of fury sends a shiver down my spine. "And stupid me. I played right into your hands by running away. What would you have done if I'd stayed?" When he doesn't respond, I raise my voice. "Tell me, Dad. I have a right to know. Were you planning to drug me when the new parents arrived to take my baby away?"

I feel Carrie's hand on my back, propelling me forward. "Come on, Angel. Let's go home. You don't want to cause a scene."

I shrug her off. I know people around me are staring, but I don't care. I've waited a long time to say these things to my father.

TWENTY-SEVEN
HARPER

I'm returning from using the restroom inside the house when I witness the exchange between Savannah and an elderly man who, I assume, is her father. I dart behind a french door and spy on them through the crack where the door meets the jamb.

Savannah's face is red with anger. "Why'd you do it, Dad? I'm sure all these people would like to know why you kidnapped my baby and put her up for adoption."

"Your mother and I did what we thought best for you," her father says in a weak voice. "You were just a kid, too young to be a parent. You had no money, no education, no future."

Savannah balls her fists at her sides. "Yet somehow, I managed to survive. I've supported myself all these years. I would've found a way to provide for my baby. But I never got the chance because you stole her from me."

Will steps between his sister and father, holding them both at arm's length. "You should continue this conversation in private. Why don't you go inside to the family room?"

"This conversation is finished," Savannah snaps and takes off with Carrie on her heels.

I rush down the hall to the front of the house, waiting at the door until Savannah and Carrie are out of sight. I drive back to town in a daze. The rumors are true. Savannah's mother, my grandmother, took me away from Savannah and arranged for my adoption without her permission. And Savannah's father helped hide me. Who does things like that? Evil people. Abducting a child is a felony. Victoria was a criminal attorney, the most law-abiding citizen I've ever known. She would never have agreed to adopt a baby under these circumstances.

And to think I wanted to know more about my family. Now I wish I could un-know this.

I need to talk to someone. I need Cody. But I don't even know where he lives. Thinking he may be on duty tonight, I drive slowly around the downtown streets, searching for patrol cars. I find a fleet of them parked outside The Nest.

Locating a vacant spot, I get out of my car and peer through the tavern's window. The restaurant appears to have been ransacked. Tables and chairs lie overturned, shards of shattered glass litter the floor, and the once proudly mounted turtles have been ruthlessly torn from the walls. There are no pedestrians inside, only police officers. I pull one of them aside as he exits the building. "What happened?"

"We're not entirely sure yet. Someone hosted a private party here earlier. We got a call about a disturbance, but when we arrived, the guests had already fled the scene." He gives his head a solemn shake. "It's a shame. They busted up the place."

"That's awful. I can't believe people would do such a thing. By any chance, have you seen Cody Porter tonight?"

"He got off duty a while ago. I believe he was headed to a party over on Sandy Island."

"Okay. Thanks," I say in a disheartened tone.

I'm headed back to my car when an explosion of fireworks lights up the night sky over the sound. I walk to the waterfront and join the people gathered along the railing.

"We have to stop meeting like this," says a nearby voice.

I turn to find Pritchard St. Clair standing next to me. He's dressed casually in a navy T-shirt and khaki shorts. "Hello! Happy Fourth."

He tips his red baseball cap at me. "And to you. I'm sorry I haven't responded to your text. Things have been a little chaotic at home. Dad took a turn for the worst, and we thought we were losing him, but then he rallied. According to the hospice workers, this is common when nearing the end."

"I'm sorry. This must be so difficult for you."

He hangs his head. "I just hate seeing him suffer. I shouldn't be here now. But I needed a moment alone to collect my thoughts."

Another round of fireworks interrupts our conversation. After the last display of color, Pritchard says, "Anyway, I was hoping to talk to Savannah before arranging a meeting with you. The more I think about it, the more convinced I am her songs would be ideal for you."

"If I'm not mistaken, I just heard one of her songs. I was at Marsh Point for a Fourth of July party earlier. They hired a small country music ensemble, and Will called Savannah up to the stage for a special request. The title was 'Lullaby Blues.'"

A sad smile crosses his lips. "I know it well. It's a beautiful lullaby."

"The last time we spoke, you mentioned you and Savannah were once close. Did you used to date?" I realize I'm prying, but I'm dying to know how Pritchard fits into the convoluted sequence of events that marked the start of my life.

"We dated in high school. I thought we would get married." His face softens, and there is tenderness in his deep blue eyes. Is it possible he's still in love with her?

"What happened, if you don't mind me asking?"

He shudders as though shaking it off. "Life got in the way. Savanah has been living on the West Coast, and I haven't seen her for a long time. I would know if she'd made a name for herself with her songs. If she's still writing music, she's likely to have a stockpile of new material."

Another long burst of fireworks signals the end of the show.

"Where'd you park?" he asks. "I'll walk you to your car."

"In front of The Nest," I say, and accept his extended arm.

"I'll stop by The Nest tomorrow to see if I can catch up with Savannah about her songs."

"I doubt The Nest will be opened tomorrow. The police were there when I arrived earlier, and I spoke with one of the officers. According to him, a private party got out of hand and destroyed the place. I imagine it will take several days to restore order."

"That's too bad. Do they know who is responsible for the damage?"

"I don't think they've figured that out yet."

When we arrive back at The Nest, the police have left, and the windows are darkened.

Stopping beside my car, I push the unlock button on my key. "Thanks for walking with me. I enjoyed our chat."

"As did I." He kisses my cheek. "I'll be in touch as soon as I've spoken to Savannah."

"I look forward to hearing from you. I hope everything goes as well as can be expected at home."

As I drive away, I sense a deep yearning for the father-daughter relationship Pritchard and I could've shared. My adoptive father, like my mother, had also been an attorney, a serious man with little time for fun. Pritchard, although subdued now with his family in crisis, would have to be vibrant and fun-loving in his job. I imagine him entertaining his clients in five-star restaurants and attending their concerts.

I consider telling him now that I believe there's a good chance I'm his biological daughter. But he'll want proof. And I can wait a few more days until our DNA is matched.

TWENTY-EIGHT
SAVANNAH

I'm seething with anger during the short drive home, unable to find the words to express my feelings. Carrie doesn't deserve to bear the brunt of my fury anyway.

Pulling up in front of Muriel's house, she takes her car out of gear and shifts in her seat to face me. "We should probably talk about what just happened. Would you like me to come inside?"

"I'd rather wait until tomorrow if you don't mind. I need to be alone tonight." I squeeze her hand. "I'm sorry you had to leave the party early on my account. You missed the fireworks."

Her lips curve in a sad smile. "No worries. Seen one firework, you've seen them all."

Entering Muriel's house through the back door, I grab Biscuit's leash and head toward town. Walking to the far end of Main Street, I cut over to the waterfront to catch the tail end of the fireworks. I'm strolling north toward the Merriweather Bridge with Biscuit trotting alongside me when I spot Pritchard ahead of me. Although his form is taller and stockier than in our youth, I would recognize his loping stride anywhere. There's a woman on his arm. I recognize the blue-and-white striped dress as Harper's. She's too young to be his girlfriend. Maybe he's representing her.

He's planning to make her a star. Jealousy tightens my chest. That was supposed to be me.

I slow my pace, letting them get ahead of me. I don't need more reminders of my life that might have been.

I'm surprised to see the darkened windows when I pass by The Nest. I wonder why the private party ended so early. Perhaps the hosts arranged for their guests to view the fireworks elsewhere.

Returning to Muriel's, I brew a cup of tea and take it to the porch. I stare out at the dark night for hours, assessing my life. If I stay in Water's Edge, I will constantly be tormented by the past. There are too many reminders here—Pritchard and Dad and Marsh Point. And while I'm thrilled to be reunited with my siblings, they, too, represent a past that is better off forgotten.

I gave it the college try. Now, it's time for me to move on. The next stop on my journey of life is the Florida Keys. If the job with Doug and Margaret doesn't work out, I'll try somewhere else. I have no one to answer to except the dog sleeping at my feet. And Muriel is due back late tomorrow afternoon. I could head out on Friday morning if not for my job at The Nest. I'll talk to Amber first thing in the morning. Maybe they can manage if I don't provide my two-week notice.

———

A CALL from Amber wakes me early on Thursday morning. When I answer a groggy *hello*, she snaps, "Get down here now! That private party Taylor booked got out of hand last night. The place is trashed. Those lousy people even tore the poor turtles off the walls."

"That explains why no one was there when I walked by after the fireworks." I glance over at the alarm clock. "It's only eight o'clock. What are you doing there so early?"

"The police called me. They've been unable to get in touch with Taylor. They received a complaint about a disturbance around nine o'clock last night. By the time they got here, everyone had cleared out."

I untangle myself from the sheets and slide up the headboard. "We need to find out who's responsible. Any clue where Taylor is?"

"Nope. I reckon she'll show up eventually. In the meantime, we need all hands on deck to clean up this place before we open."

I swing my legs over the side of the bed. "I need to shower. I'll be there soon."

"Ha. Don't waste your time showering now. You'll be filthy by the time we finish cleaning up."

"All right then. I'll be there in a few minutes."

I throw on some old clothes, feed the dog, and brew myself a large cup of black coffee. In the essence of time, I drive to work instead of walking. When I arrive, the rest of the staff has already begun the arduous process of cleaning up. I help them straighten furniture and carry the destroyed turtle mounts to the dumpster. We sweep up glass, mop floors, and wipe down walls for the next several hours. We take turns going to our respective homes to shower and are miraculously ready to serve our customers when we open at eleven thirty.

Pritchard is among the first customers to arrive. He takes a seat at the bar and looks around the tavern. "I heard The Nest took a hit last night. Aside from the turtles being gone, I would never have known."

"Because we worked our tails off this morning cleaning up." I pull out my order pad. "Do you know what you want?"

"Sure. I'm in the mood for a burger. All the way with a side order of fries and sweet tea." He returns the menu to its place between the condiments and napkin dispenser. "And if you can spare a minute, I'd like to talk to you about something."

Despite my racing heart, I respond in a tone of indifference. "Sure. Let me turn in your order first."

Hurrying to the kitchen, I give the chef the order and hide in the restroom while collecting myself. What could Pritchard possibly want to discuss with me? Did he hear about my confrontation with Dad at Marsh Point last night? Maybe he found out more about our daughter.

Feeling more composed, I return to Pritchard with his tea. "How's your father?"

Pritchard flaps his hand in the so-so gesture. "He comes and goes. I can't believe he's hung on this long."

"For everyone's sake, I hope he doesn't linger much longer." I'm unsure if this is the right thing to say, but Pritchard's face softens as though he finds comfort in my words. "What did you want to talk to me about?"

"I'm considering representing Harper Boone, the young woman you sang karaoke with the other night."

"I know who she is. Last night, she sang an impressive rendition of 'Proud to be an American' at Will and Ashton's cookout. But what's Harper got to do with me?"

He laces his fingers together on the bar. "Because of the similarities in your voices, I believe your songs might be a good fit for her. But I don't even know if you're still writing music."

"I am." I grab a lime from the bin and start slicing it into wedges. "I have all my old songs and many more new ones. You're welcome to take a look. But I won't give them to you for free."

"I wouldn't expect you to, Savannah. If your new material is as good as your old, I will make you a handsome offer. Have you ever tried to sell them?"

I shake my head. "My music is too personal. I can't imagine anyone else singing my songs." I think about my uncertain future. "But I could use the money."

"When can I see them?"

I'm not sure how long I'll be in town now. With the cleanup project, I haven't had a chance to talk to Amber. "Let me figure out my work schedule, and I'll get back to you."

"You'll need my number." He holds out his hand. "Give me

your phone."

I hand him my phone, and he types out a text to himself.

He returns my phone and asks, "So, have the police figured out who wrecked the place last night?"

"Not yet. They're waiting to talk to Taylor, the manager who booked the party. So far, they've been unable to find her. She probably went out of town for the holiday.

The front door bangs open, and Rodney barges in with Taylor on his heels.

I lower my voice and say to Pritchard, "There she is now. With her father, who owns The Nest. He doesn't look happy."

Rodney's dark, beady eyes dart around the restaurant before landing on me. "There you are!" He marches across the restaurant to me. Jabbing his finger in my face, he spits, "You're fired, and I'm suing you for the damages from your little shindig last night."

I step back, putting distance between us. "What are you talking about? I wasn't here last night."

"Liar!" he says, his fat face as red as a summer tomato. "Not only that, you've been stealing me blind. Large amounts of money are missing from petty cash."

My jaw hits the floor. I don't believe this. Taylor is blaming *me* for *her* crimes. I'm so done with this town. As soon as I can, I'm getting in my car and driving out of here once and for all.

I take a deep breath to settle my nerves. I feel Pritchard's eyes on me, but I don't dare look at him, fearing I'll burst into tears. "That's a serious accusation, Rodney. What makes you think it was me?"

"Because you're the new girl. Everyone else on staff has been here for years, and I've never once had a lick of trouble from any of them."

My gaze shifts to Taylor, standing behind him. "Taylor hasn't been here much longer than me either."

"That's beside the point," Rodney says. "Why would she steal from the restaurant when she already has plenty of money?"

My eyes bore into Taylor. "Good question. Let's ask her. More than once, I witnessed her taking money from the petty cash envelope in the safe. I've also seen her haul boxes of frozen food out of here."

Taylor tugs on her father's shirt sleeve. "She's lying, Daddy. I told you she'd try to blame me. Call the police! Have her arrested."

"I wouldn't do that if I were you unless you're prepared to see your darling daughter arrested. The police will want to see the footage from the security camera. Taylor is the one who took the money, and she knows who hosted the party last night. She booked the event. I'd be willing to bet it was one of her friends."

Taylor lets out a huff. "That is so not true."

Ignoring her, I say to Rodney, "Pull the footage! See for yourself. Your spoiled princess is the thief." I dig my thumb into my chest. "I'm the one who created new drink and appetizer menu items. Karaoke was *my* idea. I even paid for the equipment and deejay myself, you—" I stop myself from saying words unbecoming a lady.

Untying my apron from my waist, I ball it up and throw it at his chest. "I'm reporting Taylor to the police. A hundred witnesses will verify that I was at Marsh Point last night. As I brush past him, I spit back in his face, "And I quit."

As I storm out of the restaurant, Pritchard calls after me, "Savannah, wait! Are you okay?"

"Leave me alone, Pritchard. I can't talk to you right now." I'm halfway home before realizing I left my purse and car at The Nest. Fortunately, my phone is in my pocket. Turning back in the opposite direction, I call Amber, who picks up right away.

"Bravo, girlfriend! You really put Rodney in his place. He and Taylor are in the office now, reviewing the surveillance footage. I'm watching from the doorway. She's crying. Do you think he'll fire her?"

"No way. I've seen the way he looks at her. She can do no wrong in his book. She'll beg him to give her another chance."

"Ugh," Amber says. "I bet you're right. I thought we were rid of her."

"Fat chance. Listen, I forgot my purse in the breakroom, and I don't want to come back inside. Can you bring it out to me? I'll meet you in the back parking lot."

"Sure thing! I'll see you in a minute."

Amber is waiting beside my car when I arrive a few minutes later. I take my purse from her and fish for my keys.

"Don't quit, Savannah. Rodney's not a bad guy. I'm sure he'll apologize once he realizes he was wrong about you."

Finding my keys, I click the car unlocked. "I don't want his apology. And I refuse to work for a liar and a thief."

"I'll talk to him. Maybe I can convince him to fire Taylor. I don't want to lose you, Savannah. You're the best bartender we have." She grins. "Even better than me."

"That's not true, and we both know it." I open my car door and climb into my Land Rover.

Amber holds the door, preventing me from closing it. "By the way, who is the guy who ran after you?"

I assume she's talking about Pritchard. "An old friend. Why?"

"I don't know what you said to him, but he appeared distraught when he came back inside."

I start my engine. "I hate to be rude, but I have to go."

She lets go of the car door. "I understand. I'll let you know what happens with Rodney."

Closing the door, I slam the car in reverse and peel out of the parking lot.

I'm stopped at a red light on my way home when I receive a text from Muriel. *I took an earlier flight. Too much togetherness with my family. Just arrived in Charleston. I should be home soon.*

I give her text a thumbs-up. I can leave town right away since I no longer have to worry about Biscuit, and I no longer have to work out my two weeks' notice. By the time Muriel gets home, I'll be on my way to Florida.

TWENTY-NINE
HARPER

A dream I had last night haunts me as I prepare for work. I was center stage at a sold-out concert, and Victoria was down on the floor in front of me, cheering me on like a crazed Beatles groupie. The crowd went wild when I sang "Lullaby Blues," which had topped the charts for the first time earlier in the week. When the concert ended, my mother was waiting for me in my dressing room. The walls of the dressing room were painted a high-gloss, bubble-gum pink. *I couldn't help but wonder if my mother was sending me a message.*

We were alone in the dressing room, and Victoria took me in her arms in a rare show of affection. "You were brilliant, Harper. I was wrong to prevent you from seeking a music career. You're at a crossroads. But you're old enough now to make your own choices. Fly free, songbird. But choose wisely. Don't accept the first offer that comes your way. Discover your passion, the thing that makes your heart, not your voice, sing." She kissed me on the lips and vanished into thin air.

The dream continues to trouble me as I walk to work. I'm unlocking the boutique when I notice a sign announcing a going-out-of-business sale in the window of the home interior shop next door. I know the owner, Rose Cain, and she'd never mentioned she was selling her business. Lowcountry Interiors is thriving based on its seemingly endless stream of clients coming and going from the shop. As far as I know, there's no other store like it in town.

Peering through the window, I see Rose folding fabric samples at the large worktable near the rear of the showroom. I enter the store and make my way through the maze of furniture to the worktable. "Morning. I saw your sign. I can't believe you're closing the store. Is this a sudden decision?"

Rose stores the stack of fabric samples in a wall cubby and turns to face me. "I've been planning to sell for some time. My husband is retiring from his law practice this year, and I want to be free to travel with him. Bridget, my designer, was hoping to buy the business."

"Is Bridget the tiny blonde always rushing in and out?"

Rose chuckles. "She's the one. A real dynamo. Unfortunately, she and her husband couldn't make their finances work."

"Have you tried to find another buyer?"

Rose tucks a strand of salt-and-pepper hair behind her ear. "I've had plenty of interest, but none of it serious. Why? Do you know someone?"

"Maybe. Me." *Is this the message my mother was sending me via the god-awful, bubble-gum pink dressing room in my dream?*

Tucking her chin, Rose looks over her reading glasses at me. "I don't mean to be rude, but do you have the resources for such an endeavor?"

"Financial resources, yes. I recently inherited a large sum of money from my mother. But I have no experience in interior design."

"In my opinion, interior design is thirty percent hands-on experience, seventy percent good taste. Which you have plenty of based on the facelift you performed on Tracy's Threads."

I lean back against her worktable. "Ironically, I've been

thinking a lot about interior design lately. I've even considered going back to school."

Rose tugs at her chin in thought. "That's not a bad idea. You could take some online classes. Or our community college has a program." She drops her hand from her face. "All you really need is Bridget. She can teach you everything you need to know."

My mind races as I consider the possibilities. "Would you sell your inventory as well as your client list?"

"Absolutely. And we have so much business right now." Rose gestures at the stack of file folders on the table. "Everyone is building and remodeling. The business is booming. If you're genuinely interested, I'll postpone the sale for a few days while you think about it. But I would suggest you talk to Bridget as soon as possible. Keeping her on board is key."

I think about Pritchard's interest in my music career, which doesn't excite me nearly as much as owning an interior design business.

I glance at my watch. It's already five minutes after ten. "I need to open the boutique," I say, pushing off the table. "I'm definitely interested. I can let you know in a few days. I promise I'm not wasting your time."

Rose and I walk to the front of the store together. She removes the sale sign from the window, and I open the door to leave.

"I'd like to talk to Bridget as soon as possible. What times does she get in?"

"She has an appointment this morning. I expect her after lunch. I'll have her come next door when she gets in." Rose tucks the sign under her arm. "I have dinner plans tonight. If you're free, we can meet after work tomorrow to discuss numbers."

"Perfect! I look forward to it."

I have a spring in my step as I go next door to the boutique. I'm turning the key in the lock when I spot Cody down the street. I call out to him, and he spins in my direction, his face falling as though disappointed to see me. When he doesn't move toward me, I shorten the distance between us.

"I've been thinking about you, Cody. How's your sister?"

"She's fine. The lump was benign, thank the Lord. The doctor wants to remove it anyway, but all things considered, she's lucky."

"That's great news. I know you're relieved. I was looking for you last night. Something happened at Marsh Point I wanted to talk to you about."

"More family drama, I presume."

His icy tone sends me backward a step. "Ouch."

"I'm sorry, Harper. I was hoping we could be friends, but I can't just turn off my feelings for you. And I'm still angry at you for being such a flake. You sleep with me, and then you tell me you don't want to be in a relationship. You need to figure out what you want out of life. But not at my expense."

Heat radiates throughout my body, and my blood pounds in my ears. "Did you seriously just call me a flake? So, maybe I have a lot of uncertainty in my life right now. My mother died. I found out I was adopted. And I'm trying to connect with my birth parents, who are both carrying a lot of baggage. I'm entitled to be a little flaky. What's your excuse?" I plant my hands on my hips and bob my head. "Mister, I'm a good listener. I can be your friend. Oops. I changed my mind, I don't want to be just friends." I stab his chest with my finger. "You're the one who needs to figure out what *he* wants."

I spin on my heels and head back to the boutique.

Carrie has a dental appointment this morning, and I'm grateful to be alone in the shop. Too pissed off to cry, I pace the floor instead. Truth be told, I'm angry because Cody is right. I have been acting flaky lately. I was wrong to sleep with him and then break up with him. But, in fairness to me, I did see him with another woman, even though I didn't know at the time she was his sister.

I've been indecisive about more than my relationship with

Cody. I moved to Water's Edge on a whim and took a job I don't like. I'm talking to an agent about a music career, and less than thirty minutes ago, I expressed interest in purchasing a home interior business. It's the same old problem. I don't know what I want.

I stumble to the back of the store and collapse in one of the suede chairs. My mother's words ring out in my ears. *You're at a crossroads. . . Don't accept the first offer that comes your way. Discover your passion, the thing that makes your heart, not your voice, sing.*

The big question is, what is that thing? Singing? Designing? I wanted the manager job at Tracy's Threads. Yet, I've been in the position only a month, and I'm already bored. What if I spend a big chunk of my inheritance buying the interior shop and end up hating it? What if I become a big star and the grueling schedule is too much? What if? What if? What if? Once again, my inability to commit is working overtime.

THIRTY
SAVANNAH

I let Biscuit run around in the yard while I load my Land Rover. I leave my boxes of sheet music just inside the carriage house door and a note to Muriel explaining my sudden departure on her kitchen counter. Making sure Biscuit has fresh water, I lock the house and go to my car.

Muriel has come to mean a lot to me, and I should wait for her to get home, but I'm in no mood for tearful goodbyes. Despite my resolve to make a painless departure, tears stream down my cheeks anyway as I drive through downtown for the final time.

I feel guilty for leaving without seeing my siblings. We were forging new relationships. Being around them these past few weeks has reminded me of the importance of family. I hate giving up the opportunity to be a part of their lives, to watch Will's daughters grow up. Once I get settled in the Keys, I'll reach out to each of them and tell them how much seeing them again meant to me. At least I'll be on the East Coast. With only one state separating us, we can visit more often.

I'm three hours into my trip—approaching Jacksonville, Florida—when my cell rings with a call from Pritchard. I grab my phone from the cupholder and ignore the call. He tries five more times before I finally answer.

"If you're calling about the music, I left two boxes for you in the guesthouse where I've been staying. I'll text you the address the next time I stop."

"What do you mean you left them for me? Are you going somewhere?" he asks in a tone of alarm.

"I'm going to the Florida Keys to start a new life."

"So you're running away again," he says, and I envision the disappointment in his blue eyes.

"Yep. That's what cowards do."

"You are not a coward, Savannah. You stood up to that awful man and his daughter earlier today at The Nest."

"That's different. I had to defend my honor. I'm a coward because I can't face the past."

"And understandably so. There's a lot to face. I've been so angry at you all these years, I'm only now beginning to see how vulnerable you were back then. But you're a survivor. You had to be resilient to endure the awful things your mama put you through when you were a kid. You have an inner strength that has carried you through tough challenges. Now let it support you as you face the past."

"I don't know if I can do that, Pritch. You make it sound so simple." I pause for a long minute. "I came home to Water's Edge for a visit. To see my siblings. I never intended to stay forever. I figured if things worked out, it was meant to be. But things didn't work out."

"How long have you been home, Savannah? A month? That's not enough time for things to *work out*."

I don't correct him, but I haven't even been in Water's Edge for a month. "Let's just say the writing was on the wall."

"You . . . " His voice trails off, and he mumbles, "Never mind."

When the car behind me begins tailing my bumper, I move into the right-hand lane. "What were you going to say, Pritchard?"

"You may be a survivor, but right now, you're acting like a victim. Like you did thirty years ago when your mother stole our baby. Like you quit your job today on the spot instead of fighting. Don't run away to Florida just yet. Stand up for yourself. Finish your business in Water's Edge. Give it a few more months. If you still want to leave, then at least you can say you tried."

"What business?" I ask, even though I already know.

"Help me find our daughter."

"That's *your* business, Pritchard. Not mine. I've explained my position on that."

"And I'm not buying your explanation. You didn't give up your right to be part of her life. It was stolen from you. You were in labor when you signed those papers. Every judge in this country would've ruled in your favor."

When I don't respond, he continues. "And there's the unfinished business of your music career."

"What career?" I say in a huff. "That was never more than a pie-in-the-sky dream."

"You're selling yourself short, Savannah. You're incredibly gifted. And you're not yet fifty. You still have time to make a name for yourself in the industry. Coincidentally, I wasn't calling about the songs. I was worried about you, and I wanted to check on you.

"Take the songs, Pritchard. I don't want them. They bring up too many bad memories. I have to go. I'm on the interstate with a bunch of lunatic drivers. I need to focus on the road." I end the call and drop the phone in my cupholder.

My body begins to tremble, and I white-knuckle the steering wheel. Is this a reaction to my conversation with Pritchard? Or am I hungry? I haven't eaten anything all day.

I take the next exit and follow signs to Waffle House. The restaurant is crowded, but a booth by the window has just opened up when I enter. A buxom waitress, her platinum hair piled high on her head, appears at my table.

"Can I get you something to drink?" she asks, chewing on a piece of gum.

"Coffee, please."

She scribbles it on her pad. "You're in luck. I just brewed a fresh pot."

"Good! I have a long trip ahead, and I might need the whole pot."

"Do you need a minute with the menu?" she asks about the laminated menu on the table in front of me.

"No." I glance down at the menu items. Nothing looks appetizing, but I need to eat, and I don't want to delay ordering. "I'll have the grilled chicken sandwich, please."

I replay my conversation with Pritchard while I sip coffee. There is a lot of truth in the things he said. I am a survivor. I managed for thirty years on my own in Washington State. In running away, I wasn't acting like a coward. I was acting like a victim. Because I was the victim. Back then, I was the victim when my child was abducted. Today, I was the victim of Taylor's accusations.

My phone vibrates on the table with a call from Muriel. "Oh, honey," she says when I answer. "What on earth is going on? I'm distraught over you leaving."

I blurt out about my encounter with my father at the party last night and about Taylor blaming me for her crimes. "I'm at a Waffle House near Jacksonville, Florida, wondering if I was too hasty in leaving so soon. What do you think, Muriel? Tell me the truth."

"I think you're carrying a lot of baggage, Savannah. Sorting through issues as complicated as yours takes time. Not weeks, but months, sometimes years. You owe it to yourself to see things through. If you decide to move on, you'll at least be comforted knowing you gave it an honest try."

"Maybe you're right. I need to give it some thought." The waitress arrives with my food. "I'll text you when I decide."

I take a few bites of the sandwich, but I don't have much

appetite and push my plate away. As Pritchard's and Muriel's voices ring in my head, I plant my elbows on the table and bury my face in my hands.

Help me find our daughter. You're carrying a lot of baggage, Savannah. You owe it to yourself to see things through.

My biggest burden *is* my lost child. More than anything in the world, I want to find my daughter. Having Pritchard by my side will soften the blow if we discover she's no longer alive. But if she is alive and well and wants to have a relationship with us, that would be a dream come true. A dream I've never allowed myself to have.

THIRTY-ONE
HARPER

I decide to take my mother's approach to making difficult decisions. I will gather information, seek guidance, and study every option at length. I start by consulting with Victoria's financial advisor. Regina Bowden assures me that purchasing a business is feasible and instructs me to send the company's financials as soon as I have them.

I arrange Friday afternoon meetings with Rose and Bridget to learn more about Lowcountry Interiors. Trusting Carrie to lock up, I leave Tracy's Threads at five and walk next door. Rose's office is glamorous, with walls painted a high-gloss pale pink. Lamps provide accents of gold, and pillows add pops of color in shades of hot pink. Rose and I sit together in white leather chairs opposite her Lucite desk.

"Since you're a newcomer to the area, you may not be aware of our history," Rose says. "Thirty years ago, my mother and I began working as a design duo team."

"Really! That's so cool. Is she still alive?"

Rose nods. "And kicking. At ninety years old, she's in independent living at Whispering Oaks." She settles back in her chair and crosses her legs. "When we first started, we rented office space in a converted warehouse, primarily to store all our fabric and wall covering samples. But we soon realized the need for a showroom to meet with clients and sell accessories. We've built an extensive client list. We're one of the top design firms in the Carolinas and Georgia."

"I'm impressed. Tell me more."

She talks about their clients and noteworthy projects for the next thirty minutes. "We're currently working off a waitlist. We desperately need another designer. I've been hesitant to hire anyone new for obvious reasons, but I have my eye on a couple of young gals who would be valuable additions to the staff."

My heart races with anxious enthusiasm. "I'm intrigued by your success and thrilled at the prospect of continuing to grow what you've started."

Rose's broad smile spreads from cheek to cheek. "Your words are music to my ears. If you buy the business, I promise not to abandon you. I'm only a phone call or text message away. I won't interfere, but I'll be happy to offer whatever advice you need." She retrieves a sheath of papers from her desk. "I printed a copy of our financials. You should have someone look at them."

I take the papers from her. "I've already spoken with my mother's advisor in Raleigh. She's waiting for more information. If you have a digital copy, I can get them to her quicker."

"Of course. Give me your email address, and I'll send them right over." She hands me a sticky note and I jot down the information.

Rose opens her day timer. "I can't afford to drag this out, Harper. Does two weeks give you enough time to make your decision?"

"I hope to make a decision sooner than that." The lingering uncertainty about my future makes me uneasy. I am negotiating with Rose about buying her business and talking to Pritchard about becoming a professional singer. While they are two very different career paths, they both offer promise of fulfillment that excites me.

Rose stands, signaling our meeting is over. "Bridget is waiting for you. She's a talker. She'll tell you whatever I may have missed and more."

Rose wasn't joking about Bridget being a talker. On our way to The Nest for drinks, she vents incessantly about her remorse over being unable to buy the business.

When we arrive at the tavern, I'm disappointed to find Savannah missing behind the bar. After the confrontation with her father at the Fourth of July party, I hope she hasn't done anything drastic like leave town again.

Locating a booth, we order glasses of the house rosé. While we wait for our drinks, Bridget's blue eyes travel the room. "I'm sorry for what happened here on Wednesday night, but at least they finally got rid of those dreadful turtles." She removes a paint wheel from her tote and holds it up to the wall as she flips through the swatches. "I'm thinking something warm and neutral, more beige than gray." Noticing me watching her, she drops the color wheel back into her tote. "Sorry. I get carried away sometimes. My husband says I would paint our children greige if given the chance."

I laugh. "How old are your children?"

"Ages six and eight. A girl and a boy." Bridget goes on about her busy household, and by the time our server brings our wine, I'm ready to discuss the business.

"I'm not sure how much Rose has told you, but I have zero design experience. Except being the daughter of a successful attorney who redecorated our house every time the wind changed direction."

Bridget giggles. "That's more important than you might think. I can teach you a lot, but you might consider taking some design classes to get a head start. There's also the marketing side of the business. Our Instagram account has over a hundred thousand followers."

My eyes widen. "Wow. That's incredible."

"Yep. Rose handles all our social media and email marketing."

Relief floods me. Finally, something I can contribute. "I've been doing both for Tracy's."

Bridget sits ramrod straight, leaning slightly into the table. "If you buy the business, I suggest immediately hiring more staff. Rose has run me ragged this past year, and I can't keep up this pace."

"She mentioned hiring another designer . . ."

Bridget holds up three fingers. "In addition to another designer, we need two admin people to manage invoicing, check stock on products, and write up proposals. An additional support person to organize installations would be nice. Maybe you can do some of that."

I gulp back a wave of fear. What do I know about hanging drapery? "I'm sure I can with a little guidance."

Bridget waves off my concern. "You'll get the hang of it in no time."

"Why hasn't Rose hired these people before now?"

"She's been pocking profits for her retirement. Sadly, her business has taken a hit. Her long-time clients need service, and we can't accommodate them," Bridget says in a tone that makes me wonder if there is bad blood between Bridget and Rose.

"How serious is this *hit*? Will the business recover?"

"As long as we don't let things slide much longer." For the next few minutes, Bridget shares her ideas for the company's future. While she's disappointed not to be buying the company herself, she's committed to the success of Lowcountry Interiors. I admire her boundless energy and contagious enthusiasm. Not only would she make a valuable employee, but she is also someone I would be proud to call a friend.

I pay for our wine, and we walk back toward Main Street together.

Bridget asks, "What is the likelihood of you making an offer? I have a family to support, and I need to prepare myself for the possibility of unemployment."

"I can't give you a definitive answer yet. I found out about the opportunity only yesterday. But I can tell you I'm serious about the prospect. The next step is for me to discuss it with my financial advisor. I will know more the first of next week."

"I understand. I'll give you my number in case you have more questions."

As she calls it out, I key in her number, sending her a text from my phone. "Text me if you think of anything we haven't already discussed."

Bridget gives me a quick hug. Pulling away, she holds up her hands to show her crossed fingers. "I hope it works out, Harper. I have a feeling you and I would make a dynamic team. Maybe we'll end up being partners. One day, down the road when my husband is earning more money, I'd like to open a spinoff store, catering to young people with more affordable household goods."

My face lights up. "That's a brilliant idea."

She winks at me. "I'm full of brilliant ideas."

I float on a cloud back to my apartment. Buying Lowcountry Interiors feels like the perfect fit for me, more than anything else I've ever done. Including singing.

THIRTY-TWO
SAVANNAH

Pritchard stops by the carriage house after lunch on Saturday to look over my music. His blue eyes are rimmed with dark circles. His father's illness is taking its toll. When he leans down to kiss my cheek, his cologne brings back memories of the intoxicating scent of foggy mornings on the beach.

"How are things with your dad?"

Pritchard shrugs. "Some days are better than others. Today is a good day."

"Is Kate home?" I ask about his older sister, who I was close with when we dated.

"She's on standby. It's not easy for her to get away from her busy life in Texas."

I raise an eyebrow. "And your life isn't busy? You're an agent to the stars."

"She has a family to take care of." His unspoken words hang in the air between us. He would've had a family if I hadn't run away.

I motion him toward the guesthouse. "Come on inside."

We enter the guesthouse and stand at the dining table where I've organized the music into stacks by tone and mood. I place a hand on the tallest pile. "These are my favorites."

He lifts the top composition from the stack. "'Lonely Sundays.' Great title," he says and hums the first strands. Pritchard's awful singing voice is the exception to his otherwise extraordinary musical talent. Most kids complain when their mother makes them take piano lessons. Pritchard begged for more. He's exceptionally proficient on both the piano and guitar.

I hand him my guitar, and he plays the song from the beginning. As I sing along, the years fall away, and we're teenagers again. The rest of the world is lost to us. We're on a private oasis, surrounded only by the beauty of the music.

"This is incredible, Savannah. Your compositions have improved, not that they weren't spectacular before. Did you go to college? You've obviously been studying music."

His flattery brings a smile to my face. "I never went to college, but I had the next best thing, a mentor who was a music instructor at the University of Washington. Maria has an apartment in Fairhaven she keeps as her weekend retreat. We used to get together a couple of times a month to play music."

He thumbs through several more compositions. "These are truly remarkable. Whether you realize it or not, you have a gold mine here. Do you mind if I take them? I want to spend some time with them."

"Of course," I say, and together, we gather the music and return it to the original boxes.

Each of us carries a box out to his car. "Are you planning to give Harper an exclusive on my music?"

Pritchard tucks the box under one arm while he opens the trunk. "I haven't gotten that far yet. I'm meeting with her later today to discuss her music career. She seems hesitant about the prospect. I think she's worried about her age."

"I can see that. She's a little old to be just starting out. If not Harper, do you have someone else in mind?"

Pritchard stores his box in the trunk and takes mine from me. "I'm in negotiations with a young woman from Alabama. She's not ready yet, but once my voice coach finishes with her, she has the potential to be the next Taylor Swift. But don't worry. I won't make any decisions about your music without discussing it with you first." He slams the trunk and turns to me. "I'm glad you came back, Savannah. At some point, I'd like to talk about us."

"I'd like that as well. I've decided to help you find our child."

"Really? That's great news," he says, drawing me in for a hug.

His familiar embrace sends a jolt through my body, and I quickly push him away. "There's something you need to know. Dad and I had a run-in at the Fourth of July party the other night."

He nods. "I heard."

"Of course you did. There are no secrets in this town." Lowering my gaze, I kick at a rock in the driveway. "Ashton has arranged for me to meet with Dad later today at Marsh Point. I'm going to press him for answers about the adoption. He was in on Mama's scheme. He hid the baby in the guesthouse until the adoptive parents came. Even if he can't tell me anything about them, it's at least a place to start."

Pritchard squeezes my shoulder. "Thank you, Savannah. I know how difficult this is for you. Are you meeting with him alone? I would offer to come with you, but my presence might make the situation more tense than it already is."

"I agree. Besides, you have your meeting with Harper. I won't be alone. Ashton and May May will be there. The meeting is set for five o'clock. I'll let you know how it goes."

"I'll be anxious to hear." He gives my cheek a peck. "If you need me, I'm only a phone call away."

I remain glued to my spot as I watch Pritchard drive away. His animosity toward me appears to have lessened. Maybe one day, he'll be able to forgive me. He's among the most genuine, kind-hearted men I've ever known. He doesn't deserve what happened to him. While his mother was instrumental in breaking us up, my parents were the ones who stole our child and gave her away. I will do whatever I can to make this right.

I arrive at Marsh Point promptly at five o'clock, loaded for bear. Dad and May May are already seated on the veranda with Ashton, a pitcher of sweet tea on the table in front of them.

Dad eases out of his chair to greet me, and May May smiles softly.

Ignoring them both, I drop to a vacant chair beside my sister. "I asked Ashton to arrange this meeting to discuss my child." I clasp my shaking hands together in my lap. "What do you know about the people who adopted her?"

My father looks away, unable to meet my penetrating gaze. "I don't know what you're talking about?"

I lean into the table. "Like hell, you don't. You were hiding the baby in the guesthouse. Which means you probably met the adoptive parents when they came for her."

"I don't have to listen to this," he says, slowly rising.

"Not so fast, Dad. Child abduction is a felony that carries a serious penalty. After what you did to me, you deserve to spend the rest of your life in prison."

He mops beads of sweat from his forehead with a white linen handkerchief.

"Lucky for you, the statute of limitations lets you off the hook. But if you don't tell me what I want to know, I will sue you for damages."

Lowering himself back down to his chair, he stares at the glass of sweet tea in front of him.

I grab his arm, digging my fingers into his leathery skin. "Look at me, Dad. Tell me what you know about my baby's adoption."

With a loud sigh, his cloudy eyes meet mine. "Only the woman came inside. Her husband waited in the car. I remember her being attractive. She carried herself with an air of wealth and privilege. I felt relieved knowing the baby was going to a good home."

I let go of his arm and fall back in my chair. "Right. Because I couldn't provide a good home for my child. Do you remember what they were driving?"

"An SUV. A Range Rover, I think. With North Carolina tags."

I glare at him. "Think hard, Dad. Can you remember anything else?"

Dad shakes his head as he blots at his wet eyes with his handkerchief.

I look over at May May. "What do you know about what happened?"

May May's lips are pressed thin. She's so angry I can almost feel the heat radiating off her body. "Only what they told me. That you'd decided to give up the baby, and you were so distraught you ran away from home. I knew you were struggling those last few months. Everyone was being so hard on you. I had no reason at the time to suspect they were lying."

I turn back to my father. "I need to know why, Dad. Why did you go along with Mama's evil scheme?"

I wait for him to respond. When he doesn't, I answer for him. "Because you were incapable of standing up to her. All those years she abused us, and you never said a word. Because you were afraid of her." I push abruptly back from the table. "Because you're a coward."

I storm off the porch and around the side of the house. I sense Ashton on my heels but don't stop until I reach my Land Rover. I spin around to face her. "I'm not the coward. He's the coward," I say, my arm out and finger pointed at the house.

Ashton frowns. "Why would you think you're a coward? You're one of the strongest, most independent people I know."

At that moment, I feel stronger and more in control of my life than I have in years. "I'm sorry I got so upset. But I couldn't help myself."

"Don't apologize, Savannah. After what they did to you, no one would blame you if you pressed charges against him." She pulls out her cell phone. "I'm texting you the contact information for my investigator. Carter Leach is the man I hired to find you, the one you overheard me talking to on the veranda the day you got back into town. He has an impeccable reputation. If anyone can find your daughter, he can."

"Thank you, Ashton. I'm sorry to leave you with the fallout," I say, gesturing at the house.

"I can handle it. After what just happened, I'm pretty sure I already know the answer, but I have to ask if you think there's any hope for a reconciliation between you and Dad?"

"Nope. Not in a million years." I give her a quick hug and get in my car.

I call Pritchard as I'm pulling out of the driveway. "Dad couldn't tell me much about the adoptive parents except they were driving a Range Rover with North Carolina tags. Ashton gave me the name of a private investigator. Do you want me to reach out to him?"

"Let's talk first, to get our stories straight so we give the information he needs. Harper is due here soon. I'll call you after she leaves."

My adrenaline tanks on the drive home, and guilt takes control. My father is an old man, and I was hard on him. But I can't worry about him now. I need to focus on finding my daughter. Besides, May May was furious. I can count on her to take care of Dad.

THIRTY-THREE
HARPER

The British-speaking woman in my Maps app directs me to a wooded road past the Sandy Island Club. A quarter mile down the bumpy dirt drive, the St. Clair residence comes into view —a sprawling white clapboard home with a gabled roof and dormer windows. In addition to the main house are several outbuildings, two guesthouses and a garden shack. The vast property takes up the southern tip of Sandy Island, offering 180° views of the ocean and sound.

Pritchard greets me at the door and guides me through the wide center hallway to the living room, handsomely decorated in shades of blue, bringing the ocean beyond the dunes inside. We emerge onto an expansive terrace and sit down at a wrought iron table. On the table are a laptop, a bottle of opened red wine with two glasses, and a stack of sheet music.

Pritchard pours the wine and offers me a glass. "Cheers! To your career," he says, clinking my glass with his.

"Cheers," I repeat, taking a sip of wine and setting down the glass. "I'm grateful for your interest in my career. But to be honest, I have a lot of reservations about my age. I'm thirty years old. I'd like to one day get married and start a family. I don't know how that fits with a hectic concert schedule."

He sighs. "I sensed you were having some doubts. And you're right. This lifestyle is not easy. My most successful female artists have opted not to have families. Many of them aren't even married. I'm not saying you have to choose between career and family. With the help of nannies and supportive husbands, many women manage both just fine."

I nod at the stack of sheet music. "Is that Savannah's music?"

"Yes! She gave me two big boxes filled with at least a hundred compositions. With the help of a mentor, her talent has matured over the years."

"May I see them?"

"Of course." He slides the stack across the table to me. Opening his laptop, he says, "If you don't mind, I will check my email while you look at those. I'm waiting to hear from a client."

"No. Please. Go ahead."

I shuffle through the music, finding a song I like titled "Lonely Sundays." After skimming the music, I sing the first few lyrics softly. I stop when I notice Pritchard watching me with a faraway look in his eyes. "Is something wrong?"

"No." He gives his head a bewildered shake. "It's just uncanny how much you sound like her."

I assume *her* is Savannah, but I don't ask.

His computer pings with the sound of an incoming message. When Pritchard looks down at his screen, the color drains from his face.

"Is that the email you were waiting for?"

"Not from my client. But I've been waiting for this email for years. It's a long story, but I've been searching for my daughter, who was put up for adoption at birth. Usually, these emails alert me to ties with fourth and fifth cousins, but this one says close match."

My heart skips a beat. This is not how I wanted this to go. My eyes dart about, searching for an escape, but I'm trapped. I can't just get up and run away. I notice a shadowy figure just inside the opened french doors. Is someone spying on us?

Pritchard's fingers fly over the keyboard, and I assume he's accessing his account on the website. "I'm sorry, Harper. This is highly unprofessional of me. But I thought this moment would never come, and I can't wait a second longer."

My tongue is heavy, and I'm unable to speak.

He squints at his computer. "Wait a minute. Harper Boone is an unusual name." He looks up at me. "There's no picture on the profile, but you're about the right age. Where are you from?"

I gulp back fear. "Raleigh, North Carolina."

"According to this, you're my daughter. Did you know about this?"

"I suspected. I only found out a couple of months ago that I was adopted." The words tumble out of my mouth as I tell him about finding the envelope with a scrap of baby blanket and the address for Marsh Point in Victoria's desk after her death. His face is blank as he listens, and I can't tell what he's thinking. When I finally finish talking, I risk a glance at the french doors, but the shadowy figure has disappeared.

A woman screaming reverberates inside the house, and Pritchard jumps to his feet. "What on earth? Stay here. I'll be right back."

As soon as he disappears through the open doorway, I hurry off the terrace and slip around the side of the house to my car. I pound the steering wheel as I drive down the bumpy dirt drive. I handled that all wrong. I should've told him myself. I should've stopped him from signing onto the 23andMe website. Now that he knows, should I track Savannah down and break the news to her? Maybe it's better if she hears from him.

What happened inside the house that made the woman

scream? Was it his mother? Was she the one eavesdropping on us? How much did she hear? Did his father die? Did she discover him dead? Or was it a ploy to get Pritchard away from me?

I hold back my tears until I'm safely alone in my apartment. I curl up on the sofa and cry my heart out. I check my phone repeatedly for texts or calls from Pritchard. If his father died, he would understandably be tied up with his family. But what if the scream was nothing? What if his mother saw a mouse? Why hasn't he called? Is he talking to Savannah now? I tug at my hair. The uncertainty is driving me insane.

After crying for over an hour, instead of feeling unburdened, I'm even more despondent. I'm desperate for someone to talk to. Victoria may not have been warm and fuzzy, but she was always there for me when I needed her.

I pull the cashmere throw over my head, relishing the darkness. My heart aches for Cody. I need him now more than I've ever needed anyone. I fell hard for him during the short time we were together. But he made it clear he wants nothing to do with me.

When another hour passes and I still haven't heard from Pritchard, I power off my phone and go to bed.

After a restless night, I get up early and clean my apartment. To kill more time, I run some errands and load up on groceries at the market. I'm discouraged to see it's only noon when I get home. With the long afternoon looming ahead, I put on my bathing suit and drive over to the beach.

Too restless to sit in a beach chair, I walk in the surf's edge toward the Sandy Island Club. Before I realize where I'm going, I find myself in front of Pritchard's house. The St. Clair's driveway is lined with cars, and a crowd is gathered on the terrace. So, his father did die. Maybe that explains why he hasn't called.

I turn around and head off in the opposite direction. My mind races with possible scenarios. Pritchard hasn't had time to tell Savannah. Or he's told her about me, and they've decided to wait until after the funeral before contacting me. What if they're angry at me for deceiving them? Or disappointed I'm their daughter? Maybe they were hoping for a brunette. I can't help but laugh at this ridiculous idea. Another thought strikes me, wiping the smile off my face. What if Pritchard thinks I'm using him to build my music career?

THIRTY-FOUR
SAVANNAH

My days have no structure without a job. I have no idea what to do with so much free time. On Sunday afternoon, when Muriel leaves for an overnight trip to Charleston to visit a friend, I take my guitar over to her back porch. I haven't written any music since leaving Washington State, and I need to get onto paper the tune that's been dancing inside my head for weeks.

I'm only a few chords in when Carrie calls. "In case you haven't heard, Pritchard's father died last night. I thought you'd want to know."

I let out a gasp, even though I've been expecting it. "I'm sorry for them. Thanks for letting me know. Any idea when the funeral might be?"

"I heard Tuesday, but that hasn't been confirmed. I'm sure the entire town will attend. They are having a traditional funeral with church service and burial followed by a luncheon reception at their home."

"I would expect nothing less from Isabelle."

"Will you go to the funeral?" Carrie asks.

"I might as well, since I have nothing to occupy my time."

"What about work?" Carrie asks, and it dawns on me I haven't spoken to my sister since July Fourth.

"Believe it or not, I quit my job. I have a lot to tell you. Any chance you can come over? We can go for a walk."

"Sure! I'd love that. Be there in a few minutes."

After returning to the carriage house for my walking shoes, I put on Biscuit's leash harness and wait for Carrie in the front yard.

As we stroll through the quaint streets of the historic neighborhood, I fill Carrie in on the chaotic events of the past few days. She appears wounded when I admit to leaving town without saying goodbye. And when I tell her about my meeting with Dad and May May, her slate-blue eyes widen to nearly double in size.

"I don't know what to say, Savannah. He's never been a candidate for Father of the Year, but I can't believe he would do something like this to his child."

"Me either." I stare down at the ground as I walk. "I don't think I can ever forgive him, but I don't want to be the one who divides the family over this."

Carrie grabs me by the arm, spinning me around to face her. "You're my family, Angel. I'm not close to Will or Ashton or Dad. I was a mess after you ran away. Ashton was off at college, and Will was a basket case after Bert died. I was so damn angry at Mom for what she did to you, and Dad was gone even more than before. I married Tom because I was looking for a father figure, someone I could count on to care for me because our parents failed us. Having you home these past few weeks has given me a new lease on life. I'm happy for the first time in years. I want to try new things and go new places."

"You're giving me too much credit, Carrie. A lot of that has to do with your new job." I touch my finger to her chest. "And you did that for yourself."

"Maybe so. But I need you. Please don't leave town again," she says with tears in her eyes.

I throw my arms around her and hold her tight. "I won't. At

least not anytime soon. Besides, I promised Pritchard I'd help find our daughter."

Carrie pushes me away. "Seriously? Yippee!" She does a victory dance in the middle of the street. "That's the best news I've heard in a long time."

"Let's just hope we find her alive and well."

"You will," Carrie says in a genuine tone.

As we head back toward Muriel's, we talk about my potential for a songwriting career. "The money would be nice, but I can't imagine sitting around all day writing songs. I always viewed bartending as a job, a means of paying the rent. But I actually enjoy the hustle and interacting with customers."

"So find yourself another job," Carrie says. "There are plenty of other restaurants in town."

"Maybe. But the vibe at The Nest suits me. I feel at home there."

After seeing Carrie off, I fill Biscuit's bowl with fresh water and return to the porch with my guitar. I'm nearing the end of my first draft when Pritchard calls.

"I'm so sorry about your dad, Pritch. Losing a loved one is never easy, even when you've had time to prepare for his death."

"Thank you. He was in so much pain. For his sake, I'm glad it's over." He pauses a beat. "I need to see you, Savannah. Can I come over?"

His serious tone prickles my skin. "Of course. Is something wrong?"

"No. The opposite. But I want to tell you about it in person."

"Okay. But now I'm curious, so hurry. Drive around back. Muriel's out of town, and I'm sitting on her porch."

While I wait, I take my guitar to the carriage house and freshen up, splashing water on my face and pulling my unruly hair into a ponytail. Back at Muriel's, I fill two glasses of her homemade lemonade and take them to the porch. I've only sat down when Pritchard's Audi zooms into the driveway.

I call out to him, and he strides over to the porch. Planting a peck on my cheek, he collapses into the rocker beside me. "Today has been a whirlwind. There are so many people at my house. I had to wait for Kate to arrive before leaving to see you. It's her turn to hold down the fort for a while."

I move to the edge of my seat. "Out with it, Pritchard. What's the big news? I'm dying of suspense."

"With everything that has happened in the past twenty-four hours, this is the first time I've had to wrap my mind around this development," he says, rocking his chair so hard it dances across the floor.

I scoot my chair over to avoid a collision. "Slow down, Pritchard. You're going to break Muriel's rocker."

He jumps to his feet and begins pacing back and forth in front of me. "I don't know how to tell you."

I stand to face him. "Geez. Just tell me already. What development?"

His face lights up like a kid in a candy store. "Harper is our daughter."

I shake my head, sure I misheard him. "Say again."

"Harper Boone, the young woman with the amazing voice, is our daughter."

A million thoughts enter my mind at once, and I can't make sense of any of them. "Do you know this for sure?"

He gives his head a vigorous nod. "Our DNA matched on 23andMe."

"I'm sorry, but I'm not buying this. She shows up in town out of the blue and ends up being our daughter. That is too much of a coincidence."

Pritchard inhales a deep breath and sinks back down to his rocker. "I'm doing this all wrong. But I can't help myself. I'm so excited. Let's sit down, and I'll explain."

"How can I possibly sit down at a moment like this? Start talking, Pritchard. I want to hear everything."

"Okay." He takes several deep breaths. "So . . . I told you I was meeting with Harper yesterday to talk about her career. By the way, she sang a few lines of 'Lonely Sundays.' It's uncanny how much she sounds like you."

"Another coincidence," I say, although I admit our voices have similar qualities. I motion for him to keep talking. "Go on."

Pritchard is back on his feet. "Harper was never told she was adopted. After her mother died in April, she discovered a mysterious envelope in her mother's desk drawer with information that made her suspicious about her birth."

Still skeptical, I fold my arms over my chest. "What information?"

"I can't remember exactly. Her birth date and the address for Marsh Point. Everything happened so fast. Dad died, and I didn't have time to question her."

I narrow my eyes. "You mean your dad died while Harper was there?"

"Yep. Mom screamed when she found him. When I went inside to check on her, Harper disappeared. I don't blame her. It was an awkward situation on many counts."

"Back up a minute. So, when Harper discovers this envelope, she comes to Water's Edge to find out more. She meets both of us but doesn't tell us she's our daughter?"

"She suspected. But she wanted proof. So, she sent in her DNA sample."

"She does kinda look like you. She has your round face and blue eyes. And she has my curls." My hand shoots out. "I'm getting ahead of myself. I need more proof."

"I have a lot of questions, too, Savannah. But DNA doesn't lie."

I drag a hand down my face, wanting to believe it's true but afraid of being disappointed. "I'm willing to consider the possibility. But I still want to talk to Harper." I pull out my phone. "Can you share her contact information?"

"I can. But I'd prefer for us to talk to her together. Can you wait until after the funeral tomorrow?"

I frown. "Tomorrow? Carrie said the funeral is Tuesday."

"The church wasn't available on Tuesday. Mom doesn't want to wait until Wednesday, and I don't think I could've survived until then anyway. She's run me ragged today. We've been to the funeral home and the cemetery and met with the minister. She's so needy, she won't let me out of her sight. I had to sneak out of the house to come over here."

"She's milking it," I say with a straight face. I've never held back when it comes to his mother.

Laughing, he pulls me into his arms. "God, I've missed you. I can't believe this is happening. DNA aside, my gut tells me she's our daughter. I sensed a special connection between us the first time I met her."

I think back to the night we sang karaoke together. "I did, too, now that you mention it." I lean into Pritchard, letting his strong arms comfort me. My daughter is alive and well. After all these years, my burden has been lifted. Relief overcomes me, and I don't even try to hold back the tears.

"Are you crying?" Pritchard asks, kissing the top of my head.

"Happy tears. After thirty years, I finally have something to be happy about."

THIRTY-FIVE
HARPER

Monday morning rolls around, and I've heard from neither Pritchard nor Savannah. A sick feeling in the pit of my stomach warns me they want nothing to do with me. I tell myself it doesn't matter. Two months ago, I didn't know I was adopted. I didn't know Savannah and Pritchard were even alive. But myself knows I'm lying.

I'm surprised to find Carrie waiting outside the boutique when I arrive promptly at ten. She's habitually ten or fifteen minutes late. I haven't called her out on it. She makes up time by staying late in the evenings most days."

"What're you doing here so early?" I ask, holding the door open for her.

"If you don't mind, I was hoping to sneak out to attend Edward St. Clair's funeral at eleven," she says as we file into the shop.

I flip a row of wall switches, flooding the room with light. "The funeral is today? Why so fast?"

"Apparently, the church wasn't available on Tuesday. We should close the shop today since most of our customers will attend the funeral."

"Maybe we should. I was thinking of going to the funeral myself. To support Pritchard." I watch for Carrie's reaction. Savannah may have told her sister if she knows about me being her daughter.

Carrie appears unfazed as she wanders around the showroom, straightening and tidying clothes. "I didn't realize you knew Pritchard."

"We met randomly at the waterfront and have become friends based on our mutual love of music."

"In that case, you should go." She eyes my black sleeveless dress. "You're already dressed for the occasion."

"I may just attend the burial at the cemetery. That way I won't have to close the shop for too long."

"You have to at least stop by the St. Clair house for the reception," she says as she refolds a stack of colorful knit tops.

"We'll see." I send a quick text to Will, asking for his approval to close the shop for the funeral. He responds right away with a thumbs-up.

Carrie leaves the store a few minutes before eleven. I drum my fingers on the counter as I watch the minutes tick off the clock, debating whether or not to attend the burial. I need to talk to Pritchard and Savannah, but a funeral is not the right place. Around eleven thirty, I'm leaning toward not going when I spot a mannequin sporting a brimmed black sun hat. Just what I need to hide my face.

Tugging the sun hat low on my head, I grab my purse and drive the short distance to the cemetery, waiting in my car until the pallbearers have removed the mahogany casket from the hearse. I nudge my way to the front of the crowd for a clearer view of the St. Clair family. Next to Pritchard at the end of the aisle is an elegant gray-headed woman, Pritchard's mother, the woman who was eavesdropping on our meeting on Saturday. On the other side of her is a woman who looks enough like Pritchard to be his sister. I assume the man and two pretty blondes beside her are her husband

and daughters. It dawns on me that these four are my aunt, uncle, and cousins.

Scanning the crowd, I locate Savannah standing with Ashton and Will near the edge of the funeral tent. Just behind them, I spot the top of Carrie's head.

The service is brief, with a few prayers, readings, and closing remarks. Afterwards, I join the convoy of cars headed across the Merriweather Bridge to Sandy Island. As I approach the St. Clair compound, parking attendants direct me to the expanse of lawn to the left of the driveway.

Grabbing a mimosa from a passing server, I go to the familiar stone terrace where I met with Pritchard. Although it was less than forty-eight hours ago, it seems like a lifetime. I stand near the knee wall, hoping to find a moment alone with him. The sun is hot, and sweat soon trickles down my back. The black sun hat was a bad idea. I'm considering going inside to cool off when I notice Pritchard break away from a group of women and move to the edge of the terrace, staring at the ocean.

I walk up behind him. "Pritchard, I'm so sorry about your father."

As he turns toward me, a broad smile spreads across his face. "Harper! You came. I'm glad to see you."

"Are you? I wasn't sure. When I didn't hear from you, I thought maybe you . . . I wasn't sure what to think, honestly. That maybe you were having doubts about . . . you know. Me."

His bushy brows become one. "Oh. Gosh. No. I didn't mean to worry you. My mother has kept me on a short leash since my father died. Planning a funeral of this magnitude in two days has been challenging."

My shoulders sag in relief. "I can't imagine."

"All things considered, I thought a text message or phone call would be inadequate. I wanted to see you in person. We decided to wait until after the funeral to reach out to you. I'm hoping the three of us can have dinner together tonight."

My heart skips a beat. *We? Three?* "So Savannah knows?"

A voice behind me says, "Yes, I know. Pritchard told me, and I am positively thrilled."

I slowly turn to her, but my voice is tight, and I'm afraid to speak.

Savannah places a hand on my face, thumbing my cheek. "You're lovely. You look so much like Pritchard. You have his beautiful blue eyes."

When she draws me in for a hug, I burst into tears. "I'm sorry," I sob. "I've been so emotional these past couple of days."

Savannah doesn't respond, and when her body trembles, I suspect she's also crying.

"What're you crying for? You haven't seen Edward in over thirty years."

The harsh voice causes Savannah to freeze. "Brace yourself," she whispers to me. "This is liable to get ugly."

Freeing herself from our embrace, Savannah spins around to face Pritchard's mother. "Actually, Isabelle, I'm crying because I just found out this lovely young woman is my daughter." She hooks an arm around my waist. "*Pritchard's* daughter. *Your* granddaughter."

Isabelle doesn't bat an eye. This is not news to her. She overheard my conversation with her son. Her lip twitches as she gives me the once-over. "You're a fool, Savannah. This young woman is an imposter, an opportunist, showing up here on the heels of my husband's death. Don't you know she wants money? She's after Pritchard's inheritance."

Pritchard steps forward, coming to our rescue. "That's enough, Mother. You're way out of line."

I'm aware of others watching us. Through the sea of faces, I spot Cody's. I can't read his expression. I have no idea what he's thinking. Is he as mortified as me? Pushing away from Savannah, I elbow my way through the onlookers to the edge of the terrace.

I'm almost at my car when Savannah catches up, grabbing me

by the arm. "Don't let her get to you, Harper. Isabelle is a spiteful bitch. Pritchard tolerates her because she's his mother, and he's an honorable man. But he knows how she is."

"I don't need money, Savannah. My mother . . . my adoptive mother left me plenty."

"Nothing that woman says concerns me. Least of all money. Pritchard and I are both so grateful we found you." She takes me by the shoulders. "We've been given a second chance, and I can hardly wait to know you. I'd love nothing more than to leave here with you now, to spend the afternoon on the beach, filling each other in on our lives. But I think we should wait for Pritchard."

I inhale an unsteady breath. "I agree, we should. I need to get back to work anyway."

"Then we'll wait until tonight. We'll have a lovely dinner, just the three of us. We'll be in touch once we make a reservation," she says, hugging me one final time.

I watch her go. I'm surprised when she doesn't return to the reception. Instead, she gets in her old-model Land Rover and drives off.

I fall back against the side of my car as my new reality hits home. The earth has shifted, and my life has forever changed. I have a brand-new family. Cousins and aunts and uncles. I wonder what my relationships with Pritchard and Savannah will be like. We're all adults with less than twenty years of age between us. Will we be friends? Will we spend the holidays together? Will Pritchard walk me down the aisle when I get married? Will Savannah stay with me when I give birth to my first child? No one will ever replace Victoria, who impacted my life the most. But I'm no longer alone in the world. I have a family. My family. My flesh and blood.

THIRTY-SIX
SAVANNAH

I'm the first to arrive for our seven o'clock reservation at the Sandy Island Club. Pritchard appears shortly after that, and by the time Harper joins us at seven fifteen, a bucket of bubbly is chilling beside the table.

While the server pops the cork and fills three flutes, Pritchard peruses the appetizer menu and orders the calamari and shrimp ceviche for us to share. As an afterthought, he says to Harper, "I'm sorry I didn't think to ask. I hope you like seafood."

"She's not our daughter if she doesn't like seafood."

Despite my teasing tone, Harper's face falls as though wounded. "If you need more proof, I can have additional DNA testing."

I place my hand on hers. "No, honey. That's not necessary. All the proof I need is in your eyes."

Harper removes a yellowed envelope from her clutch. From the envelope, she hands me a slip of paper. "You should see this anyway."

I read the scribbled writing. *Darby Baby. January 9th. Marsh Point. One hundred Pelican's Way. Water's Edge, South Carolina.* I hand the slip of paper to Pritchard, who shakes his head in disbelief. He's thinking what I'm thinking. My mother must have been planning for months in advance to steal our baby.

"This was also in the envelope," Harper says.

Tears fill my eyes at the sight of a scrap of yellow flannel. I run my finger across the ducks printed on the fabric.

"I gave you that blanket for the baby," Pritchard says.

I nod. "I remember. Along with the little rubber duck."

Pritchard picks up his champagne flute. "Well, that seals the deal for me. Not that I ever had any doubts. To our reunion," he says, holding out his glass.

As the three of us clink glasses, I add, "To second chances."

"To both of you for bringing me into this world," says Harper, and we all sip champagne.

The bubbles tickle my nose, and I set down my glass. "Start talking," I say to Harper. "I want to know everything about you."

Harper giggles. "That could take some time. I'll start with the highlights." With the flute in hand, she sits back in her chair. "As you already know, I grew up in Raleigh. My father died when I was young." She cast Pritchard an apologetic look. "My adoptive father, Stanley. I hope you're not offended when I refer to them as my mother and father. It's difficult to break that habit."

I smile at her. "No offense taken, sweetheart. They raised you. They *were* your mother and father."

"Thanks for saying that." Harper lowers her gaze to the table. "My mother, Victoria, was a hugely successful criminal attorney. Even though she worked all the time, she was an excellent mentor and provider. She made certain I minded my manners and got a top-notch education." She fingers the corner of the yellowed envelope. "Finding out I was adopted was like locating the puzzle piece that makes sense of my life. Victoria and I were different in almost every way. I tried living up to her expectations. But I never could. And now I know why. We weren't cut from the same cloth."

The server arrives with our appetizers, and we share a laugh when all three of us order the same grouper entree special.

As she forks calamari onto her cocktail plate, Harper says, "Now it's your turn. I want to hear more about your lives. I've already met your siblings, Savannah. I'm crazy about Carrie. Will is a super nice guy. And I'm looking forward to getting to know Ashton better." She looks over at Pritchard. "Was the woman seated next to your mother at the funeral your sister?"

He nods. "That's Kate. Her daughters, Shelby and Grace, are your cousins. Because they live in Austin, Texas, I don't get to spend much time with them."

I sense Harper's disappointment about her newly discovered family. "I'd like us to get off on the right foot, Harper, which means no secrets. Regarding our families, Pritchard and I have more than our share of ghosts in our closets. I want you to know your family history. But there will be plenty of time to talk about that later. Let's not go down that dark path tonight."

Pritchard's lips part in a smile. "I wholeheartedly agree."

"Whatever you think is best. But do you mind if I ask about your relationship? Were you in love?" Harper asks in a way that tells me she already knows some of our background.

I smile over at Pritchard. "We were. I was a senior in high school, and Pritch was a freshman at Alabama. Our parents were against us getting married. They thought we were throwing away our lives. We were planning to elope and set the country music world on fire."

I'm relieved when Harper doesn't ask why we didn't elope, why we put her up for adoption instead.

"Is your music what brought you together?" Harper asks, forking a shrimp into her mouth.

"In a manner of speaking," Pritchard says, his eyes meeting mine. "Music has always been my passion. But I fell head over heels in love with Savannah when I heard her sing in a high school musical."

"Pritchard is a music savant," I say, my eyes still on his. "At age three, he learned to play the piano from ear. And he's proficient with several other instruments."

Harper's mouth falls open. "At age three? That's unbelievable. I play the guitar, saxophone, and violin. But not from ear. And I'm rusty. I haven't picked up any instrument in years."

"We'll have to do something about that," I say. "We can have a guitar jam session."

Pritchard jabs a piece of pretzel roll at Harper. "Brace yourself, Harper. Savannah has mad guitar skills."

Harper's expression grows somber. "Now seems like a good time to tell you I've decided not to pursue a music career. I've given it a lot of thought, and it seems too risky at my age. I don't think I could handle traveling all the time. I need stability in my life." She places her hands on the table as though bracing herself. "So, I've decided to go in another . . . safer direction. Tomorrow, I will be making an offer to buy Lowcountry Interiors."

"Good for you!" I press my hand against my chest. "And for me. This means you'll be staying in Water's Edge."

Harper beams. "That's the plan. I know virtually nothing about interior design, but I plan to take some classes, and Bridget, the current designer, is staying on board. I'm terrified out of my mind, but this feels like a good fit for me."

"Congratulations!" Pritchard says in an enthusiastic tone. "For the record, I think you're making the right decision. The music industry can be a grind. I'm happy to help if you need any business advice."

"That means a lot, Pritchard. Thanks. For now, Victoria's financial advisor is coaching me."

"In light of this development, I'm taking my songs off the market," I say to Pritchard. "My music is too personal. I was okay with it when Harper was the one recording them. But I'm not comfortable with a total stranger singing them."

"That's fair, Savannah. It's your work to do with as you see fit."

I wink at Harper. "Who knows? Maybe one day, you and I will release some of the songs together as duets. A mother and daughter duo."

"Once I've brushed up on my guitar skills, we can start a garage band," Harper says with a mischievous glint in her eye.

"Yes!" I say, coming out of my chair a little. "Or I'll open a nightclub, and we can perform live to a packed house on Friday nights." I catch Pritchard watching me and settle back in my seat. "What? Did I say something wrong?"

"Not at all. Your eyes are sparkling diamonds. Is opening a nightclub a longtime dream of yours?"

"I'm not sure. For the past thirty years, I've been afraid to dream." My gaze meets Harper's. "But now that my biggest dream has come true, I feel like the sky's the limit."

Pritchard offers me a high five. "That's the Savannah I remember." His smile fades. "I'm envious of the time you two will be spending together. Sadly, I have to return to Nashville tomorrow."

Harper pokes out her bottom lip. "So soon? We only just found each other."

"Unfortunately. I've been neglecting my clients these past few months. Not only do I need to put my life back on track, I need a break from my mother," he says in jest, although I can tell he's serious. "But I'll be back and forth, helping Mom settle Dad's estate."

My heart sinks. Nashville is nine hours away. It won't be the same as seeing him every day. Did I misunderstand the vibes he's been sending off these past few days? I don't think so. Our connection is still powerful. There are sparks between us. My future looks less bright without him in it.

THIRTY-SEVEN
HARPER

I walk on air as I enter Lowcountry Interiors on Tuesday morning. I hold my head high as I present Rose with my carefully thought-out, handwritten offer. She scowls at the number for thirty seconds before lifting her elegant shoulder in a shrug. She knows this is the best she'll get, a nest egg for her retirement while her legacy lives on.

"We'll begin due diligence right away," she says. "If you can swing it, I'd like to close at the end of the month. At least by the end of the summer."

"That gives us most of July. I should be able to make that happen. I'm super excited, Rose. I promise to take excellent care of your company." I extend my hand to shake, but she brushes it away and hugs me instead.

"I have faith in you, Harper. Lowcountry Interiors is in good hands."

When I return to the boutique, Carrie is waiting at the door. "Well? How'd it go?"

"She accepted. I'm the proud, soon-to-be owner of Lowcountry Interiors."

"That's wonderful news. Congratulations."

Carrie was beside herself when she arrived back at work after the funeral yesterday. She told me all about the night I was born—the ice storm and how special it was for her to witness my birth. She left out the part about my abduction. I suspect Savannah will eventually tell me the truth.

As she follows me to the checkout counter, Carrie peppers me with questions about when I'll close on the business and who will take my place as manager at Tracy's Threads.

I glance at my watch. "I'm meeting Will in a few minutes to turn in my notice. We'll talk about that then. I hope you don't mind holding down the shop a little longer."

She waves me off. "Of course not. Take as long as you need."

"I'm going to suggest to Will that he promote you. How do you feel about being the manager?"

Alarm crosses Carrie's face as she steps back from the counter. "No way, Harper! I'm not ready for such an important position."

"Give yourself some credit, Carrie. You're doing a wonderful job. Truthfully, I believe you're perfectly suited for the position."

Carrie softens as she moves back to the counter. "Really? In that case, talk to Will about it. If he agrees, maybe I'll give it a shot."

"I can't imagine him not agreeing." I place the folder containing my Lowcountry Interiors documents under the counter and sling my purse over my shoulder. "I'll just be down the street at Corner Coffee if you need me."

I beat Will to the coffee shop. I order an iced coffee and locate a table for two by the window. When Will arrives, he pulls me to my feet and into his arms.

"Welcome to the family, Harper. I spoke to Savannah a few minutes ago. I'm overjoyed for both of you."

"Thank you, Will." I push away so I can see his face. "Or should I say, Uncle Will?" I flash him a mischievous smile.

He scoffs. "Will is fine. You're not that much younger than me."

I laugh. "True."

He gestures at my cold brew on the table. "I see you already have a drink. Let me get a coffee. I'll be back in a second."

When he returns, I tell him about my new business endeavor, and he congratulates me. At first, he doesn't seem keen on the idea of promoting Carrie. "This is the first job she's ever had."

I cut my eyes at him. "As if being a stay-at-home mother isn't a demanding, thankless, round-the-clock position."

His hands shoot up. "All right, already. You sound like my wife."

"Seriously," I say, absently toying with my straw. "This job has given Carrie confidence, and she's really come into her own these past few weeks. Besides, the customers love her. Some of them refuse to let me help them anymore."

"I've noticed the change in her as well. Carrie and I don't exactly get along. Maybe this will help improve our relationship."

"Maybe so. I truly believe she's capable of managing Tracy's Threads. Otherwise, I wouldn't recommend her."

"Fair enough. I'll give her a shot." His phone pings, and he reads the text. "I'm sorry, Harper. I hate to cut this short, but I have a crisis at one of my job sites."

I wave him on. "Go. With your permission, we'll start looking for a new sales assistant."

"That'd be great." He kisses the top of my head. "I'm truly so happy to have you in the family. Maybe you'll be the catalyst that brings us Darby siblings back together."

"No pressure there," I say with a chuckle, but inwardly I'm flattered.

I leave the coffee shop and head back toward the boutique. I walk slowly as I absorb the morning's events. I'm so lost in thought, I'm startled when Cody steps in line beside me.

"There you are! I've been looking all over for you."

I glance over at him. His smiling face makes my heart dance

across my chest. I hope this means he's forgiven me. "Hello, Cody."

"I owe you an apology, Harper. I underestimated what you were going through in trying to connect with your biological parents. Yesterday, when I saw how Isabelle St. Clair treated you, I wanted to smack the smug look off her face. You deserve better than that."

"I'm the one who owes you an apology. I'm sorry I've been so fickle. I've had so many changes in my life, and my emotions have been all over the place."

"And understandably so. With your mother dying and finding out you were adopted. I should've been more sensitive to your needs." We stop walking and face each other. "Do you think we can start over? Will you give me another chance, Harper?"

Stepping toward him, I tap my finger on his chest. "You're the one who should be giving me another chance."

He places his hands on my hips. "Since we're both at fault, let's call a truce and move forward together. Will you have dinner with me tonight?"

"Maybe. Are you sure you're ready for commitment? Because I like you too much for anything less."

He laughs. "I'm not the one with commitment issues." He draws my body closer to his. "The question is, are *you* ready for a serious relationship?"

"Absolutely! I'm totally ready to be exclusive. But only with you." I hook an arm around his neck and pull his lips to mine, completely oblivious to the people passing us by.

THIRTY-EIGHT
SAVANNAH

I spend much of Tuesday morning visiting area nightclubs and eateries in search of a job. Only one is hiring bartenders, but the restaurant's elegant atmosphere is too staid for me. I'm walking home from the waterfront when Amber calls.

"Get over here fast," she blurts. "Rodney fired Taylor, and he wants to see you."

"Slow down, Amber. Why did he fire Taylor? Did he finally figure out she was stealing from him?"

"Actually, Taylor confessed, and then she quit. She's going back to school to become a nurse. Can you imagine her taking your temperature? Anyway, where are you? Can you come now?"

I'm still sore about the way Rodney treated me, but I need a job, and I enjoyed working at The Nest. "I can be there in a few minutes," I say and take my time backtracking my steps to the waterfront.

The Nest is hopping with the lunch crowd. Every seat in the house is occupied. Amber, who is pulling draft beers, inclines her head in the direction of the kitchen. "He's waiting for you in the office."

I greet my ex-coworkers as I make my way behind the bar and

through the kitchen to the office. Rodney jumps up to greet me. "Savannah! Thanks for coming so quickly."

He holds my arm as though I'm an elderly woman as I lower myself to the chair opposite the desk.

He returns to his seat and clasps his hands on the desk. "I assume Amber told you Taylor has decided to go back to school."

"She did. But what's that got to do with me?"

"I'd like to offer you a job as manager," he says, grinning like a Cheshire cat.

Manager? I expected him to offer me my bartending job back. I sit back in my chair, forcing myself to take a deep breath, to not jump at the opportunity. "That's an about-face if ever I've seen one. Why would you hire a thief?"

A flush creeps up his neck. "About that . . . I owe you an apology. Turns out I was wrong about the missing money."

I wait for him to continue, but when he remains silent, I prompt him. "So, where did the money go?"

His face beams red. "Turns out Taylor borrowed it. But we've worked out our differences. I was wrong in forcing her to take over the business when managing a restaurant is not her passion."

I cross my legs. "Okay, so why me? Why not Amber? She's been here much longer."

"Because you have a vision. I approve of the decisions you've made and the ones you've suggested. Both Taylor and Amber agree that you're a better fit for the job."

I inspect my fingernails. "Go on."

Rodney twiddles his thumbs. "The Nest is way overdue for a facelift. We'll come up with a reasonable budget, and you'll have full authority to make decisions regarding the decor. Hire a decorator if need be. The only thing I ask is that you maintain the vibe."

"The vibe is what makes The Nest a success. I wouldn't dream of changing it. How do you feel about bringing in live entertainment?"

He screws up his face. "Is that really necessary? Our customers are loyal, and they don't expect that."

I uncross my legs and sit up straight. "And herein lies your problem. You're taking those loyal patrons for granted. If a glitzy new nightclub opens up down the way, they'll disappear." I snap my fingers. "Just like that. Happened at the last place I worked. It's vital to your future success to keep up with the trends for food, drink, *and* entertainment."

He throws up his hands. "Okay! Fine! Have your live entertainment." He leans back in his chair, the springs groaning beneath him, and folds his arms over his ample gut. "I'm getting older, Savannah. I don't want the hassle of the day-to-day operations. As long as you keep up the bottom line, I'll be happy."

"I need to think about it." I get to my feet. "I'll let you know in a couple of days," I say, leaving him gaping at my back as I exit the office.

I totally want the job. But after the way he treated me, I'm not going to make it easy on him.

Amber is waiting on a customer when I emerge from the kitchen. I wink at her as I pass by, letting her know everything went well.

My mind races with ideas as I stroll home. Maybe I'll hire Harper's new firm to help with the decorating. I'm ready for the challenge of a new position. I'll still have plenty of interaction with the customers, but I'll have control over my hours, and I can be creative with the menu offerings. Live entertainment is a must. I can see Harper now, making her debut performance with a few of my songs.

I arrive back at Muriel's to find Pritchard leaning against his Audi in the driveway. "What're you doing here? I thought you were leaving today."

He pushes off his car. "I made it an hour outside of town before it dawned on me. Why would I leave town now when you're back and we've found our daughter?"

My stomach does a somersault. "But what about your career?"

"I can work remotely. I'll still have to spend a fair amount of time in Nashville. I'll keep my apartment there and maybe buy a small house here. I've missed being on the coast, and I'm ready to make Water's Edge my home base."

Pritchard's phone rings, and he glances down at the screen. "Excuse me a second. I need to take this."

He walks to the edge of the driveway, out of earshot. His call is brief, and when he returns, his expression is grave.

"Is something wrong?" I ask, frowning.

"That was my dad's estate attorney. He wants to read Dad's will tomorrow morning while Kate is still in town. He warned me there are surprises Mom won't like."

"Uh-oh. Are you going to tell her in advance to prepare her?"

Pritchard cocks an eyebrow. "And risk the wrath of Isabelle? Not a chance." He runs his fingers through his hair. "No way can I continue living with Mom. You don't happen to have a spare bedroom I can borrow while I find somewhere else to live?"

I close the distance between us. "I have a spare bedroom." I place my hand on his cheek. "But I'd rather you share mine." Standing on my tiptoes, I press my lips lightly to his. "I've missed you, Pritch. I've never felt about anyone the way I feel about you. We were good together once. I believe we can get back what we lost. Will you give me another chance to make it up to you?"

He wraps his arms around me, pulling me in close. "I thought you'd never ask."

———

WITH ASHTON'S BLESSING, I arrange a family cookout at Marsh Point on Saturday night. The flexibility of my new work schedule will allow me to work most of the day so I can take the evening off. Since starting as The Nest's manager on Wednesday, I've begun revamping the menu, arranging live entertainment for the coming weekends, and discussing remodeling with Harper. She has good taste, and I love the ideas she's suggesting.

I invite everyone in the family to the cookout, including my dad and their significant others. Not that I care to see Dad, but it's the right thing to do. I refuse to be the one who divides our family.

When dinner is ready, before Will says the blessing, I gather everyone for a brief word.

"Thank you all for coming tonight. Some of us are strangers to one another, but I aim to remedy that in the coming weeks and months. This family has experienced our share of hardships over the decades. I hope this cookout will begin a new era of better days ahead." I reach for Pritchard's hand. "I'm eternally grateful to have Pritchard and our daughter back in my life." I smile at Harper, who is standing nearby with her new beau, Cody. "As well as every single one of you."

Ashton comes to stand beside me. "I'd like to add a word if I may. I spent a lot of time with Mama during her illness, and she was acutely aware of the damage her alcoholism caused this family. Because I'm the oldest, I believe Mama was counting on me to mend the rift in our family. Ironically, Savannah, the one she hurt the most, has reunited us." She gives me a half hug. "Welcome home, little sister."

My voice is tight, and the tears are just beneath the surface. "I never thought I'd say it, but I'm thrilled to be here."

Ashton continues, "I wasn't sure what to think when I inherited Marsh Point, and I spent considerable time pondering Mama's message. I often spoke to her about my desire to restore Marsh Point in those last years. I believe she intended for me to restore our beautiful home to her original glory. Not just for me but for all of us. I don't consider myself the owner of Marsh Point, but the custodian." She sweeps a hand at the second floor of the house. "We have plenty of bedrooms. The door is always open for all of you whenever you need a place to retreat. Now!" She claps her hands. "Say the blessing, Will. I, for one, am starving."

A grinning Will steps forward. "Yes, ma'am. But first, I have an announcement to make. Julia is pregnant. Come January, we will have a new member of the Darby clan."

The family erupts in cheers and whistles, and everyone rushes to congratulate Will and Julia.

After serving our plates, we migrate to the veranda. Some of us eat at the table and others in rockers. The younger ones sit with their legs dangling over the side of the porch, and the small children picnic on a blanket on the ground.

After dessert, as the sun descended toward the horizon, I grab my guitar and sing a few of my favorite original songs. At Pritchard's request, Harper joins me for several duets of today's top country songs.

I don't speak to my father until everyone is leaving, and he thanks me for including him and May May. "I did it for the others, not for you. You stole thirty years of my life, and I'm not sure I can ever forgive you for that. But for the family's sake, I'm willing to try."

Before he can respond, I turn my back on him to speak to someone else. *Baby steps.*

The men insist on helping Ashton clean up, giving Harper and me a few minutes alone.

"This place is amazing," Harper says as we stroll out to the end of the dock. "I can't imagine what it was like growing up here."

I smile. "There were some happy times mixed in with the bad ones. I'll eventually tell you about the past. You should know your family history. But I'm warning you, it isn't pretty."

"I'm a big girl, Savannah. I can handle it. Knowing the good and the bad will help me understand *you* more."

When we reach the end of the dock, I turn to face her. "One thing you need to know now. I did not willingly give you up for adoption. My mother tricked me into signing the papers. She told me I was signing a release form, allowing the doctor to deliver you. When I woke up the next morning and discovered you were gone,

I freaked out and ran away to Washington State, where I stayed for thirty years."

"Thanks for telling me, Savannah. I can't imagine how hard that was for you. There's no sense dwelling on the past when there's nothing we can do to change it. I'm so fortunate to have found you. The three of us are still young. Hopefully, we'll have many happy years as a family going forward."

"I'm counting on it. We have a lot of making up for lost time to do," I say, looping my arm in hers as we retrace our steps back down the dock.

"Do you think you and Pritchard will get married?"

"I certainly hope so. There's never been anyone else for me. Even though we've only been back together a few days, being with him feels right." I lean into her. "Now, tell me about you and Cody. Are you two serious? A police officer would be a blessed addition to this family."

Harper giggles. "He's a good guy. I've struggled with commitment issues, but Cody and I are a good fit. This may sound corny, but he completes me. Without him, I don't feel whole."

"I know exactly what you mean." Ahead of us, up at the house, the soft glow in the windows is a beacon of warmth, twinkling in the darkness, reflecting on the tranquil waters of the sound. "Since Ashton opened her house to us, maybe we'll have a double wedding on the lawn."

A dreamy expression passes over Harper's face. "A mother-daughter wedding. How much fun would that be? I can't think of anyone I'd rather spend my big day with."

"Me either." I rest my head on her shoulder. "Although it might get a little complicated for Pritchard being both a groom and the father of the bride."

Harper's melodic laughter fills the night air and makes my heart sing.

———

I HOPE you've enjoyed *Songbird's Second Chance* and the Marsh Point series. Are you curious about the surprises in Pritchard's father's will? Check out my new spinoff Sandy Island series for feel-good family drama set at Palmetto Point.

You might also enjoy my other family drama series: Palmetto Island, Hope Springs, and Virginia Vineyards. I hope you'll stop by my store where you'll find these series and more bundled together for an affordable price. Shop Ashley Farley Books Now!

ACKNOWLEDGMENTS

I'm forever indebted to the many people who help bring a project to fruition. My editor, Pat Peters. My cover designer, the hard-working folks at Damonza.com. My beta readers: Alison Fauls, Anne Wolters, Laura Glenn, Jan Klein, Lisa Hudson, Lori Walton, Kathy Sinclair, Jenelle Rodenbaugh, Rachel Story, Jennie Trovinger, and Amy Connolley. Last, but certainly not least, are my select group of advanced readers who are diligent about sharing their advanced reviews prior to releases.

I'm blessed to have many supportive people in my life who offer the encouragement I need to continue my pursuit of writing. Love and thanks to my family—my mother, Joanne; my husband, Ted; and my amazing children, Cameron and Ned.

Most of all, I'm grateful to my wonderful readers for their love of women's fiction. I love hearing from you. Feel free to shoot me an email at ashleyhfarley@gmail.com or stop by my website at ashleyfarley.com for more information about my characters and upcoming releases. Don't forget to sign up for my newsletter. Your subscription will grant you exclusive content, sneak previews, and special giveaways.

ACKNOWLEDGMENTS

ABOUT THE AUTHOR

Ashley Farley writes books about women for women. Her characters are mothers, daughters, sisters, and wives facing real-life issues. Her bestselling Sweeney Sisters series has touched the lives of many.

Ashley is a wife and mother of two young adult children. While she's lived in Richmond, Virginia, for the past twenty-one years, a piece of her heart remains in the salty marshes of the South Carolina Lowcountry, where she still calls home. Through the eyes of her characters, she captures the moss-draped trees, delectable cuisine, and kindhearted folk with lazy drawls that make the area so unique.

Ashley loves to hear from her readers. Visit Ashley's website @ ashleyfarley.com

Get free exclusive content by signing up for her newsletter @ ashleyfarley.com/newsletter-signup/

Made in United States
Troutdale, OR
04/19/2024

19294614R00152